ACKNOWLEDGEMENTS

We would like to thank editors Connie Vader Rinehold and Andrea Barilla. Both are personable and professional, a terrific combination.

This is a work of fiction. It is not intended to define or reflect on any cultures, people, or groups of people and should not be considered a resource.

CONTENTS

When the peace treaty is signed, the war isn't over for the veterans or the family. It's just starting.

—First Lieutenant Karl Marlantes

.

PROLOGUE

Two startled hikers stared upward as the rescue helicopter burst over the trees lining the lower edge of the meadow, its searchlights glaring on the ominous rise of Mt. Humphreys above the Arizona plain. It maneuvered toward the far edge of the bristlecone pines, a giant dragonfly in frantic flight. To the Native American, the dragonfly symbolized resurrection and renewal, a thought lost on Russ, the elder of the two hikers. He winced at the deafening sound of the blades slicing through the mountain air. The whole scene felt like a bump to an ancient, unhealed wound. Russ instinctively ducked, even as logic spoke of no chance of contact. His generation had gone to war accompanied by that repetitious whopping sound, a drumbeat that alarmed the enemy while bringing hope to trapped and wounded comrades.

Twilight approached, threatening a successful rescue. Russ steadied his injured companion, whose labored breaths etched regret on the elder's face.

Near the summit a silent explosion pulsed illuminating light into the body of gathering clouds, their outlines dark. *Lightning,* Russ thought. *No good.* Still shaken, he gripped his nephew and continued their hobble toward the parking lot yet a mile or more away. They had fully expected to be in Flagstaff hours ago, but Colton's injuries had slowed their descent.

"It looks like some sorry fool is having a bad day," Colton muttered between shallow breaths.

"And you're not? Yeah, at least we were able to trek out. I'll have you at the hospital in time for dinner." Russ's tone offered no sign of sympathy—not that he didn't have any, but at the moment he was out of sorts.

"Can we sit for a minute, Uncle Russ? I need a break."

Colton grew limp in Russ's arms. Russ lowered his nephew onto soft pads of grass. He stepped back, studying a physically broken young man not much older than he had been when he was cast out into the world, emotionally broken, so long ago. The young man heaved his shoulders and gasped a labored breath. Stepping back, Russ stretched, relieving the strain in his back. The clamor of the chopper faded as it became a mere bright speck above the bristlecone in its search for other ill-fated hikers.

This trip had been at the younger's invitation, a pup wanting to run with the big dogs. The plan was to trek up to the highest point in Arizona, followed by a descent to the lowest point—in the bottom of the Grand Canyon. Russ had surprised himself when he accepted the invitation. It had never been in his nature to allow for any requests from others, and he didn't even know this kid named Colton—hadn't talked to Colton's dad, his brother Gary, in over thirty years. Gary's narcissism had not allowed space for Russ to voice his own opinions. Russ found himself searching for answers for a questioning nephew during their ascent.

"Uncle Russ, I'm sorry about all this . . ." Colton looked up at his uncle, eyes scrunched in not-so-hidden pain. "What are you going to do?"

"I'll do what I do, head into the canyon."

"Do you plan to go it alone?" Colton's voice exhibited sincere concern.

"There are plenty of people on the trail; I'm never alone. People doing the same thing are a friendly bunch, especially while indulging in a challenge."

Russ had no intention of hooking up with other hikers. Catching himself in his own lie, he thought, *Hypocrite. Why do I always do that? Always cloaking the truth.* The advice he offered Colton had been learned in the school of hard knocks. He had never nurtured the loves he had been offered; instead, he had deliberately poisoned them with shaded statements, hidden feelings, and intentions.

It has been said that glorious natural wonders inspire a belief in a creator and in supernatural forces. Russ still welled in an intense exhilaration, a feeling he dare not express, for his words would only fumble. Hours had passed since he had stood at the top of Arizona. Now he rested in this quiet meadow, yet he still bore the power of the moments at the summit, even as a conflict raged in his soul.

The mountain rose in grand rocky splendor above the old-growth forest of aspen framed in Douglas fir, ponderosa pine, and spruce. The thick and sweet valley air choked him, a severe contrast to the frugal yet crisp offerings endured at the near fourteen thousand foot summit.

"Do you believe in God?" Russ's eyes never strayed from the summit.

"Haven't given it much thought, Uncle Russ. Why?"

"Just thinking, that's all. Never mind." Russ paused. "But if there is a God, do you think He does things in a natural way and manipulates all, with the forces at hand, or is it a supernatural force?"

"I don't know."

"Of course you don't. We mortals are the ones that struggle with nature. God doesn't."

Russ scrutinized the salmon-pink twinges that formed where the red earth pecked the blue sky. Another Arizona sunset rapidly drawing in threatened the clarity of day. Russ carried a grudge for the night, but the night never seemed to care as it descended day after day all these years. The evergreens turned to dark silhouettes against a quickening rage of red on a canvas swirling in shades of pink, grey, and blue. He turned to Colton.

"Granny Jacobs told me that the secret to a long life was to always keep moving. That's my intention. Make it yours."

Russ looked back toward the loose debris of a once-mighty volcano. Mt. Humphreys had once towered over twenty thousand feet. If anything is forever, mountains are, but this one had been on par with Mt. Rainier and Mt. Fuji before it blew out in a Mt. St. Helens type cataclysm eons ago. The loose rubble of that long-ago event had flipped Colton as he leaped from boulder to boulder.

His wound was not of a visible nature—no blood or protruding bones. The fall had broken ribs near the heart, and that concerned Russ. A bruised heart is a serious thing.

No, even mountains are not forever.

HAVASUPAI

The dragonfly, in almost every part of the world, symbolizes change and change in the perspective of self-realization, the kind of change that has its source in mental and emotional maturity and the understanding of the deeper meaning of life.

CHAPTER 1

Alongside Route 66, in a tavern known as the Lodge Pole Inn just outside of Flagstaff, Arizona, Russ raised a cool glass to his parched lips. Its contents quickly quenched his thirst, unceremoniously marking the midpoint of an adventure gone wrong. He glanced at his reflection in the window-turned-mirror by the darkness outside. An older man glanced back. He hardly recognized himself, and didn't feel as old as his reflection looked.

When had it happened? He had always been a health fanatic, yet somewhere along the way he had aged. His brother Gary, Colton's dad, wouldn't even recognize him for sure. It had been a lifetime since they had spoken. Russ sipped the contents of his glass as an argument boiled inside him. Bravado and doubt. It had always been this way, alone in the struggle to decide if he was a maverick or a fool. Never once did he delve into a discussion about it with anyone. He glanced back at his reflection, this time accepting the image, knowing he had earned it.

The tavern, somewhat of a museum adorned with antiques and memorabilia of the Old West, offered him a refuge from the hospital scene and a place to drown his guilt. The dinner crowd was long gone, and the night lizards had not yet arrived, affording him time to think. A stranger in these parts, he didn't bother to look for a friendly face. Intentionally, he avoided them.

The bartender, a wholesome looking twenty-something, made small talk with patrons seated along the sparsely occupied bar, hawking for tips. She was somebody else's pain in the neck. Relationships were work, even temporary ones. And work caused blisters, and blisters caused pain. Even though Russ's skin was too thick and calloused to allow for even the smallest of blisters on his heart, he still avoided the pain of relationships.

An unfair assessment based on his own failed relationships. *Shame on me,* he thought. His fateful fall had not occurred during the conquest of a mountain. A younger Russ would have dallied with the bartender, he was sure. If age was good for nothing else, it did eliminate temptations, unless you're a fool and he was not. He thought of Colton leaping from boulder to boulder before he fell. Russ's fall had occurred attempting a much more dangerous endeavor—*amour*. He was becoming a crotchety old man who had misspent his youth, as so many do. He lifted his mug and took a gulp.

"You seem awful serious, mister. This is happy hour—smile!" The bartender slammed down a fresh mug that startled Russ out of his self-absorption.

"Happy hour? Oh, I suppose I'm just tired."

"Too tired to smile? They say smiling takes less energy than a frown. The night is young. By the end of happy hour, I'll have you smiling. My name is Kelly, by the way."

"Well, Kelly, I'm feeling old, as in 'too' old."

"Old? You're only as old as you feel, they say."

"Well, 'they' say a lot of things. You sure are persistent. I've been hiking for four days."

"A good two-step will limber you up."

"It's been a long time since this boy has done a two-step."

"It's like riding a bike; you never forget. I'll drag you out there myself if I have to!"

"Is that right?" *Was this girl for real?*

"My beau's band is playing tonight, so he won't be available for dancing."

"You drive a hard bargain."

"I just love life, that's all. Where'd you hike?"

"I was up on Humphreys."

"That's a great hike! That alone ought to make you smile. Did you do the saddle with Agassiz Peak? Really, when I reach the summit I get giddy. It's the same every time." Her arms flailed about, and her face glowed like a clear sky anticipating sunrise. Russ watched her crystal-clear blue eyes dance and suddenly felt shame for his gloom.

"Yeah, it was pretty exhilarating. We hiked all around the base for three days before we made our ascent. The weather on the mountain finally cleared on our fourth day, and we headed up. On our way down it clouded over again, and we had a lot of lightning. Scary stuff." Russ's voice exuded enthusiasm, and his heart lightened for a moment.

"I was there earlier this year. Snowbowl was going full tilt, and my beau and I were doing a little extreme skiing. You feel like you're on top of the world. *Dook'o'oosliid*—the mountain held to the earth by sunbeams—as the Navajo say." She smiled, wiping the bar in long strokes with a towel and swaying almost dance-like. "I love it up there. It's sacred to the Navajo. We respect the mountain, but a lot of people leave litter behind and don't appreciate its history."

Russ lifted his beer in a pause. "Reaching the summit was awesome. The entire trip was great, until my hiking partner fell."

"Oh no! Is she okay? Did they call in a rescue? I saw the chopper just before sunset."

"The chopper wasn't for us. My nephew was able to walk out. The doc said he's got broken ribs and a bruised liver 'n spleen—and a crushed ego. His wife drove up from Phoenix. She'll take care of him. She's a good kid."

"Kelly! Can't a body get a beer around here?" came a shout from the other side of the room.

"Hey, can you hold that thought? I have to set up a couple rounds." Kelly turned to work her way down the bar.

As she walked away, Russ saw it as an opportunity to make his "two-step" exit. The door was that close. Downing the last of his drink, his gaze combed the objects hanging on the wall—implements, paintings, and photos of scraggly characters. Native Americans, known in less sensitive days as Indians and mountain men, colorful, rugged, and romantic adventurers, rowdy fellows who spoke their minds in a way that let men sort things out. Sometimes their words ended in physical contact, but in the end the air was clear and feelings refreshed. Those were the days before the speech police and word twisters. Images of such characters filled movies when he was a boy and had set his spirit in motion. Always courageous and self-reliant, he had believed, but now his own reflection caused doubts about what really drove them.

Some, he speculated, were on the run, a fear of civilization possibly, a thought that he had never pondered before. Heroes to his generation, now rarely discussed as the new millennium approached and a generation of cyber-geeks lived out their days in virtual reality and virtual safety as they escaped into a world of fantasy. Suddenly, a fear of an overly controlled society and the growing bar crowd motivated Russ to run. On the edge of his seat he hesitated, and in that single moment, fate shifted gears.

The crowd had doubled in the last twenty minutes, the noise quadrupled. The band tuned up on a stage in a far, dark corner. The sweet little barmaid, too busy to listen to his drivel, doted on the younger crowd. Nameless faces chattered away at each other with no one really caring what the other had to say. Russ was yesterday's crowd, and to this crowd he was yesterday's man, as ancient and foreign as a buffalo hunter or a cowboy. As he perused the distant band, he wondered, *Which one is her beau?* Then he settled on, *Who cares?*

A "been-there-done-that" feeling came over Russ as he looked around the scene. *Irrelevant—me, this place, and these people.* It was the kind of thinking that came with age, when you realize how meaningless and hopeless it all seemed. There was even a passage in the Bible that said, "All is for naught."

"Test, test!" a loud squeal interrupted a guitarist who scrambled to tweak the feedback. He strummed a few disconnected notes. Tall, lanky band members with weathered faces under ten-gallon hats posed and strutted. *Rednecks, caricatures of good ol' boys*, Russ mused with a smirk. He set down his empty glass and turned to leave, but his path was blocked by a stodgy man bellying up to the bar.

"Excuse me, fellow," the man spoke in a foreign accent.

"No, excuse me. I've been going to leave for some time and realized how late I'm running."

"Hey Grumpy, where you headed?" Kelly's clear-as-a-bell voice made Russ jump. He turned to face her.

"I promised I'd make you smile. And you're my dance partner tonight!" The bartender picked up Russ's glass.

"Well, Kelly, that's my dilemma. Where am I headed? I need some air, I'm really not in the mood to smile or dance, and another beer will put me over the line of no return." Russ placed a twenty on the bar. "Keep the change."

"Route 66, man—for this Belgian. I'm looking for the America I saw on TV when I was a child," the foreigner interjected, his eyes wild with a sense of romanticized adventure. Russ gave the man a quick glance before the bartender recaptured his attention.

"Good luck with that," Russ muttered.

"Come on. I'll pour you a fresh one, and you tell me about it. Think of me as your therapist. Life's too short to be a grump, pappy." The girl said the words, but Russ knew she had no real sense of how short life was.

"I can work it out better if I stay sober and go it alone." How many times before had Russ fallen to the alternative? It had never worked.

Her lips pouted and she batted her eyes jokingly as she placed his glass under the tap. It was innocent and well-intended; Russ had no delusions beyond a youthful spirit trying to lift his, and he had to begrudgingly appreciate her effort.

"One for me also." The foreigner held up his thumb above his beaming grin.

Kelly nodded and smiled at Russ. "One more, just to finish your story. Sorry I got busy. Really, I'm interested in your story. Being a hiker myself . . . you know what I mean? Don't you feel a family connection with other hikers? Really, that's who I am. Who you see here is just what I do to get by." The bartender set two drafts on the bar. How many times had Russ said that to himself when he worked in the refineries?

"Yeah, gotcha," Russ responded. "Alright then. Well, I have reservations to hike into the canyon at Havasupai. I'm not sure I want to go it alone. My nephew and I wanted to hike to the highest and lowest points in Arizona. That's the story."

"Go for it! I love it down there!" Kelly encouraged.

"You've gone into Havasupai?" Russ wasn't really surprised.

"Many times. I love it."

"I think you love it everywhere. It's the guilt of going without my nephew, I think." Russ really wasn't sure what his problem was, but guilt was a part of it. He surprised himself with his candor. It wasn't like him. He felt his guard drop, allowing a stranger to know he had feelings.

"Excuse me, what's *Havasupai*?" the foreigner inquired.

"They call it Hawaii, Arizona style. It's one of the most beautiful places on earth. The water is a vibrant blue-green, the vegetation is lush, and there you'll find the kind of waterfalls of dreams." Kelly's eyes stared off as if her mind replayed an adventure into Havasupai. "It's part of a reservation and as sacred as the mountain." She shrugged. "The Indians have been back-and-forth owners of it as the Feds reneged on their word way too many times. The hike is a challenge, but one you'll never forget. There are secret places down there, and if you're lucky, you'll stumble onto one."

The Belgian hoisted his drink. "Secret places? I read about your government and the natives. Wounded Knee. The natives give up their weapons, and then get massacred. Good that some managed to get some of paradise." He drank and set down his mug. "Good for them." The foreigner perched on a barstool. "It's a long way from Antwerp," he mumbled.

Russ and Kelly looked thoughtfully at the foreigner. Neither offered a response but both reflected on the truth in his words, neither wanting the conversation to turn morbid.

After an impromptu moment of silence, Kelly spoke up. "One of my favorites is in an old calcite mine. There are vertical and horizontal shafts, so it is treacherous going. The main shaft burrows right through a room-sized geode that is plastered in crystals. When you enter, your light sets the room aglow." She rested her elbow on the bar. "I won't tell you how to get in there because it is dangerous if you go alone. There are old timbers laid across pits that seem to have no bottom. That whole valley is riddled with old mine shafts. The mines and men who worked them amaze me."

"I think you just convinced me." Russ lifted his beer. A sense of wonder at the world of nature stirred in him. It had been what he felt when he first received the invite to hike with Colton. These days Russ struggled with holding onto feelings. Repression and suppression had left him detached from his feelings for so long that a use-it-or-lose-it syndrome had developed.

"You remind me so much of my dad."

"Wow, that's what old guys like to hear."

"Silly, that's not what I meant!" Her eyes flirted innocently with Russ's for just a moment. "Hey, let me call my dad or some of his friends to see if anyone can go with you. If you don't want to go alone, I may be able to hook you up. My dad would jump at the chance; I'm sure of it. He'll show you the geode room. You two would love each other! He's a hoot!" the bartender bubbled.

"No, don't do that. Being alone doesn't scare me, really." Movement at the end of the bar distracted Russ, so he used that to divert the conversation. "What's that Indian doing down the bar?"

"Indian? You mean Native American, don't you?" Kelly retorted.

"Whatever . . . What's he doing?" Russ shifted his whole body to divert her focus. The Indian stood between two patrons at the end of the bar. He gently nodded his head, eyes closed. His hands gestured, forearms extended. He appeared to be in a trance as he chanted. He wore buckskin-colored cloth trousers; a red-and-white print shirt; and a worn, black felt hat with a single feather tucked into its band. Slung over one shoulder was a pouch with a dragonfly-shaped clasp on the flap. His skin resembled weathered rawhide. He was lean in build, but by no means frail.

Russ glanced at the photos on the wall and snickered to himself. *What? Did you think you might see a blank space where this apparition had popped off of the wall?*

Intrigued despite himself, Russ felt an odd kinship with the man. He shook his head and looked away. His mug was half-full. He'd finish it off and then call it a day, before melancholy got the better of him.

CHAPTER 2

"Chief Thunder Cloud? He'll make his way down here," Kelly said in a quieter tone. "He does a rain dance, hoping you'll buy him a beer to call off the *Kachinas,* the rain spirits. He comes in here occasionally. My boss says he's been doing it as long as anyone can remember. People say he's ninety years old and change." Her expression sobered as she glanced at the Native American. She flicked her bar towel at an imaginary smudge. "Some say he offends his culture by doing what he does. The truth is, I'd bet the old guy knows more about the old ways and his culture than anyone. He's truly a keeper of his people's heritage. Maybe he drinks to drown the spirits that haunt him or something. His day has passed. It's a shame because his type adds so much color to life."

"He looks like he's right out of one of the pictures on the wall, or some sort of apparition," Russ said. His own day, too, had passed. He was irrelevant.

She sighed and continued as if Russ had said nothing. "They say his tribe has rejected him. The younger members don't want to bother with the old ways. It's sad when people turn their backs on their heritage, but we are almost in the twenty-first century. Look how dumbed-down our schools have made our own culture. They teach multiculturalism, but when someone displays their culture, they're accused of being a stereotype . . . or a joke. Go figure."

Russ raised his head, seeing her with new respect. Smart girl. Twenty-something going on a hundred.

"I was hoping I'd see an Indian while I was in America, and now I've seen one doing a beer dance," the foreigner quipped. "We have a real-life Indian posing for a photo. Now there are no droopy-drawered Indian punks, texting."

Kelly frowned at the tourist, then turned to Russ.

"You two keep talking. I'm going to make some calls." Kelly turned away before Russ could convince her he'd rather go it alone, even though, admittedly, he found comfort in her offer and appreciated her concern.

"Wait—" Russ called, a last plea that faded in a whisper. "Aw, I don't want her trying to find a hiker to go along with me." He turned back toward the bar and focused on his beer. "So much for a fast getaway," he muttered.

The Belgian was more hopeful. "Maybe she gets someone to hike with you, and you make a lifelong friend. Maybe her daddy is a lot like you, like she said."

"I've got more lifelong friends than I can keep up with now, both of 'em." Russ was not a collector; he traveled light. Everything he owned fit into two large backpacks. If he stumbled upon an old associate in some outback it instantly became like old times, but he never sought out fellowship.

"My friend works with computers," the Belgian said. "He says that one day friends will only be in your laptop. No flesh-and-blood real friends. Hell, I'm a longshoreman; computers won't contain *my* friends." The foreigner's comment passed without a retort from Russ. "I was told that Indians like that one exist only in the movies, that they all use computers and run casinos now. My friend tells me one day I will travel Route 66 on a virtual trip without leaving Antwerp. It would not be the same," the Belgian observed, again ignored by Russ. "You know, I can hike, but there is no time . . ."

Movement out of the corner of Russ's eye startled him. It was the apparition from down the bar. His face resembled sunbaked stone chiseled by the wind. Deep ruts surrounded lonely dark, crystal eyes, too piercing for those of an alcoholic, staring beyond Russ.

The phantom stepped well within Russ's space. His hands pushed ever so slightly up and down while his torso turned in place. His open palms exposed a pronounced set of lifelines set and marked by time. With outstretched arms, he raised his powerful hands over Russ's head, then suddenly thrust them down toward his sides as his mouth opened to let out a monotone chant. His expression never changed. His hands kept rhythm to his chanting as they made short, jerky chops in front of his chest. This display was different from what Russ had observed prior, what Kelly had called a rain dance.

"Better buy him a beer," the Belgian tourist urged.

"Hey, Chief—settle down. When 'Gidget' gets back, I'll buy," Russ offered.

The chanting and dance continued, unaffected by Russ's offer. Kelly darted about the far end of the bar, having trouble keeping up with the surge of fans that began packing in to hear the band.

"He won't stop until it's on the bar in front of him," the Belgian speculated.

"Wow, this is so weird. Does he understand English?" Russ asked. "This doesn't look like the same dance he did down there. I don't think this one is about getting a beer."

"Might be putting a curse on you for trespassing on sacred ground. I saw that in one of your American movies, one with that Redford fellow . . ."

"I don't believe in curses." Russ got off his barstool to increase his comfort zone.

Kelly worked her way back down to Russ, apparently catching their conversation. "That's the first time I've seen him do that particular dance. Here, Chief." Setting down a cold one for the chief, she angled her head to watch him.

The stone-faced old chief gave a slight nod of thanks and then pushed the glass away, stern with those distant eyes, as if he saw far more than the rest of them.

"I've never seen him turn down a beer before." Kelly wiped the bar and continued to stare at the chief. She leaned in and confided, "Chief rarely speaks. He has talked with my dad some, though. Chief told him that he believes that the truth needs few words, that life is to be lived, not talked. He had been orphaned, and was raised speaking only his native tongue, though he became proficient in English." She drew a few more beers. "He was raised by a shaman in a time long before the passage of the American Indian Religious Freedom Act in 1978. He learned the ways of his people, their wisdom from this mentor. His shaman was a renegade named Rearing Horse who taught many religious practices specifically banned by the federal government; he was also a keeper of the powerful Buffalo Pipe."

The Belgian looked hard into the chief's eyes. "Excuse me, fellow . . . I came here from Belgium, and I want to know if you think 'Indian' is offensive? Shoot, this here is the Will Rogers Highway. Give me the truth—like Will Rogers."

The chief stared into a realm beyond the walls of the tavern without responding.

"Is Native American better?" The Belgian's eyebrows arched as he sipped his beer, waiting for a response.

"*Diné*," the chief uttered.

"*Diné*? Why do you say that?" The Belgian looked for guidance from Kelly.

"He's telling you that his people are the *Diné*. He is probably offended by both 'Indian' and 'Native American,'" Kelly offered.

The chief picked up his beer and lifted it to his lips, then stopped, looking directly at Russ. "You have walked the *Nuva'tuk-iya-ovi* where the Kachinas dwell. I sense this, and yours was not a walk of desecration, for your spirit seeks. I see a distressed heart that must be healed. My dance was a healing dance."

Suddenly, Russ felt naked. He glanced between the chief and Kelly. The bartender's lips parted slightly and she gazed at **Russ**, waiting for a response that failed to come. **Russ** picked up his glass and drank until his beer was gone.

"I'll be damned," Kelly uttered.

"Last week in the land of the Cheyenne Sioux, I rested on Coffee

Butte. In each of the four points of the compass I saw a vigorous herd of Buffalo. It was a good omen. The time of redemption is near." The chief set his glass lightly on the bar.

With a snort, Russ slid his mug toward Kelly for a refill. No way was he leaving until the chief had his say.

Russ, the Belgian, and the chief shared another round, then another. Between rounds, Kelly dialed up another potential trail mate despite Russ's protests and without success. Her father had departed for a skydiving event in California, and his friends either didn't answer or were already committed. Russ watched the chief nod as the glass touched his lips, never changing expressions, never contributing further to the conversation or offering to buy a round. Russ and the Belgian shared stories of world travel and wanderlust. It was a flavored talk, a truth base loaded with spice, more for entertainment than fact, but in this they spoke the same language, and none of it mattered. As Russ recounted his stories and listened to the Belgian's enthralling adventures, something sparked, reviving his spirit. It might have been Russ's story about encountering the jaguar in the Amazon, but then again it could have just been the beer.

The crowd grew, sandwiching the trio closer to the bar and within earshot of other patrons. Russ caught skims and grins as the people surrounding them eavesdropped on their stories. Russ glanced at the old chief to see if their talk was having any effect on him. Not once did his expression change, yet he seemed reluctant to move on to another patron. *Why do I attract the crazy types . . . and why am I waiting for the old guy to speak?* Russ wondered as he walked to the men's room. *There's one in every bar, and they always gravitate to me . . .*

Russ stood at the john and listened to the muffled sound of breaking glass, screeching chairs frantic on the old wooden floor, and what must have been a heavy table crashing onto its side. What the heck? He burst out of the men's room into a scene of chaos. The music had stopped, the merriment had stopped, the small talk had stopped, and there was a moment of silence before—

"I hate Indians!" Russ saw huge, tattooed arms waving above the crowd. Russ glanced toward the Belgian but saw nothing of the chief. He looked down toward the floor and spotted the worn felt hat with a single feather tucked into the band. He pushed forward into the pack surrounding what must have been the chief on the floor.

Vaulting over the bar, Kelly showed her athletic prowess as she bounded off stunned patrons to aid the old chief. But she was no match for the three hundred pound lug that hulked over him. She frantically slapped the giant on the back, yet he remained unfazed.

Without a thought, Russ rushed into the chaos. He seized an outstretched arm that had just propelled a rock-hard fist toward the chief's face. His timing superb, Russ deflected the blow. Tumbling to the floor, Russ found himself crushed as if in a vise. Hot, foul breath blew hateful words into his face. Russ struggled, but with each twist the force about him tightened until he could no longer breathe.

"I hate drunken, freeloading Indians, but I hate Indian lovers more!" The words spewing from his assailant's mouth were muffled due to the blood pounding in Russ's head. He tried to turn his head to find relief but couldn't. He forced his words out, all he could manage before his air was gone. "Aargh, you'd have killed him . . . he's old . . ."

Distant voices called for his release. With his face squashed to the floor, all Russ noticed were a dozen shuffling cowboy boots and the odor of the stale, beer-crusted floor. He struggled one last time, to no avail. Straining to look up, he saw the emotionless stare of that damned old Indian hovering over him. The sound of a drumbeat pulsed as Kelly continued to pound on the back of Russ's assailant. Fairly certain he was about to black out, Russ believed he might never regain consciousness. He heard a faint, metallic click. Was that his ribs breaking? Suddenly, the death grip released, and Russ's breathing eased. He blinked as the colossal bully rose to his feet.

Apparently, the bully had felt the cold steel against his temple. The law of the Old West was alive and well, and Kelly's boyfriend was its enforcer. *The cowboy way.* The bully fell spread-eagled on the floor and whimpered like a pup.

"Partner, you interrupted an otherwise perfect performance," the bandleader said through gritted teeth. "You're the unwelcome one, not the Indian." The cowboy's voice was monotone and deliberate. "Shooting you would be a pleasure, but if I don't you'll suffer longer, you wasted piece of buffalo dung."

The bully contorted his face to view the steel against his temple.

"I don't carry to kill, but I will," the cowboy said. "Now get up slowly and walk out the door, and don't ever show your face here again. This is between you and me as it stands, so don't make the mistake of notching it up any. Now move it."

"Dang, here's a story that won't need much added to it." Russ looked up and there stood the Belgian, his hand extended to help him to his feet. Russ closed his eyes. All he wanted to do was catch his breath. He heard the bully lumber toward the exit. Russ bent forward, resting his hands on his knees. Several people patted his back as the crowd dispersed.

Russ nodded to the cowboy. He'd been mistaken in his earlier assessment of the band. They *were* real cowboys. Lately he seemed wrong most of the time. Moments passed as a second silence fell over the crowd. His ribs, bruised but not broken, ached as his lungs inflated. The bully was gone, squeezed out by the crowd and dispatched by the cowboy. The cowboy hugged Kelly and whispered, "You alright, honey?"

Russ reached for the old Indian's shoulder. "Old man, are you alright?"

The old Indian broke his stare and turned toward Russ.

"You saved his life," the old Indian declared in a monotone voice.

"What?" Russ retorted. He stepped back.

"You white men all stick together. I was about to drop him when you got in my way."

"Tell me you didn't say that."

"It is true, but now you will never know." The old man turned away.

"No, I'll never know." Russ shook his head in disbelief and glanced at Kelly. "It looks like people are making for the exit."

"It's over; the band is done. We're all going home with no last call!" shouted Kelly, turning to peck her cowboy on his cheek.

Russ turned to Kelly's beau. "Thanks for stepping in." Russ offered the cowboy his hand and felt the strength instilled by hard work.

"Glad to oblige. Besides, this little gal was beating him to a pulp, and I had to stop it." He placed his hat back on his head and squeezed her again.

"Did you hear what this old Indian said?" Russ whispered as he watched the old man walk to the bar to retrieve his beer.

Kelly snickered. "Forget about it."

"In our culture silence speaks, sometimes louder than words, and the truth needs few words," the chief uttered in a firm tone.

"Yeah, well, I've got to get up early if I expect to hike into Havasupai." Russ brushed sawdust off his pants.

The Belgian held out his hand, brandishing a business card. "This will be a great story back in Antwerp. My biggest fear is that no one will believe me—real cowboy action with an Indian added in to boot. Mister, my name is Carel Boudewijn. If you are ever in Europe, look me up. Here's my address and phone number. Really, look me up. You could verify all this for me. We'll have a great time. What's your name?"

"Russ. Russ Jacobs."

"It was a pleasure meeting you."

"Thanks for the offer, Carel. You never know. I might just take you up on it." Russ shook his hand. "I've been to Switzerland and Italy but never ventured north."

"Take him up on it. You'll have a wonderful time. The people in Europe love Americans. If you can manage to be a *friendly* tourist, they'll treat you just fine," Kelly offered.

"Another place you've been?" Russ raised one eyebrow toward her.

"Absolutely. Backpacked and jumped trains all over." She leaned into her cowboy's chest. "Hey, about Havasupai, I'm sorry. I called everyone I know trying to find someone to hike with you, but everyone is tied up."

"That's alright. Going it alone is my normal way, and it's

probably better for me."

"I will take you."

Kelly's eyes lit up, and Russ turned to face the old Indian staring back at him.

"You go to visit the people of the blue-green waters, the sacred waters of truth?" the chief asked.

"I'm going into Havasupai, and I don't need any old Indian tagging along." Russ did not feel very charitable toward the old chief at the moment.

"It is the valley of the people of the blue-green waters. I will take you," the chief insisted.

"Old man, I understand that it's a long, hard hike," Russ countered. "I doubt you are in a condition to keep up with me. Thanks, but I'll go it alone."

"You need protection," the Indian said.

"Protection?" Russ snorted. "You sure have some ego."

"You can't fight flesh-and-blood white men, let alone the spirits of my people."

"Look, we're talking about a hike down into barren landscape where it's 120 degrees in the shade. We aren't going into battle."

"It is the land I know. There is no need for you to describe it to me. You have never been there. I need to go to the blue-green waters. It's settled. Tomorrow we go."

"Forget it, Chief. Good night, all," Russ said and finally headed to the door.

"He needs me," the old chief informed Kelly.

She nodded in agreement. "Yep. He needs you."

CHAPTER 3

Morning arrived much too quickly. The tent smelled of stale alcohol. Russ's mouth was dry as the desert air, and his tongue felt thick. He grabbed a clean pair of jeans, unzipped the tent flap, and struggled to crawl out of the cramped quarters of his two-man tent. He emerged slowly and slipped on his jeans one leg at a time. He did a little hop that shook his head a little too hard as he sucked in his gut to close his fly. The smell of pine straw warmed by the morning sun filled his lungs. As he breathed in the sweet morning air, he realized how tender his chest still felt after the constrictor's death grip last night. He squinted bleary eyes in the bright Arizona sun, and dry grass crunched beneath his bare feet. It felt wholesome. The campground was near empty except for a few rigs with air conditioning.

"White man sleeps too late."

Russ jumped and raised his arm in an act of defense. Still punchy from last night's fight, Russ clenched his fist. He struggled to focus on the darkened silhouette eclipsing the rising sun.

"Bad nerves?" the voice continued.

There sat the old chief, cross-legged on top of the campsite's picnic table. Russ moved slightly so that the sun was not directly behind the voice. He finally made out the hardened face of the old Indian.

"How did you . . . ?" Russ blinked, his hand cupped above his eyes.

"I am Indian tracker." The voice was self-assured.

"I drove here. What kind of tracks did you follow?" Russ shook his head and sensed weirdness to it all.

"White men are predictable; there are only so many options for them."

"Is that right? Well, what kind of option do Indians have? One option might be for you to head home."

"Home is where I am headed; I will travel with you."

"No, we are *not* traveling together."

"Havasupai, it is my home. It is a sacred place, home."

"Havasupai is just dirt, rocks, and hot air. It is just a challenge, not home and not sacred to me." Russ took a bite of a granola bar.

"It is all the things you say; it is just rocks and dirt, but it also touches your spirit. It is home."

"It doesn't matter what it is; I'm going alone. It's a long drive just to get to the rim of the canyon, and then a very strenuous hike to the Havasupai region."

"You never went to war." The old chief looked into Russ's eyes.

"No? What makes you say that? What does that have to do with anything? You're just trying to change the subject." The statement was pointed, not spoken in general terms, and Russ felt its jab. Again, Russ felt naked, as he had last night when the old man mentioned his wounded heart. He also still felt hungry, and searched in his pack for a piece of jerky and a hardtack. He made an offer, gesturing to the chief to take a piece.

"No thank you, I just had an egg sandwich . . . I can tell that you lack fighting skills." The old man's eyes wrinkled with a grin, and Russ rolled his own eyes with a shake of his head. Somehow he had pictured this old relic reaching into a stream, pulling out a trout and eating it raw.

"What is that look for?" the chief asked.

"Never mind. Lacking fighting skills, that's not what you meant, was it?" Russ saw through the old man.

"Why does the question bother you?" Chief tilted his head curiously.

"Never mind. Let's stick with my fighting abilities. I saved your hide back at that bar, you ungrateful old coot." Russ bit down hard on a piece of jerky, ripping it.

"You should feel honored. The white man should have felt grateful; I felt only disappointment," the chief responded.

Russ nearly choked on a bit of hardtack. "Honored? Disappointed?"

"I let you impress that woman who serves the beer." The chief chuckled as he reached for a piece of jerky.

"What? You were about to be crushed. I never try to impress anyone, old man, and I gave up on women a long time ago. I was just saving your mangy butt!" Russ began to fuss with his gear, readying it to be packed.

"I am a warrior; I have been proven in battle many times. There was no need for you to rescue me."

"At one time you may have been a warrior, but that day is gone." Russ stopped himself. He'd crossed a line. The chief did deserve respect if in fact he had served in a war.

"She is very pretty for a white woman. She reminds me of a squaw I had once; I think it is the way she smiles. Do you have a woman?"

"I did a long time ago . . ." Russ caught himself. "Wait a minute. We're not talking about my women, and I don't want to hear about yours either. Let's talk about last night. What was all the fuss about?"

The chief silently stared off toward the highway, watching a car glide past. The muscles in his cheeks flexed, and his teeth gritted. Moments passed while Russ let his question stand, waiting for a reply. He began taking down his tent but kept glancing at the chief.

"Young white woman insulted me," the chief finally muttered.

"A woman insulted you?"

"She said I was a disgrace to Native Americans. She said I played a stereotypical Indian. Then her man said he hates all Indians, stereo or not. He did not impress me as bright. I consider myself a human being, of the *Diné* people. Am I a disgrace to human beings?" The chief gave Russ a hard look.

"Well, Chief, your style went out before I was born, and I don't really think we can eliminate hate in this world. We live in a world of hypersensitive feelings. You have to walk like you are tiptoeing on eggs. It's not you; it's our times. The world is turned upside down. We've traveled through the looking glass."

The chief took a long breath and turned toward Mt. Humphreys. He ran his fingers through his long hair. Russ didn't mean to insult him. He felt all the frustrations of the world of word games. He hoped it might make the chief go away. Finally, the chief turned, his eyes molten, burning Russ with the heat of his glare.

"I am a human being. I carry the heritage of my people in my heart. Young Native Americans are proficient in texting, computers, and all such nonsense. I have even seen some wear the look of the clown with their pants pulled down below their butt. They have no soul. They eat the flesh of white man's meat that has no spirit—flesh of creatures raised in pens—and they drink of this thing called pop culture, which has no substance. Now I am told that I am stereotypical. These young ones are the stereotypical homies with no class or balance. I am the last to hold the great knowledge of my people, but none want to hear of it. This makes my heart sad. I see into your heart and know that you have a great emptiness, a wound that needs healed. But you too reject my offer."

Russ stood speechless, holding his rolled sleeping bag. It all seemed so weird; he'd just met this man last night, and for all he knew he was some escaped crazy. Yet, here he was, engaged in a conversation that he felt deep in his soul. All Russ wanted was to hike into the canyon, see its splendor, and move on; he didn't want to be involved. Yet there was something strange in the chief's insight; this crazy man knew things about him. How was it possible? The old man spoke vaguely, and yet Russ could sense the old man knew more. Part of him wanted to find out what it was about, but the reasonable part of his psyche told him to run, and run fast.

"Well, time moves on. Hell, it's almost the twenty-first century, and I gotta run."

"Run from the truth, and you will stumble. The truth of the

twentieth century is still the truth in the twenty-first century. I speak the truth, what I feel, and my tongue is straight. Tourists, I tell them what they want to hear. You are not a tourist, I can tell. Don't misunderstand my words." The chief's eyes cooled; he took slow, deliberate breaths and seemed relaxed.

Russ's tension eased.

"Well, honestly, I'm running late and don't have time for small talk." Russ stuffed his tent and sleeping bag into the trunk of his rental car.

"Humph . . ." The old chief grunted as he turned away. "My talk is not small. I know you are no tourist. You did not climb the mountain as so many do, to enjoy the view. You went there to look into your heart, to find your spirit. Maybe to heal it. And I think you have been at this healing a long time."

Russ's hands clenched the open trunk lid, and he rested his head on his outstretched arms. He felt a frustration not only with this old man but also with the torment churning inside him. Russ suppressed his thoughts and feelings for everything he did. He didn't dwell on why he climbed mountains and hacked through jungles. He did want to confront his reasons, but he had always told himself the same cloaked lies he told his women. Russ closed his eyes but saw visions on his eyelids, visions of past adventures, misadventures, and lies. He slammed the trunk lid closed.

"Look, you're too old to go where I'm going, and my spirit and troubles are none of your concern." Russ was impressed with the old man's insight, but he didn't need the burden of being responsible for an old coot who might expire at any moment. Still, Russ felt strangely drawn to him.

He surveyed the old character who sat looking off toward the prairies, picking his teeth with a dry piece of straw. Russ was unsure of where the actor ended and the real man began, both in himself and in this Indian.

"I have been where you go many times, and now, once more, I go. Listen to my thoughts: Your people put buffalo into pens, then show their children and say, *see the buffalo,* but what they see is not a buffalo; it is merely meat. The spirit is not there. It is not a buffalo. If you want to see a buffalo, you must walk through his herd and feel his hot breath, smell his odor, and feel anxious that he may charge." The chief turned and looked into Russ's eyes. "*Then* you can say that you have seen a buffalo."

Russ froze. For just that moment the chief's eyes were wild and wolflike. There was more to him than just an old man in the skin of an Indian. Russ sensed a fire about him, even with his advanced years.

"Tourists come to our sacred lands and drive by, or they hike so they can tell all their friends where they have been, but really they have been nowhere. They never experience its spirit. They come, but are never really here. I think you are different. I think you want to capture a spirit—your spirit. I think you need me to guide you through the sacred land of my people to find your way. My body is old, but my spirit is still strong and can still overcome things that a strong body with a weak spirit could not."

CHAPTER 4

The old man sat, still picking his teeth with the straw of grass, looking far off into the distance. Russ wondered what the chief saw; he saw only the vast plain beyond the pines. Not wanting to argue or even respond, Russ tossed his day pack into his rental car and figured he would just drive off, leaving the old man to sit on the picnic table. No more words exchanged, Russ hopped into the driver's seat.

"I will show you a shortcut," the chief declared. Shocked by the voice beside him, Russ flinched and spun his head to the side as he clenched the steering wheel so tight that his knuckles turned white.

"How the—when did you get in the car? I saw you on that table a second ago."

"Drive." The chief gestured toward the main road. "You were shocked that I ate an egg sandwich; you probably thought I eat raw fish from a stream." Russ's jaw slacked. He felt a chill even in the Arizona heat.

"You can't hike with me! I'll drop you off at your teepee, how's that?" Feeling defeat, Russ dropped the shifter into drive.

"Just take me to the trailhead," the chief commanded. He crossed his arms on his chest and closed his eyes. "You are not what I first thought."

Russ felt the jab. He had been trying to shake the old man, but as the chief reflected back his real image, Russ was crushed by his own self-centeredness. It was all so convoluted and confusing. Russ struggled with the rejection. Released, and yet disheartened, Russ mulled over potential conversations in silence, listening to the resonance of the rubber on the road. He rejected them all.

"How old are you, Chief?" he asked.

"I was born this morning with the knowledge of all my other days. I am only as old as this moment."

"You talk in riddles." Russ took a deep breath.

"God is reborn in the hearts of men over and over, only to be crucified again and again. It is the way of men." The chief raised one eyebrow and glanced at Russ out of the corner of his eye. "Jesus said, 'Forgive them Lord, for they know not what they do.' He didn't mean it for just that day, but for all the days men crucify Him. Even now, they know not what they do. Each day I am born anew, but even with the wisdom of days gone by, each day I stumble and fall, for I am flawed. But tomorrow I may live again." The chief closed his eyes.

"What's the use? Fine, but you're on your own at the trailhead," Russ muttered through gritted teeth. The chief beat him at every turn. Since the moment they had met, the chief had outthought, outmaneuvered, and outwitted him. Russ again pondered the words he just heard.

"All my life," the chief murmured without opening his eyes.

"What? All your life?"

"On my own . . . all my life . . . way too long." The chief grinned, then turned a half-opened eye to peek at Russ with satisfaction.

"How old *are* you?" Russ repeated in a pleading tone.

"I am ancient. I have lived longer than most. How old do I look?"

"My guess is eighty-something, but not because you look it. You don't look eighty, but you have to be. I mean, based on some of the things you've told me."

"Well, then. Let's just say eighty-two."

"Eighty-two," Russ repeated in amazement. It dawned on him that he was facing a man from his father's generation. "My father would be eighty-two if he had lived," Russ said aloud as he glanced at Chief.

In Russ's mind, his father had never aged. Struck down in his prime, he lived in Russ's memory with the vitality of a fifty-two-year-old. So much time had passed since that fateful night, the night that robbed him of the chance to reconcile with his father.

Leaving the Flagstaff region at the chief's direction, Russ soon turned onto a fairly wide, well-maintained gravel road. Pulling to the side, Russ unfurled his map to verify the chief's shortcut. A lanky, grizzled cowboy worked nearby, mending a barbed-wire fence.

The only sign of man for miles around was the fence; the cowboy; and his dusty, worn-out pickup truck. The desolate track stretched out as far as the eye could see, without any other sign of life. Parched skeletons of mescal and Parry's agave danced in waves of heat. The only shade appeared on the face of the cowboy, cast by the brim of his Stetson. A mistaken turn in this country could mean death. A vague line on the map looked like it might be this road, and if so, it did lead directly to the Havasupai reservation.

"Hey! Excuse me!" Russ shouted out to the cowboy.

The cowboy looked toward Russ but didn't speak; his gnarled hands continued twisting the barbed wire with pliers. His eyes lurked somewhere in the shadow of his hat; the only visible feature of his face was the tip of his nose as it extended beyond the shadow. He appeared deaf or completely dispassionate.

"Can you hear me?"

The Stetson slowly nodded once.

"Does this road head over to Havasupai?" Russ asked in a pleasant tone.

The cowboy turned away without a response. His broad shoulders and back blocked his work from view as if to hide some secret technique.

"Did you hear me? Does this road lead to Havasupai?" Russ spoke louder, but still held a pleasant tone.

"Don't know where this road leads, never had a need to travel it. Far as I know it goes straight to Hell."

"What? You really don't know where this road goes? You look like a local to me." Russ let out a nervous chuckle.

"You heard me right. There ain't nothin' out there but Injuns and dust, and too much of both." The cowboy turned back toward Russ and pointed his pliers at him. "I wouldn't try it alone if'n I was you, and if you do make it . . . well, let's just say . . . never mind."

"Never mind what?"

"I said more than I need to already."

"I'm not alone; I got the chief here with me."

The cowboy lowered his head to peer in Russ's window; his eyes were cold.

"You been in the sun too long, better get going back to town. A lone man can die out here. If you choose to proceed, I'd shut off your air so's you don't overheat." The cowboy stood straight up and stepped back toward the fence.

"Thanks for the advice." The words were not lost on Russ, but he chose to ignore them.

This place could kill a fool without a blink. Tires spit gravel as Russ headed down the endless ribbon of dirt road. The pavement disappeared behind him along with the cowboy and his truck. Only the barbwire fence marked the presence of man as it ran with the road, its pickets ticking off blurred seconds as they whizzed past. It fenced in empty, worthless land as far as Russ could determine. Undulates of heat, barren moonscape, and loneliness were what he faced, and he found no comfort in the companionship of a geriatric Indian, even one with seemingly mystical powers.

"Chief, I hope you know what you're talking about."

The old chief stared out onto the vast chaparral. "Years ago I walked this route, alone. I know what I am talking about. I am at home in the desert. I might still be able to walk it, but riding suits me just fine."

"It seemed like that cowboy couldn't see you, Chief. He was kind of a creepy guy." Russ felt surrounded by creepy people. In this desolation, it took only two to feel surrounded.

"He couldn't see me. I didn't want to be seen. It is the art of invisibility."

"You didn't want to be seen, so he didn't see you? You don't think so? Well that's creepy too." Russ glanced repeatedly between the road and the chief as if to verify that he could see him, that he was real.

"It is in man's nature to be blind; rarely does he look beyond himself. This one's eyes were not sharp; they were dulled by hate. Hatred puts a person at a disadvantage. I used it to my advantage, that's all," the chief retorted. "Invisibility protects very well. Have you never experienced it?"

"I'd have to say no."

"You are a lucky man if you have never stood in line at a checkout and had the clerk ask the person behind you if they needed help, or went to a gathering where no one acknowledged you when you spoke. It is just that you were not in control of it. That is the difference. It's natural, not mystical."

"Invisibility? I guess." Looking over at the chief, Russ felt drawn by his mystique. The old man looked straight ahead, yet it was as though he looked at Russ without using his eyes. No, he looked *into* Russ somehow. Even in the intense desert heat, a chill ran through Russ. The chief closed his eyes, but that gave Russ no comfort, for he still felt watched. Without the air conditioner the heat was insufferable, and he couldn't believe the old Indian could think about sleeping.

"Aaah" was the chief's only response before Russ heard him snore.

CHAPTER 5

The once-wide ribbon of gravel narrowed to one lane after thirty miles, then turned so rough that fifteen miles per hour was a push. Ten more miles and the road became nothing more than two parallel tracks in the grit. "Four Wheel Drive Only Beyond This Point" read a sandblasted and weathered sign.

Stopping the car, Russ walked up a small mound to scout the territory ahead. The sun overwhelmed him, drawing on his shoulders and reaching through the top of his hat. Far off to the north the plain appeared to melt into what Russ assumed was the Grand Canyon. Dried brittlebush, canyon ragweed, desert lavender, and a sparse setting of prickly pear and yucca spread across the dusty, red soil. Russ kicked at the soil, knowing that inches beneath the dust an endless rock layer stretched out.

On the flats toward the north an invisible finger tickled the dust, rousting it to take flight. An invisible force swirled ever faster. A spiraling cloud of dust suggested a creature hundreds of feet high, the birth of a dust devil. It rushed across the plain, frantically trying to sustain itself, but collapsed as quickly as it was born. Witnessing a birth and a death on the wind left Russ feeling insignificant, a fallible creature on the edge of an unforgiving, endless universe, his own time growing short.

The sun-drawn surface seemed incapable of supporting life, and yet Russ watched as a Chuckwalla darted from under a brittlebush just a few feet from him. The clear blue sky stretched unblemished to the horizon. Once more Russ witnessed a set of twin dust devils rise and fall.

Russ cupped his hand over his brow. The sun's glare neutralized the effectiveness of his sunglasses. The tracks of this trail disappeared on a dry, rocky hill about a quarter mile ahead. Four-wheel-drive vehicles indeed—the compact rental car did not seem adequate for the challenge. Between where he stood and the barren hill, Russ could see deep ruts cut in the soil, deep enough to hang the car up on the frame. *What is over the hill? What if I get there and can't turn around?* Turning around now would mean this day would be lost to hiking. Continuing might involve being stranded without adequate food and water. Distance seemed to have more meaning when calculated in terms of a four-day walk, two days' worth of water, and 12 hours a day of cloudless, brutal skies. A breeze like that from the exhaust of a forced air furnace ruffled Russ's hair, a dry heat, the kind that sucks the moisture and often the life out of any exposed organism.

The chief leaned against the hood with his arms folded across his chest. He looked at home, his demeanor one of complete composure, while Russ was on the verge of a meltdown. The sheer enormity and emptiness of this land never ceased to astound him. Russ thought it strange that he felt the way he did. He was a seasoned traveler and had rarely felt overwhelmed, yet now he did.

"Devil's Claw," Chief muttered. The words inexplicably annoyed Russ—not the words themselves but the sound of Chief's voice. "What?" Russ looked puzzled and briefly glanced back over his shoulder—not long enough to see anything, if there had been anything to see.

"Devil's Claw." The chief twisted his hand without unfolding his crossed arms; his index finger pointed at Russ's feet.

Russ looked down. On his shoelaces and socks clung strange pods with long tentacles, spiny little devils. Russ tried kicking them off, and then finally bent down to pick them off.

"Devil's Claw . . . that's a good name . . . what a pain," Russ complained as he gingerly untangled them from his foot.

"They're known as 'hitchhikers.' That's how they move about the desert. Hitching rides with large animals."

Russ refrained from a comment about their likeness to someone he was dealing with, but he gave the chief a look, suspecting that the old man knew his thoughts.

"I call it 'ihug.' Some say it is the unicorn plant. Where you see an annoyance, I see food. Knowledge of such things is the difference between life and death." The chief grinned. "That is what makes the desert so special. You learn to appreciate God's miracles, for they are subtle. In the big forests, you are among so many that you often take them for granted."

Again, Russ restrained his comment.

"I think we need to turn around, Chief." Russ flipped his keys in the air and caught them backhanded.

"It says four-wheel drive beyond this point?" The chief pointed to a weathered sign.

"That's right! So we go back." Russ swaggered toward the car, finally feeling in control. He made an instant decision to drive Chief into Flagstaff, dump him somewhere, and take the paved road to Havasupai in the morning.

"And how many wheels to head back?" The chief stood firmly against the front of the car. Russ placed his hand on the fender but quickly retrieved it from the searing-hot surface. Russ shook his hand briefly to cool it down. Chief's facial expression brought him up short.

"What?" Russ asked impatiently.

"You don't have four wheels." The chief pursed his lips.

"No?"

"You've only got three wheels."

"What?"

Chief nodded toward the wheel on the driver's side. Taking off his hat, Russ slammed it to the ground. The front tire was flat. Fine dust plumed into the air with a kick from Russ's boot. The heat was getting to him—no, it *had* gotten to him, and he acted out of character. He looked at Chief, embarrassed by his outburst. He closed his eyes to clear them of sudden double vision. His knowledge of survival in the backcountry had been usurped by his excessive drinking the night before.

"Give me the keys; I'll change it," Chief offered. "You just sit and breathe deep to relieve your stress."

"No. I'll do it. You go sit down. When I'm done, we're heading back." Russ struggled to regain his pride, but like quicksand, the more he struggled the deeper he sank. He had not been drinking enough water, and the effects were obvious. His skin was dry and red, and he wasn't sweating. His head ached. He had been telling himself it was just a hangover.

"No. The canyon is right over there." Chief nodded his head toward a vanishing point on the horizon.

"Chief. I originally said you weren't coming with me. In my mind it was settled. I was going alone."

Chief looked off toward the place where the plain melted away. He showed no reaction to Russ's words. He handed Russ a water jug, then signaled him to sit down.

"Not only are you here with me, but I keep doing things your way. What is going on?" Russ stammered. He felt a little confused and weak.

"You are just a wise man for that. Now you must drink water and rest. You are on the verge of a serious condition. Alcohol from last night has worked to dehydrate you. Drink."

"What? Look at this place! We're a hundred miles into nowhere. If we break down or get stuck, we'll only last a couple of days. We already have a flat tire. So how wise is that?"

"Ha. You can only last a couple of days? Did you think the canyon was in a shopping mall? This is where you are wise. I am here to take care of you."

"No, no . . . I . . ."

"We are here; therefore, this is somewhere, not nowhere. We make it what it is. I make it my home. You make it your threat. Sit, breathe . . . please sit. When a man panics, he fades like a dust devil. The desert provides plenty. We will be all right; trust me."

The old man sat at the edge of the road in the shade of a lone whitethorn acacia. He crossed his legs and held out his hands palm up as Russ dropped to the ground beside him. Russ thought the old goat must have some sort of hypnotic way about him, for he could not resist the command. Russ filled his mouth with water, swished it around, and let it trickle down the back of his throat as Chief had instructed. The key was to drink slowly, to do everything slowly. He knew this, yet he had let himself succumb to the allure of an alcohol-induced retreat from reality.

"Close your eyes. Slowly breathe in the desert spirit's smell. With your mind, see the redness of the land. Taste the fruits of the desert. Hear the silence of peace . . . Aaaaajaaa, aaaajooo . . ." Chief's low-pitched chant relaxed Russ almost to the point of sleep. His heart rate dropped, his breathing slowed, and the dryness in his mouth was quenched. He continued to take small sips of water that he slowly let drain down his throat; it occurred without thought. It was an automatic function as much as breathing or the pumping of his heart.

Opening his eyes after an indeterminate time, Russ saw Chief seated in the passenger's seat, staring stone-faced out the side window. The spare was installed on the back, the rear tire rotated to the front. Russ sat perplexed, then looked at his watch. Forty-five minutes had passed. He felt refreshed and in control of himself.

"We should go." Chief motioned to Russ to get in but did not look at him.

"How did you change the flat?" Russ gasped.

"It is done. What does it matter how? I'm an Indian, not Amish. I know cars inside out. Now take me to the trailhead. We are not turning back." Chief turned toward Russ.

"Right! Yes! We'd better get going." Russ looked at Chief, amazed and refreshed with self-confidence as well as confidence in Chief. Russ jumped up and ran to the driver's side of the car.

"Yes, and ride the high ridges of the road. Don't drop into the ruts, or our frame will hang up. Picture us floating over the ground. My fate is in your hands, paleface, and I am feeling too old and feeble to walk." Chief's monotone voice seemed surreal. He gave a wry grin, then closed his eyes.

"The secret success of a rain dance is timing." Chief never opened his eyes.

Without uttering a word, Russ drove the car forward over the small hill and up the rocky slope while straddling the deep ruts. Soon the worn road was replaced by white markers painted on large, flat rocks. At times Russ slowed to adjust for changes in the terrain, but made steady progress. He straddled and then inched over pointed boulders that could rip the oil pan and listened for any sound of contact.

Ten miles of vehicular rock-climbing found them dropping down toward a familiar-looking set of parallel lines in the red desert dirt. It looked just like the road they had left before entering the rocks. Soon the road widened, and a cloud of red dust rose behind them on a path leading to an intersection with a paved road. An arrow-shaped sign announced "Havasupai" and pointed to the right. Relief overwhelmed Russ as he spun out onto the macadam and sped toward his destination.

"Good work. I never had any doubts. Did you?" Chief asked.

"No, none whatsoever." Russ looked straight ahead, his hair blowing in the hot breeze.

Chief simply grunted.

"Chief, I'll sign you in on my hiking reservation—no pun intended. But after that we part company."

"Roger that, *Kemosabi*. You have proven to me your ability to take care of yourself."

Russ shook his head in disbelief at the old chief's high opinion of himself.

CHAPTER 6

Pulling in at the trailhead parking lot, Russ parked and then sorted through his gear. He wanted only necessary weight. He looked at his tent and his sleeping bag. A tent offered shade, and it zipped shut to keep crawly things out. The bag only offered warmth, and there would be enough of that, even at night, this time of year. He left the bag, cinched his pack to his back, and walked toward the trail check-in hut. He completely blocked out thoughts of Chief. He would sign him in and be done with him.

The lot was nearly full; there would be plenty of hikers to hook up with for safety if he chose, but he knew he wouldn't. Chief sauntered along behind Russ, his strange pouch slung over his right shoulder. Hiking into the canyon would take days at his pace, though it was only eight miles down to the village.

"Afternoon, can I help you?" asked a dark-eyed young woman dressed in a formfitting ranger uniform. Her straight black hair framed an inviting smile. The brilliance of her white teeth accentuated her dark, flawless complexion.

"Hi, um yes, I have a reservation to hike." Russ removed his pack and placed it beside him.

"You're getting a very late start. The sun will be at full strength. Most people prefer to start while the sun is low. Under what name?"

She poised her hands over the keyboard.

"Huh?" he said, distracted by the chief approaching him from behind.

"Your reservation. Under what name?"

"Oh, probably under Colton Jacobs, my nephew. He made all the arrangements."

"Where is he?" Her eyes narrowed, and a line formed above the bridge of her nose.

"Hurt. He had an accident on Mt. Humphreys. We had planned to do this together, but he won't be able to make it."

"Sorry to hear about your nephew. Is he going to be alright?" She had a skeptical look on her face.

"Oh yes, I got him down and to a hospital. His wife will take care of him."

"That's good, but now you will be alone? It's not advised to hike solo. I won't stop you, but I suggest you team up with someone on the trail." She started typing into her computer.

"That is my plan, but there is also this old chief. I told him he could use Colton's spot." He aimed his thumb up over his shoulder. "We aren't really together," he added.

"Excuse me? All I see is an old stray dog." The ranger raised her eyebrows and strained to see another person. She rose up out of her seat and leaned across the counter.

Russ spun around to scan the parking lot. The only sign of life around the hundred or so parked cars was an old stray dingo-looking dog. Russ stepped out of the hut to get a better look, but found no sign of Chief. The only building was the check-in shed. The edges of the lot ended in a sheer drop, and the back of the lot was chiseled out of a cliff face.

"Well, I guess it's just me then."

"I need a driver's license and a credit card. Mr. Colton Jacobs has a Russell Jacobs listed on the reservation."

"That would be me. Here." Russ handed her his ID and credit card.

"Okay. Here's your permit. Carry it with you all the time; you are in the Indian Nation now, and there are members of the tribe who don't appreciate visitors." She reached over and retrieved a printout from the printer. "This is a list of rules. Now, remember, you will be under the jurisdiction of the tribe police. They are serious fellows. Don't leave your equipment unattended. Here's a map, and always keep in mind that the pack animals have the right of way, so get out of their way."

"Thanks for the insight."

"One more thing. Do you have plenty of water? I know it sounds stupid, but I have to ask. You would be surprised by the number of people who think they can make it on a liter."

"Absolutely. If I carried nothing else, it would be water."

"There are springs in the canyon, but we don't recommend counting on them."

"I've got plenty," Russ assured her.

"Yes, but make sure you drink it. It's weird, but the more dehydrated you get, the less you crave water. It can get you into serious trouble. Drink it before you crave it."

CHAPTER 7

Russ thanked her and set off down the trail. He hadn't taken a hundred steps when the flash of sun on something off to the side of the trail caught his eye. He stooped to get a better look. The dragonfly pin on the chief's bag was staring back at him. He stood and scanned the area, then called out, "Chief? You here, Chief?"

"What did you find?" the ranger called out, but Russ refrained from answering. Instead, he briskly walked back toward her. The stray dog followed close behind, wagging its tail. "What did you find?" she repeated in a lower tone.

"This bag belongs to the Indian that I said rode with me from Flagstaff. It seems strange because he was very protective of it. It was stashed in the rocks at the beginning of the trail. It wasn't just dropped. I'm a little concerned. It would be bad enough for that old man to be wandering about, but without his pack—well, it doesn't make sense." Russ handed the pack to the ranger. "What do you think?"

"I'll put it in my office for safekeeping, but first I want to get on the radio and report this to the tribal police. Would you mind waiting while I do that, just in case they have any questions? It won't take long."

"No, I don't mind waiting." Russ leaned against a post of the porch. The screen door squeaked, then slammed shut. He could hear the static and squelch of the radio, then garbled communications. Russ watched the old stray, still perched where he had ordered it to stay. It had never looked anywhere but at Russ. The screen door screeched and slammed again as the ranger stepped outside.

"The report is filed. They'll be on the lookout for him. Do you mind if I walk to the first bend in the trail with you?" The ranger looked concerned. "I doubt he could have walked out of range in this amount of time. I also want to look over the edge, just in case he might have tripped or slipped off the side. It has happened."

"Let's have a go at it. I'm already way behind schedule." They walked to the trailhead, and the ranger stepped to the very edge. Her movement unnerved Russ. He stood back a couple of steps as she inched along the edge. She shook her head, and the sheen of her long black hair glistened in the sun.

Russ walked ahead, looking for signs that might indicate a stumble or a slip but saw no trace.

The ranger stepped back onto the trail, and they walked toward the first bend. "I couldn't see anything down there. It doesn't mean he's not down there, though. These cliffs have ledges and crevasses that can hide a lot, depending on your vantage point. Hopefully, we'll see him stumbling along down below. I might need your help getting him back up."

"At this point, nothing else matters. If I never get started today, I don't care. I'm in no hurry. It's not like I have any place to be anytime soon."

"This heat is brutal. You're going to be tortured on this hike."

"If I don't go down today, then I'll just sleep in my car tonight."

"Sorry, no overnight camping in the parking lot. The only camping allowed on the reservation is down at the campground or in the lower valley."

"Are you kidding me?" Russ looked at her in a pleading way.

"I'm dead serious." She had an impish grin. "If I catch you, I'll fine you. I leave here around five and get back around seven. I can't speak for the police, but I doubt if they'll look in your car. They usually just do a drive-through, so they probably wouldn't see a person if he slid down on the seat." She gave Russ a wink.

They peered around a point in the cliff face. The precipice reached hundreds of feet over their heads and dropped twice as far into the canyon. They could see the trail switchbacking for a mile and a half along the cliff face until it disappeared around another point. There was no sign of hikers, no Chief, but a rider on horseback rounded the point below with pack animals in tow. He moved quickly up the grade toward the ranger and Russ. While the pair stood and waited for his approach, the ranger once again stepped to the edge and searched the rocks below.

Russ wanted to grab her arm but resisted; he knew it wouldn't be appreciated. Instead, he backed up toward the upward side of the trail and leaned against the rocks. He wanted to be on the inside as the pack team approached. The ranger joined him the moment before the packhorses arrived.

The rider on the lead horse looked weathered and unbreakable. His outsized hands clutched the reins with an authority the beast surely respected. He wore a black felt hat much like Chief's, a light-blue denim shirt, and black denim trousers. His hair hung to mid-back and was as black as the horse he rode. He slowed to a halt next to the ranger. The rider sat unfazed by his position on the precipice, but once more Russ struggled to contain himself. As much as he loved adventure, he could do without this particular peril.

The ranger held her hand against her brow to shade her eyes from the sun as she looked up at the rider. "We are looking for an old man walking alone. He wouldn't be far down the trail. Have you seen anyone?"

"No, I saw no one." The horse danced on the edge of the cliff.

"It's a bad time of day for a ride up the trail."

"Humph, yes, but it is an emergency. The helicopter is out for maintenance. I will rest the horse, then go back down. Big money talks, and I listen."

"That's dangerous. Big money is talking?"

"The Japanese made it worthwhile. They made a big offer to bring them what they need."

"Well, be careful. Would you watch out for an old man?"

"Yes." The rider shook his reins, nudged his mount's ribs with his heels, and was off, the pack animals in tow. The smell of hot horseflesh filled the air and mingled with earthy dust.

"Watch out for him on his descent. When you hear him coming, put yourself to the inside. If someone goes off the edge, no one may realize it for a long time." The ranger gripped Russ's elbow.

"Gotcha. Believe me, I am warned."

Russ watched the horses as they lumbered up the trail, half lost in a cloud of dust.

"It doesn't look like there's much point in me going beyond here. Are you going to be heading on down or coming back up with me?"

Russ pondered for a moment as he looked down the trail. The view was intoxicating, the heat was excruciating, and the trail looked lonely. He sighed in resignation. "I think I'll keep going. It was nice walking and talking with you."

"Look for the Watchers; when you see them, you are near the village."

"Watchers?" It sounded mysterious. She meant it to sound mysterious, he was sure.

"Two great stone spires that tower over the canyon. Our legend predicts that one day they will fall. When they do, the canyon will be sealed forever, and no one will enter or leave." Her eyes widened to accentuate her tale.

"Ha, I hope it doesn't happen this week." Russ chuckled as she gave him a wink.

"You take care of yourself. I wish I was on duty when you're scheduled to come up, but those are my off days."

They shook hands and Russ started back down the incline, the dog trailing behind him.

CHAPTER 8

Russ whistled a tune that he would repeat over and over as he walked: the "Colonel Bogey March." He chuckled to himself. Why this tune? Then it struck him—the horseman was on an errand for a group of Japanese tourists—*The Bridge on the River Kwai*.

The solar radiance had already punished him for staying out too late last night; now it upped the ante. The trail offered no mercy, no sign of shade for as far as Russ could see. His mind flashed images from *The Bridge on the River Kwai*. He had empathy for the men working in the tortuous heat on an epic mission of futility. It had nothing to do with the Japanese. This was not the caressing sun of home; this sun turned unprotected flesh into rawhide.

With squinted eyes, he looked back but saw no sign of Chief, the stray dog, or the horseman. Alone, he also saw no sign of other hikers on the trail ahead. In the stillness, he heard his own breathing, his heart, and the crunch of the soil beneath his feet. Whistling helped him with his sudden feeling of aloneness. He realized that it was the first time in days he had actually been all by himself.

He wiped his brow with a dampened kerchief, and the evaporating residue felt cool on his skin. The heat was getting to him. The ranger warned him that the afternoon sun would punish him. It was too hot for where his mind had wandered. He wanted happy thoughts to lighten the burdens of the hike. He stopped and stood on the outer edge of the trail. A spectacle unfolded before him, full of dramatic contrasts, a story millions of years old. He sipped his water appreciatively. His life had little meaning compared to the history of Havasupai.

The canyon spectacle intoxicated. Sheer cliffs of exotic colors and textures rose in layers toward a cloudless, azure sky. The bartender had said she wasn't a bartender but a hiker. In that moment, he understood what she meant as she had offered to refill his mug. The canyon offered up its own drink—a libation of the senses. Despite interrupted thoughts, leg cramps that knotted in muscles still tight from Humphreys, and ribs tender from the bar fight, he plodded along, putting one foot in front of the other, drinking of the splendor of the rocks. Occasionally, he sipped a little water, but always it was spiked with canyon concentrate.

He looked back on the trail, expecting to see Chief or perhaps a younger hiker catching up with him, but there was always . . . no one. It seemed a shame to imbibe in all this wonder unshared. These were the times when he regretted not having someone permanent in his life . . .

The swift approach of a horse-mounted Indian at full gallop leading a string of ten packhorses on the narrow trail snapped Russ to attention. Instinct and adrenaline alone threw him against the steep cliff face. The Indian passed without acknowledgement. Horse sweat and saliva splashed Russ's face as the packhorses raced by within inches of him. Rocks tumbled from the ledge on the low side of the trail, knocked loose by pounding hoofs on the precipice. So quickly did it happen that Russ questioned it as an illusion, a time warp of some kind. The lingering dust and hoof prints told him it was real, and he wiped the moist residue on his face with his sleeve.

The trail was barely wide enough for a man; it was crazy to take it at full tilt on a horse's back. But the trail belonged to the Havasupai, and horses had the right of way. Russ realized he was a meek visitor in a beautiful yet dangerous land. Had he moved to the outer edge, he would have been knocked off into the abyss, no one knowing where he had gone.

Shade from a large outcrop became Russ's first well-deserved resting point. Leaning against a rock, he looked around, sipped water, and mulled over a question: *Why am I doing this?* To which he eventually replied, *Simple. To feel the pain.* Yes, Russ wanted to feel alive through healthy pain. His grandfather once told him that what doesn't kill you makes you stronger, and Russ lived it. That's why he climbed Mt. Humphreys, and that's why he trekked down into the canyon. It was the edge, doing something that not everyone else would do. He spit a mouthful of water at a scorpion climbing on a small ledge; it fell at his feet, and he crushed it.

Out of the corner of his eye, he saw the stray dog from the parking lot barrel down the trail toward him. His teeth clutched a strap attached to a bag. Chief's bag. How did he get that? Russ jumped to his feet, arms spread and legs stretched across the trail. The mangy critter fanned left, then right, and then let out a burst of speed along the cliff's edge.

Foolishly, unthinkingly, Russ dove toward the mutt, grasping for the bag, but he landed late on the edge of the sheer drop. His fingers clutched the dirt as he slid spread-eagled on the ground, pebbles tumbling from the edge, a thousand-foot fall only inches away. He lifted his head to see the dog panting, its chest heaving and its tongue lolling. Russ did a double take as the dog's mouth formed a smile, his eyes revealing a devilish look. Chief's bag lay neatly between his front paws as Russ clung to the one solid rock near his landing point, one leg dangling in open space.

The mongrel appeared to assess Russ's condition and position. Slowly, Russ bent his arms to raise himself up. Teeth gritted as he strained to his knees. He looked back over his shoulder and shuddered at the sight, a sheer, unforgiving drop. Russ turned, lowered his head, and bared his teeth with a low growl. The stray mutt likewise held his torso only inches above the trail, his body on spring-loaded legs, mimicking Russ. Suddenly, the canine burst forward, feinted to the left, tucked his hindquarters and tail tightly into his abdomen, and scooted to and fro in a sort of teasing dance that barely missed Russ. Then, without warning, the dog stilled midstride with a hard look, only to spring back into his dance, its ears flopping wildly. Without shifting from his position, Russ extended his hand toward the bag, only to be beaten to the punch by the exuberant pooch that dragged the bag four more feet away.

In hopes of distracting the dog, Russ poured water into a cup and placed it on the ground as an offering. Slowly, the mutt crept toward the water, crinkling his nose to acquire a scent. He lapped at the water with his wary eyes trained on Russ, poised to spring away should a false move be made. He drank until the empty cup tumbled over.

The dog stared at him for a moment, then leapt over Chief's bag, spun around, and ran full speed down the trail, his paws kicking up dust. Picking up the bag, Russ looked toward the next bend in the trail as he watched the dog sprint out of sight. He decided he would carry the bag until he got to the tribal store to turn it in, or until he saw Chief once again.

To know the length of a mile or a minute, one needs only to hike alone into a burning hole in the ground. Mile after mile, Russ slogged along one step at a time, arguing with himself to turn back. Turning back would mean going uphill. He saw no advantage to that. Stopping for another break might lead to quitting, so he sipped water continuously as he walked. The few pounds in Chief's pack felt like a hundred. Russ was curious about the contents of the bag, but he was also too honorable to invade another man's belongings. His toes played with a stone inside his shoe. Nothing seemed to make any sense at this point.

CHAPTER 9

Jumping back instinctively, Russ spotted a coiled rattler, or at least an illusion of such, in the path. A horned head swayed back and forth above a tightly wound spring. A twitch of its tail produced a sickening sound. Russ stood dumbfounded, frozen even in the hundred-plus heat. The viper sat three feet away, its senses honed in on Russ who stood, frozen, within its strike zone. Russ heard the low growl of the dog. Woozy, he shifted his weight ever so slightly.

Instantly, the rattler lunged toward Russ's midsection, with mouth agape and fangs extended, in adrenaline-slowed time. Sharp pain. Russ arched his back, retracting his abdomen. His arms rose as if to do a reverse two-step. The serpent fell at his feet. Adrenaline pains pulsed through his body.

"Grab him behind his head! Quickly now, while he's outstretched!"

A voice sounded from some other dimension, the words echoing in Russ's head without producing a physical response. Russ looked down at the snake, but no thought processed in his mind to obey such a command. A hand flashed between Russ's ankles and snatched the snake. Russ remained frozen, stunned by the sudden attack.

"You need to show him that we are the hunters, not the hunted," a voice proclaimed.

Turning around, Russ found himself face-to-face with Chief, rattlesnake in hand. Chief stared with cold eyes into the snake's two elliptical orbs.

"He could be our supper," he mused. "They say they taste like chicken, although I wouldn't know. I don't eat chicken."

"Chief, where did you . . . how did you . . . my God, man!"

"Do not ask. It matters not." Chief stood naked as the day he was born, holding the deadly rattler. Taut skin stretched across ancient muscle and bone. His nakedness revealed scars that appeared to be from mortal wounds, long swaths that must have formed over gaping penetrations. A burn scar covered his entire right shoulder.

Russ stepped back, increasing his comfort zone, forgetting why his questions were important. There was a naturalness in it all that transported Russ back to the hippie era and its "get stoned, get naked" mantra. So Chief's appearance was in no way shocking or grotesque, other than the scars and the obvious pain that he must have endured. Russ wondered why, but in the short time he had known Chief, he had decided that anything might happen.

Chief held the snake over his head and began to chant. Dancing slowly in a circle, he raised then lowered the snake, his voice changing tone and pitch. Backing farther away, Russ watched in awe as Chief performed his ceremony. Holding the snake above his head, Chief lowered it to his open mouth, grasped it with his teeth midway along its torso, and then let go. The viper's business end was free to strike, yet it only slightly twisted, its tail making no sound. Chief turned a full circle before securing its head and tail with his hands. Slowly, he lowered the snake to the ground and released it. It slithered between two rocks, and like a spaghetti noodle being sucked by a child, it was gone.

"I call to the Kundalini in the lowest center of the earth and to Man to awaken. It carries to the four corners of the earth that White Brother is not forgotten and must come forth. Do you feel the movement of Chakras?"

"I feel numb. My stomach is churning." Russ looked out across the canyon abyss.

"Chakras," Chief whispered.

Russ stood speechlessly and watched an eagle catch a thermal near the far ridge as Chief retrieved his bag. Very slowly, Chief removed items of clothing from the bags and examined them as if he thought there might be some hidden threat lurking in a crease. Gently, he laid each item one on top of the other on the ground before removing the next. When his clothes all lay at his feet, he further examined the remaining contents of the bag. He removed a velvet sack and dumped a fistful of gold coins into his hand. He clutched them with an iron fist, and then restored them to the sack. He donned the clothes, the same ones he had worn earlier in the day. Seven miles from the parking lot, and the old Indian showed no sign of wear. *An eighty-two-year-old alcoholic Indian, miles down into this canyon and stark naked, saved me from a rattler* was all Russ could think of as he slowly shook his head.

"Chief, you were freakin' naked. What's up with that?"

"It is the natural way. It means nothing. Do dogs wear clothes?" Chief responded matter-of-factly.

"Well, you aren't a dog. You have a lot of scars. What happened?"

"White brother, you do not understand. There will be a time though. I will not speak of my scars except to say that many suffered far worse than I; therefore, it is best to just let the scars speak for themselves. Now I ask you to help me with this thing I must do. You will help me, and in doing so, you will help yourself."

"You are so right; I do not understand. What in the world can I do to help you, and what makes you think I need help?" Russ tightened the straps on his pack, shifting his shoulders.

"We only have a mile to the village. We will walk together now. It is your spirit that will help me; you have the spirit of a warrior, yet it is clean. I have waited long for this time." The old man threw his bag over his shoulder.

"Clean? What does that mean?"

"There is no blood on your spirit. You have no kills." Chief started to walk.

"No . . . I've never . . ." Russ stood his ground without following.

"Then you will be able to do things that I cannot." Chief continued to increase the gap between them.

"I don't believe that." Russ took a couple of brisk steps to catch up.

"You will see. What do you know of war?" Chief asked.

His question was an arrow that hit its mark.

Russ hesitated. "Firsthand, nothing—but my father served for five years during World War II. The only time I ever saw him weep was when he tried to speak of it. It told me a lot because he was a hard man, and yet he sobbed."

"Yes, your father. He wounded you? I think you will see his reason soon." Chief nodded.

"He wounded *me*? Why would you say that? Maybe *I* hurt my father. You like to think you can see into people? Well I think you just guess, and then talk in vague terms." Feeling offended by Chief's comment, Russ went on the offensive. "You're a fake. You probably aren't even a chief." Russ walked ahead.

Without another word, Chief stepped up his pace to the village, his walk strong. The trail had begun to offer shade from a thin line of honey mesquite trees. In time, Chief spoke.

"These honey mesquite trees offer nourishment in their pods. You must be careful, though, and only harvest from the tree, not the ground. On the ground they may have a fungus that will cause insanity and death." Chief continued to walk.

"Good to know." Russ looked at the black pods scattered about on the ground, half embarrassed by what he had said and taking note of the wisdom being imparted.

"This land we are in was taken from the Havasupai by the great white father known as Roosevelt. He is known as the one who created the national parks, but there was a price exacted from the native peoples." Chief's face had a drawn look.

"I know the white man did a lot of bad things to the Indians," Russ interjected.

"You may know of some of the things that were done, yet you know nothing. To know it you must feel it—the hurt. It was all foolishness; the land never belonged to the Indian, and the Whites have no power to take it. It belongs to the Great Spirit—then, now, always. Men are fleeting creatures who only use what they find while they are here. The Great Spirit must find all this fuss to be the fuss of fools. What I call the Great Spirit is the same one you call God. God sees all of us as brothers, and as brothers do, we hurt one another, and God is saddened by this." Chief paused thoughtfully. "There is no future if you live in the past. There are talkers who like bringing up the mistakes in history to churn anger and hatred in the peoples of today. I say, let the spirits rest. Live today one moment at a time."

Chief's words made sense; Russ nodded his head in agreement. He looked around at the ancient rocks that were ancient before man had set foot in the valley. He wondered how many white men and Native Americans had argued and fought to control it. Russ knew that different tribes fought over territories too, but he didn't comment.

"I will tell you this: all men share guilt in their treatment of others. In our schools we teach the evils of the white Christians; I believe that all cultures have evil men who walk among them, as evil or maybe more so than a white Christian. The first white men came because they wanted to escape the evils of their land. They brought with them their Bible, and it spoke the same beliefs of my own people. The white man came seeking freedom—not to harm my people—but the evils of their leaders followed them. There are those who condemn all whites, but their words are false. There are those who offer no guilt to the Native Americans, but their words are also false. The black man blames the white man for enslaving him, yet black men captured and sold their own brothers to the whites.

"Most men only want to hunt and feed their children and to love their wives and be loved. Evil lives in some men who gain power—and then all men suffer. This is the truth." Chief stood with his arms crossed.

Russ remained silent, mesmerized by the cadence of Chief's voice and the wisdom of his words.

"I was young when I left my village to serve in the white man's army." Chief stared out toward a sheer cliff that rose up from the other side of the canyon. "We are short-lived creatures, when you consider the formation of this canyon."

"You took the words right out of my mouth; I was just thinking that. Why would you even consider serving in the white man's military, and why pick me to help you? I'm a white guy. Can't one of your own people help you?"

"So called 'White Men' have laid down the words of the Great Spirit for all men. White Men are just men like any others, but the words they wrote when they separated from their king spoke from a place beyond men. It is our duty to protect the words. If the leaders fall short of them, these men must be replaced. There are those who would renounce God and offer The State in His place." Once again, Russ was caught up in Chief's words, in the truth of them. Content to walk along the trail and listen to Chief, Russ breathed deeply of the air and drank in the magic of nature around him.

"We have a generation that has been educated to believe that the Constitution is just words on a piece of paper. What they are not told is that it is our hearts that give meaning to everything. These young people who accept these teachings have hearts that pump sugar water. The words are what make us free; they are the treasure of all peoples. You cannot enslave a proud people. Strip a man of his pride and he will forge his own chains. When the *Diné* had pride, they were useless to the white man . . ." Again, Chief paused to gather his thoughts.

"There was a time when words were chiseled in stone. Then words were put to clay tablets, copper, cloth, animal skins, paper—and the words were passed from generation to generation. Now we write our words in a cloud, and they are subject to the winds. The meanings are changed, and words are deleted and added at will. This is not good for our children. Although we have much information, it becomes used against us." Chief sighed.

"The 'words' are why I chose to serve. As for you, a man's spirit has no color. It is your spirit I ask for help. Men muddle with superficial differences and confuse religion for God to gain advantages over one another. If you believe in Love, then you believe in God and His promise." Chief stopped walking and met Russ's gaze.

Russ stared back with a whole new level of respect for the man. "You're amazing, Chief."

"Rearing Horse prepared me to be a fierce warrior, one like few had ever seen in modern times. He taught me the ancient ways, the ways of the "skinwalker." My dreams were those of a warrior, but my people no longer walked the warpath. I was young with the heart of a wanderer."

"A skinwalker?" Russ asked gravely, as if he were about to be let in on the secrets of the universe. *Skinwalker must be Diné for naturist . . .*

"Yes, I had missed the first great battle of the white man. Out here in those days we didn't have satellite dishes for our televisions as we do now. This was a very isolated land. I did not hear of it until I joined the US Army and was sent to the Philippines before the start of World War II." Chief studied Russ's face and sensed an opportunity. "Indians got TV long after the white man. The *Diné* waited with bated breath for generations to see and hear white-man wisdom. When the white man finally figured out how to send a signal, our people felt great pride in the knowledge that they had been defeated by a courageous, independent people with great spirits. We watched Matt Dillon, Rowdy Yates, Roy Rogers, and the Cartwrights, but then the signal began to change. Around-the-clock news and reality TV showed us that white culture was conflicted and filled with perversion and wickedness. Our people watched all of this, and soon we felt ashamed that we had really lost our lands to an inferior lot. Our young men took to drinking and became abusive. When we reflected on it all, it was decided that now was the time for revenge on the weak white men, so we built our casinos." Chief had a twinkle in his eye and an impish look as he laughed and winked at Russ.

"You got me Chief; you got me. I don't know what to make of you." Russ laughed.

"Don't make anything of me. I am a human being enjoying my life." Chief grinned proudly, pleased with his own cleverness.

"Right, do you have anything else to share?"

"When Bataan fell," Chief took on a serious look, "I did not surrender but hid in the mountains with a band of guerrilla fighters until MacArthur returned. I could sneak into the Japanese camps, make a kill, and be gone without triggering any alarms. The Japanese called me 'The Ghost' and put a price on my head. I watched from the bush as my comrades were beheaded, bayoneted, skulls fractured, and shot. There was little I could do except seek revenge at night—one enemy at a time. The Japanese were brutal, but nature with its plagues also took a toll with malnutrition, dysentery, malaria, beriberi, dengue fever, lice, bedbugs, and depression. Many longed for the comfort of death. I had no weapons against these horrors.

"When that war ended, I joined the Merchant Marines and traveled the world until the Korean War started. I enlisted in the Marine Corps and fought at the Battle of the Chosin Reservoir."

The old Indian looked for a reaction in Russ's face, but his companion returned a blank look. Russ was speechless and slack-jawed in the presence of this man. He thought about his own missteps when he was young. He had always felt guilty about shirking his responsibility of serving in the military. Now, he was face-to-face with a man who humbled him.

"Do you know of this battle?" the old man asked in a reverent tone.

"A little, I think." Russ's gaze shifted as he vaguely remembered reading a story about it once, but the details were elusive. None of the history classes in school had mentioned it. They had skimmed over the Korean War.

"Korea—they call it the forgotten war. It was bitterly cold in November 1950. I was a scout for the First Marine Division. We were outnumbered. My kills were all up close and personal. The Chinese were ill equipped but sent wave after wave of soldiers until we were out of ammunition. Countless ones just froze to death. There were so many dead in the river you could walk across on their bodies. They won't teach that in the schools."

Chief's eyes told of the horrors he had witnessed. His shoulders heaved as he tried to catch his breath. There were no tears in his eyes. His emotions went beyond tears. Gathered once more, he continued to speak.

"Rearing Horse gave me great advantages over my enemies. The powers entrusted in me made me a collector of the souls of each man I killed. It is the way of the skinwalker. Most skinwalkers go insane before they find redemption. Collecting souls is like eating honey mesquite from the ground."

Chief went quietly to the edge of the trail and gazed across the canyon.

"Skinwalker, what is it?" Russ asked with hesitation. He felt as if he had heard enough and that actually Chief had probably said enough.

"No, you will see in time. *'Anaa'jí*, so my soul may rest. This you must help me with. It takes a special spirit. Yours is such a spirit. I felt it at the Lodge Pole Inn." *'Anaa'jí* must take place in a special place. You are pure of heart like some of the knights of the white man's dark ages. I feel comfort in your ability, but I wonder, you are of an age that should have taken you to Vietnam. Yet you were not there. You are healthy enough that you should have been drafted. How is it that you were not?" Chief looked at Russ's eyes and watched them shift.

"Personal, Chief. I don't feel a need to explain it to you." Russ turned his head in shame.

"All will be known and . . . the truth is, you see. We do not need to know the truth for it to be the truth. The Lord offers us a focal point beyond the bounds of man. The Great Spirit knows the truth, all the truth. Rest your heart; I don't judge you."

"This entire day has convinced me not to doubt anything. *'Anaa'jí?* What'd you say?"

CHAPTER 10

The old chief grunted and walked out ahead without a word. The shadows on the canyon walls grew long as they neared the village of Supai. The village lay just across the bridge. The barren landscape had begun to transform into a lush, green oasis with a canopy of cottonwoods. The whinny of horses in a fenced pasture, along with barking dogs, announced their arrival. The blue-green waters of the Havasupai River cascaded over the red rocks of the canyon floor, roiling in a white froth. A cool mist from the falls drifted overhead. Chief stopped at the river's edge to perform a chant, as Russ settled on a rock to witness the spectacle. The chant droned on. Chief danced in place and stared off toward the water's source.

"Hey Chief! It's been half an hour. We need to get to the village. It's going to get dark before we make the campground." Russ stood to move on.

The old chief did not respond.

"Old man, I think that you're one of those skinwalkers that went crazy. Hey! You didn't eat one of those honey mesquite pods, did you?"

Russ leaned in front of Chief, looked at his eyes, and waved his hand in front of him. There was no response to his gesture. Chief's eyes stared off into some distant space, the chant continuing through closed lips. Russ thought it almost looked like a seizure.

"See ya, Chief! You are on your own. You are where you wanted to be, in the Havasupai."

Russ turned to walk the trail toward Supai. The sky had turned a darker shade of blue. In the distance were two stone spires illuminated by the fading sun against the dark, dramatic sky. It was a haunting, mystical spectacle—the Watchers. Stone spires, pinnacles that rose above the canyon and truly created the feeling that they were, in fact, looking down on the canyon. Russ glanced back at Chief one last time before he left him to his chant and headed toward Supai and the camping checkpoint. He walked along the trail until he came to a bridge across the river. He paused on the bridge to admire the crystal blue-green waters flowing through the valley. Paradise, he thought—the contrast of color, the obvious life-giving fluid, and a lush oasis in a barren land. He was still within sight of Chief and watched as the old man continued his ceremony. The sun had dropped low, and the changing of the tint in the sky had begun. It was time to make for a campsite.

He stopped in the village store and purchased a bottle of water. Small native children stood at the counter, staring at glass jars filled with penny candy. Russ handed the clerk two dollars and signaled the children to indulge. They grabbed their loot, and out the door they went with a laugh. The screen door screeched, then slammed behind them. When Russ stepped out into the canyon, he did not see or hear any sign of the children—only a couple of old men sitting on a bench under a tree and a young woman approaching with a shopping basket. Russ turned and walked toward the sound of the first large falls.

One sorry soul sat on a rock alongside the trail, his face contorted in anguish. Beside him sat two young women dressed as if they had just stepped out of the early seventies. They had long, flowing hair adorned with wild flowers. They wore peasant dresses, their figures lean and athletic. The young man on the rock swayed with his head tilted back. As Russ approached, he became aware that the man's feet were bare of skin, the red, raw meat oozing blood. Beside him lay a bloody pair of sandals. Russ had never seen blisters like those. He looked at the women's feet and saw they wore practical athletic shoes.

"Do you need help?" Russ inquired.

The man with the bloody feet sat up straight, his legs straight out to keep them out of the dirt, and looked soulfully at Russ.

"I'm cool, man; I'm good."

"Well, I'd say you are about eight walking miles from good."

"Bad trip man, really bad, we kind of did this while . . . we were . . . we were kinda stoned. I didn't even know I had feet until we chilled. By then it was like, too late. I ain't going nowhere like this. My man is over at the lodge working on things."

"I've got bandages, salve, and moleskin in my bag, but I don't recommend wrapping them. The salve will help prevent infection, though." Russ slipped his bag off his shoulder and rummaged through it until he found the salve. He handed it to one of the girls. She looked uncertainly at the broken man. He gave her a nod, and as gently as possible, she began to apply it. His face contorted in anguish but he remained silent, his teeth locked behind compressed lips.

"Thanks, man; that's real cool of you," the would-be hiker whispered when his friend was done applying the salve.

"So what's your buddy trying to work out for you?" Russ asked.

"A helicopter ride out of this stinking hole. We got no cash, so he called his mom. She's loaded and an easy touch. She'll arrange for a magic carpet ride back to Oz, and we can all get on with it. We're from L.A. This here ain't us."

"Why did you come here, then?" Russ had a flashback of the ranger at the check-in. He watched the boy's eyes.

"We heard rumors that we could score some great dope down here."

Russ saw no clue that he was lying, and with what he was saying he sounded believable.

"Well, sounds like you're covered, but I'm from flyover country, so what do I know? I guess I'll be on my way." Russ stood and slung his pack over his shoulders. His compassion whisked away on the evening breeze; he saw the kid's feet as well deserved and no lesson learned. He managed a weak smile and an insincere "good luck," but as he walked away, he felt they all had set their destiny for a tragic end in the not-too-distant future. *Everything had a price in this world, "cool" being the most expensive and of least value*, Russ thought as he walked away. The trio reminded him of so many of the people he had known in his youth who squandered their lives on drugs and sex. He looked back at those days as a death party and was glad he had only been an observer. Over the years, he had come to know many fine people whose lives were cut short through accidents and disease. He had little use for those willing to take life for granted and toss it away.

The campground was a short jaunt down the canyon from the village. Russ walked until he saw Navajo Falls. He stopped to refresh at the sound of gushing water. Walking on, he came to an observation spot at the top of Havasu Falls and looked down on the valley, the campground and pools formed by hardened calcium carbonate. Pools filled with blue-green water, water that contrasted with the red rock of the canyon walls. He had been told of the wonder, but still, he had no idea of the splendor he would behold. He stood slack-jawed, not quite capable of taking in the view but trying to form a permanent imprint in his mind. It was one of those moments that should last forever.

Finally, he resumed his walk down the path into the campground to look for an empty site. The sites were sparsely set, allowing for privacy. It seemed idyllic, and campers were busily going about their needs, looking at maps, snacking on camp food, and chatting. The campground sat beneath a canopy of cottonwoods that offered protection from the Arizona sun. The litter-free grounds were neat and clean. The only thing missing were campfire rings, as fires were forbidden. Halfway into the grounds, Russ spotted the site he would occupy.

He slid his pack from his shoulders and stepped off the trail into the site. A fluffy, yellow stray that looked to be mostly golden retriever crawled from beneath the picnic table, tail wagging to greet him. He appreciated the nonjudgmental welcoming. Russ slowly offered his hand to the mascot for a sniff of approval, and once confirmed, scratched behind its ear. "Old Goldie," he whispered. The dog whimpered when Russ's hand crossed its shoulder.

"What's the matter, boy?" Russ crouched down, separating

tufts of fur around the dog's shoulder. A two-inch twig protruded from reddened flesh. He consoled Goldie, then gently grasped the twig. The dog panted, then pulled in his tongue stoically. The twig came out easily and Russ examined it; two inches had been in flesh. Puncture wounds are deadly things. Russ bathed the lesion in the antibiotic lotion from his pack.

"Good boy; you were a pretty tough guy. What happened? Did you run into a dead branch chasing a bunny? I guess we'll never know." Goldie panted in a smiling way as Russ patted his head.

As he set up his tent, a pressing darkness overwhelmed the canyon. The voices of the other campers died out, and suddenly it was as if he were alone.

He sat on his picnic table, imagining that it was a hundred years ago and he was the first explorer to venture into the canyon. The canyon walls melted in the darkness, and the only sound was the tumbling waters of the falls. He slipped off his boots, $200 kickers he had bought just for this hike, but even though he had worn them in for weeks before the expedition, his feet hurt. He pulled off his socks and massaged his feet. His toes hurt the most—downhill hiking works on the legs and feet more than climbing. He flicked on his flashlight to take a better look at his toes. His toenails were black, bruised from being smashed against the toes of his boots. He kneaded his insoles as Goldie sniffed his shoes, socks, and even his feet. His feet were actually in great shape he thought, not like those of the kid back up the trail.

It would be a moonless night, a sky filled with billions of stars. Russ sat at the picnic table petting his new friend and sharing bits of jerky with him. A sudden silver streak in the black sky caught his attention just before it faded. Another silver streak—only this time Russ saw it from the moment it appeared until it fizzled out near the rim of the canyon. He had seen two shooting stars. Silently, he made two prayerlike wishes and said good night to Old Goldie by giving him a scratch behind the ear. Russ slipped inside his frail refuge, pausing halfway in to stargaze for a moment. He was too exhausted for much more.

Curled up in a fetal position, Russ tried to sleep, but his head bounced with thoughts of the strange man, Chief, and the three hikers he had offered to help. His thoughts were disturbing. He half-hoped he wouldn't see the chief again, but then half-hoped he would. He thought of the lives that the young hikers were wasting getting high and how they were so willing to use someone else to escape a situation of their own doing.

His thoughts eased as he focused on his last vision of the night sky. The resonance of the distant river whispered for him to be still, and he slept. But his sleep filled with strange dreams and ancient Indian rituals that had no logical basis in his experience; yet what wondrously vivid visions they were. Russ's eyes popped open and his heart raced to the blood-curdling cry of a night predator: a puma.

Russ listened for another scream or a footstep outside his tent, but heard only the beating of his heart. He armed himself with the only weapon he could conjure: a flashlight. Gingerly, he unzipped his tent and peeked out into the moonless night. It was as if his eyes were shut, for he could not make out the outline of a single object. He heard a whimper and flashed his light in the direction of the sound. Large glowing, soulful eyes stared back. The mutt shook from fear and hunkered beneath the campsite's picnic table. "Goldie," Russ whispered. Again, the shrill scream sounded in the opposite direction of Russ's focus, and he swung the light around in time to catch the demon slip into the brush. Russ emerged from the tent and retrieved a large branch from a debris pile he had earlier collected when clearing the site.

Mountain lions were opportunists that would avoid situations that might bring them harm. Predators seemed well aware that a wound would jeopardize their survival chances by limiting their ability to hunt. Russ felt his best protection was aggression. He stood, armed only with a tree limb, and shouted challenges at the puma—daring him to attack. There was only silence, but as Russ's eyes adjusted to the night, he caught movement in the underbrush. He let out a scream of his own, and with his arms raised high so as to appear large, he charged the beast. It turned tail and ran off toward the river. The rest of the campground was silent, dead to the world. Russ turned back to his tent and went to sleep.

It wasn't long before the morning sun warmed his tent, awakening Russ with the smell of hot nylon. He dragged out to sit at his picnic table. The mutt nuzzled its nose into Russ's hand as if grateful for his protector's act of courage during the night. Russ scratched him behind his ear and offered comforting words. He thanked Goldie for backing him up. He ate dry cereal, tossing a few bits to the dog, and sipped bottled water. Other campers moved about in nearby sites while Russ wondered if any of them were aware of the night visit of the puma. Other stray dogs moved among the campers and begged for bits of food. In the morning light, all seemed right with the world, and the night visitor took on the guise of a dream.

The canyon walls rose abruptly in all directions, dwarfing nearby trees, yet with the radiance of reflected sunlight, Russ could see the sparkle of Havasu Falls. The red-rock cliffs could have been in a valley on Mars. There was nothing Russ needed to do, except to relax. *Relax,* he thought. *Lie back on the picnic table and breathe easy.* The night terror grew distant in the morning light. He ripped a piece of jerky and let the juices it generated soften it in his mouth.

Breathing easy—the tenderness in his ribs had faded—Russ mulled over the events of his trip, wondering how Colton was making out with his broken ribs, internal injuries, and a much-bruised ego. A slight breeze of cool earth-scented air washed over him, air-cooled by shaded rocks and a fount that splashed alfresco from a nearby crevasse. The harshness of the surrounding land emphasized the value of such a feature. There was much to see, do, and feel in this extraordinary valley, but Russ savored this moment of peace. The smell of warmed earth, vegetation, and water sounds soothed him. The muffled voices of strangers mixed with the swishes of the river flowed together to hypnotize and create a bemused trance.

He thought about his two wishes on the shooting stars. One he felt he would never realize its outcome, for it was for the injured hiker and friends, that they may find a better path and mature before they die. Strange that he probably would never see or hear of them again. The other was for Chief, that Chief might find the one he needs to help him overcome his obsession with redemption. That wish, he hated to think, might manifest around him.

Be careful what you wish for, he thought.

CHAPTER 11

"White man, you abandoned me to the darkness last night."

"What?" Russ popped up into a sitting position on the picnic table and tried to gather his thoughts. His heart pulsed in his ears.

"You walked away from me on the trail." The chief sat on a fallen log at the edge of the camp.

"I told you I was leaving . . . you never answered me. You were in a stupor or something."

"I asked for the blessings to enter the valley of the blue-green waters. I asked for the forgiveness of the spirits of the blue-green waters for trespassing."

"That was very thoughtful of you; I just paid my camping fee. Here, have a bit of jerky."

"No thanks, I ate breakfast up at the village lodge. They have a little diner. There is much in life that you do not appreciate. You need spiritual help."

"Chief, I . . . never mind. I figured you hooked up with some of your people last night. I am pretty certain that you can take care of yourself."

"These are not my people, but I get by, live off the fat of the land. I slept at the lodge. At my age, the ground is too hard."

"What? I thought . . ."

"You jumped to a conclusion. You thought because I am an Indian and they are Indians that we are the same people. I am not of this tribe. My tribe does share sacred places with these people. Our ancestors fought each other for access to the sacred places. We are at peace now because of our common threat—Washington. The words of our founding white fathers are supposed to protect us from the government overreach, but it has failed many times. It is to one of these sacred places that we shall go."

"Look, I'm chillin'. I'm kinda enjoying not being caught up in anything but the beauty of this place. Why don't you stroll over to some of those other campers and bother them for the day?"

The chief took on a sick, green look and dropped into a squatting position to stare at the ground.

"Hey! Are you alright, Chief?"

"You are my last hope. You are the one. Here I will die and spend eternity with the spirits of my dead. Without your energy, there is no hope."

"Hold it! Don't you be guilting me out. You ain't my problem." Russ threw up his hands and ducked inside his tent, changing into shorts and packing up for the day. The chief seemed to shrink as he squatted in the center of the campsite.

"Chief, I'm sorry for that remark, but you just hiked into this canyon; you want me to believe you're weak? You just did something that most of the population can't or won't do."

"I embodied a stray dog. The dog brought me down here, *yee naaldlooshii*."

"That's crazy. Yee naadloship or whatever."

"That's the way of the skinwalker, *yee naaldlooshii*. We can transmute ourselves into the spirit of another. I walked in the skin of a stray dog. That is why when I took human form I was naked."

"That's crazy." Russ stopped packing his stuff and gave Chief a challenging look.

"Crazy because you don't understand. We are all energy. We all project what we want others to see in us. Do you believe that?"

"Yeah, I can understand that much."

"Well, the skinwalker takes it to another level. We reach a level where we touch the spirit of other creatures and not only project their image but transform our energy as well. There is spiritual energy for each living creature; we are all receptors for a specific spiritual energy. Each of us filters it in our own way and then projects it to others. It is the way of things. It is not crazy."

"Chief, you make me crazy. I don't know why I like you, but I do. I really just want to be left alone to enjoy this canyon. Just give me today. I need to recharge. I've been hiking a long time."

"It is your right. I cannot force myself on you. I will tell you that if you follow me, you will experience things you have never dreamed of. You will come away a richer person."

"Look, I need time to think. You know, Chief, you really don't know me; I have faults."

"Yes, please think. It is best. Your spirit must do this in peace. Did you sleep well? I think there might have been a demon on the prowl last night."

"Did you hear or see it?" Russ once again gave Chief a long look.

Chief grinned and raised one eyebrow. "I know this about you. You showed great courage in the face of danger and darkness. The puma could have taken you out, but you stood your ground. I also know that you did not remove anything from my bag when you carried it for me; my clothes were the way I packed them, and my coins were of the same number. This speaks well of you. You are not a thief."

Russ gaped at Chief. "Wait a minute . . . how the heck? No . . . no, it's not possible. You were here and saw the puma come into my site?" He wanted to believe that Chief witnessed the puma come into his campsite.

"You were tested last night by the cat, and you showed your courage. How I know is not important." Chief formed a wry, telling grin that left no doubt in Russ's mind that the chief could indeed do impossible things.

Chief rose and walked toward the bush without another word.

Russ picked up his pack and headed toward the river for a swim. Water fell from the cliff into a natural pool of blue-green, releasing a cool mist that drifted toward the variegated foliage on the shore. The droplets split the intense desert sun into an arched spectrum, energy transformed. The rainbow framed the falling water as the sunlight struck at just the right angle.

He set his pack on a rock that he could view from the water and waded into an inviting spot where the water was nearly chest high. Russ slid onto his back and floated in wonder of it all, in wonder of Chief. Who was he to question any of this?

Tourists waded in the shallows at the foot of the falls and swam in the deeper areas. Russ alternated between swimming and floating as he steered across the pool toward the base of the falls. Never had he been in a more magical and mystical place. When he reached the far shore, he climbed onto a rock and lay in the sun, listening to the thunder of the falls. He drifted off and slept.

He was awakened by the sound of laughter and screams from a group of youthful campers in their late teens or early twenties climbing the rocks nearer the falls. Russ sat up and watched.

They took turns diving into the froth of the falls from a shelf of travertine twelve feet above the surface of the pool. First a muscular-looking guy, then a skinny guy, and finally one that didn't look as if he could have walked the trail into Havasupai. Three girls giggled and danced on the shelf as the boys egged them on, coaxing them to jump. All three finally jumped while holding hands. There were probably a total of twenty campers playing in the pool.

Russ worked his way over to the travertine shelf and poised for a dive. He looked every bit as muscular as the first diver, his body lean and knotted. But Russ's dive was less than perfection, his legs crooked and spread. His chest smacked loudly, and the younger divers all cheered as he rose to the surface. Russ offered a victory wave, and then broke into a breaststroke. One dive would be enough; he had proven himself.

Russ swam back to his resting rock and sat in the sun. Across the water he saw the chief surrounded by a small group of people. Chief sat on top of a large rock. Russ could see his arms in motion as he pointed in different directions. It was obvious that Chief was giving a lecture on the Native American's history in the valley. At times, Chief rose to his feet and did a little dance, only to sit back down and wave his arms again. His admirers eventually found seats of their own, obviously engrossed in the tales and the stories that flowed like the water of the falls. Russ smiled and lay back to enjoy the warmth of the sun-heated rock. Here he would spend the day in renewal.

When Russ again sat up, Chief's audience had changed. Some had moved on, being replaced by new ones. Chief was now in photo-opportunity mode and posed with members of his listening audience one by one with the falls as a backdrop.

What a ham, Russ thought. The old man relished the attention. To the strangers he was not irrelevant; he was part of what they had come here to find—a stereotype, a story. It all seemed like harmless, good fun.

Russ's stomach growled almost as loud as the puma. He checked his watch. It was eleven o'clock. The crowd around Chief was dissipating, and so Russ did a low dive into the pool and swam toward his pack. When he climbed out of the water, the old Indian was waiting for him.

CHAPTER 12

"The food at the lodge is pretty good?" Russ asked as he patted himself dry. He felt restored.

"Plenty good. Competes with your jerky."

"What do you say I buy you lunch?" Russ raised one eyebrow.

Chief grinned. "I thought you lived on jerky and hardtack."

"Today is extraordinary; let's go have a good meal." Russ shouldered his pack and nodded his head for Chief to follow him. Up the trail toward Havasupai was a different walk than yesterday.

Halfway up along the falls trail, Chief stopped and looked back down the valley. Russ stood beside him staring at the wonder of the falls, the blue-green pool below, and the cottonwoods. Could Eden have looked any better? "I ran into a man once who told me he did not believe in God," Chief said, and paused. Russ listened, knowing there would be more.

"He said he might believe if God would do a miracle for him." Chief took a deep breath and sighed. Again he paused and looked about him.

"I told him he was like a man standing in a lake demanding that God show him just one drop of water." Chief turned and started up the trail again. Russ followed without a word. Then Chief stopped cold in his tracks with Russ nearly colliding into his back. Chief turned to face the falls again. "Nice setting for a mall, don't you think, white man?" Chief broke into a broad grin, proud of his humor.

Russ glanced between the falls and Chief. He had to laugh as they resumed their hike toward lunch.

Soon they arrived at the lodge. On the porch sat the injured hiker, alone, his feet naked of shoes and skin. His legs were outstretched and resting on the deck rail. He looked miserable.

Russ walked by without acknowledging him. His magic carpet ride must not have materialized yet. Upon seeing him, Russ felt nothing. He saw only a fool, a fool who didn't even plan for a way out of the canyon, and the fool showed no recognition of the one who had offered him salve.

There was only one vacant table, and they took it. It was a pleasant setting, and the two men sipped coffee as they waited for their order. A big-eyed girl of about eight at a neighboring table glanced at them.

Chief returned her glance. Her face disappeared beneath her flowing hair, then, slowly, one eye peered out before disappearing again. She seemed entranced by the chief.

Russ was reserved. He practiced caution around children and respected a parent's suspicion of strangers, especially men. Chief lit up at the girl's fascination. The girl's mother watched her daughter without a word as the girl's father rattled on about his business deals, totally oblivious of his daughter or his wife. The wife smiled at her husband and gave an occasional nod toward his self-absorbed rhetoric. Finally, the mother held up her hand toward her husband.

"Hold that thought." She rose and approached the chief.

"What . . . ?" Her husband turned to watch her walk away.

"Excuse me, gentlemen. I wouldn't do this if you were eating, but since you haven't been served yet, I was wondering if I could take a picture of my daughter standing by you. She is obviously intrigued by you." The mother had a camera in hand.

"My pleasure, if you're sure I don't scare her." Chief grinned and sat up straighter in his chair. "Teach her well, for there is a mother and a grandmother in her."

The woman looked at Chief and offered a smile as she mulled over his words.

"She's shy, but not afraid. Honey, come over here." The mother waved her hand in encouragement, and the little girl shyly walked over and stood by the chief.

"I have two sons. I never had a daughter." Chief smiled.

The little girl looked up at him. Her eyes danced about, first taking in his hat, the character lines of his face, and then his long, grey hair. They posed, and the mother shot again and again until she was sure she had the perfect shot. The mother thanked Chief, and the little girl shook his hand. When the mother and daughter returned to the table, the father fussed in a low but nonthreatening voice and picked up the check. The little girl glanced back over her shoulder as the family walked toward the register.

"That was nice of you, Chief."

"Yes. I saw that family last night as I checked in. The father was talking then as he was just now. The mother and daughter looked bored, but I saw the little girl look at me. My silence seemed to speak to her." Chief thought for a moment. "It is not that I will be part of her memory of this place, but about what I represent—a proud, independent, and free people. Hopefully it will inspire her to learn the ways of my people. I think her father doesn't appreciate what he has."

After a substantial and flavorful lunch, the two men ambled back down the trail toward the campground. Russ parked beneath the shade of a fringe of cottonwood at the edge of the water, removed his boots, and soaked his feet while Chief wandered about the campground, working the crowd. Looking at and listening to the falls, Russ wished he had found Havasupai in his youth.

"White brother, you see the colorful spirit of Havasu?" Chief's voice slipped through the veil of Russ's dreamy slumber.

Rolling around to look behind him, Russ spotted Chief squatted on a rock along the shore just a few feet from him. His head was tilted back as he focused on a rainbow, the colors vivid and luminous, reaching across the face of the falls.

"When I see rainbows, I think of my wife." Chief did not look at Russ. His gaze was locked on the falls.

"How is that?"

"The day after she died, I saw a rainbow. It was unexpected, for it was not a rainy day. My wife loved rainbows. I called her Rainbow Woman to tease her. I took that rainbow as a sign. It was her way to let me know that she was fine and had crossed over." Chief continued to look at the rainbow.

"Rainbow Woman, that's a nice thought." Russ was sincerely touched; he knew his mother and father had used pet names for each other, too.

"Have you ever loved a woman? Love—truly love, not lust." Chief waited as Russ gathered his reply.

"Sure, I think so. Why?"

"If you have truly loved, then you know the way of spirits, for only spirits love. When spirits try to touch, it is the body that gets in the way. Spirits in love try to mingle, but the body separates them. This is a special experience that is lost on those who practice only lust. Lust is of the body—momentary, empty—while love is eternal. Sadly, the world has put more emphasis on the physical while the spirit is laughed at."

Chief sat with his eyes closed. The thunder of the falls rumbled. Russ moved closer and mulled the words of the chief.

"Tell me about your wife, Chief."

"She is the one who kept this skinwalker sane. Women are more in touch with the ways of the spirit. Women possess the one gift that the Dark Spirit can never give, and that's the gift of life. It is a good way. My woman had a strong spirit. My mother gave me physical life. My woman gave me spiritual life."

A satisfied grin appeared on Chief's face with lingering thoughts of his woman, who he longed to join with again. Their reunion was what drove him. It was for this purpose that he sought his redemption.

"Chief . . ."

"Yes? Now that I have explained this, do you know if you have ever loved another spirit?"

Russ had never spoken of it to anyone. This would be the first time he would try to find adequate words. "Yes . . . yes I have, but I was not loved in return. At first she loved me, but for her, it didn't last. I still love her."

"That is sad. Being with someone and yet being alone is worse than just being alone. When was this?"

"Long ago, when I was just out of high school . . ."

Chief sat silently, contemplating the falls, waiting for Russ to offer more, but there was silence. "Ah, you were a boy too young for love."

"When I married her I didn't feel like a boy. I loved her very much, with all my heart. She was very beautiful, prettier than any woman I've known."

"Maybe you did not love the girl." Chief looked at Russ directly.

Russ's gaze focused inward, on his soul.

"No, I loved her more than anything. I would have died for her. I would have done anything for her."

"You speak in a tongue that only reveals her as an object of your desires. You have said nothing of who she was. She was more than just beautiful. You loved her image, but that is not love. You loved who you wanted her to be, yet her true spirit eluded you. You loved perhaps an image she projected, yet one without substance."

"You never met her; how can you judge her? I have loved her all these years . . ." A perspective Russ had never considered began to dawn into truth.

"You have loved a fantasy. My judgment is of you, not of her. Find no shame in it, other than that you wasted so much of your energy, your life, focused on a false spirit. She never loved you back? In the beginning, she probably gave you the impression that she did, and maybe you treated her differently and acted like someone you weren't. You both tricked each other maybe, but when she began to see the real you, she rejected you." Chief paused, nodded slowly. "You may have both walked as skinwalkers. The world is full of skinwalkers. When you are young and the summers are warm and you feel what you think is love—that is easy. In winter is when love is proven."

"She was pregnant. I was excited and wanted a son, but she wasn't thrilled with the prospect."

"Yes, when reality set in. For her, the images of you faded."

"Her friends all went off to college and she married me. Her friends would visit and talk about their adventures and parties. She became very depressed."

"Fantasies with which you could not compete. But then the child, you loved your child. Did she give you a son or a daughter?"

"No . . . I have no son or daughter . . ." Russ's voice trailed off. The old man saw the pain on Russ's face.

"Well, you matured," he said softly, so as not to bruise Russ with a harsh observation, "and I believe that you can understand what real love is. I won't ask you any more questions. You did love an image; you never loved who that girl really was."

Russ knelt by the water and dunked his head. He shook his head back with soaked hair and water flying. The water hid a tear and cleared the lump in his throat. He stood, then waded out into deeper water where he plunged into a deep hole. He knew he had never allowed himself to love anyone after his wife. With a kick from the bottom, he emerged into a full stroke, swimming to the middle of the river. Rolling onto his back, he gazed at the falls, the rainbow against the blue-green effect of calcium carbonate in the water. The fluid look of travertine smoothed the sharp-edged walls of the cliff face. Russ submerged then reappeared time and again as he gave consideration to the wisdom of Chief. The truth. How could he sort out what the truth was at this point? Did it even matter? Whatever the truth was, his life had been a journey away from the time and place that he had loved freely—hoping, knowing, and dreaming that everything was going to work out somehow. What Chief said made sense. All these years maybe he *had* been living a lie . . . Thinking about Rainbow Woman, he swam toward the boulder upon which Chief sat.

"How do I go about helping you?" Russ asked in a quiet tone.

"We must follow the river to where it meets the great Colorado. There we will find a sacred place that only I and God know of. The other knowers have all passed. It is the only place where I can free my spirit. Along the way you will have to retrieve some things I will need at the sacred place. I cannot accomplish these tasks, for they must be done by another. Only one who is clean, such as you."

"It sounds like an exorcism. Maybe you need a priest," Russ suggested. "Really, I've heard of Catholic priests doing things like this."

"I am aware of exorcism. This must be done in the ways of the *Diné*. This is something I am sure of. You will be my envoy to the fourth world."

"You got a list for this envoy?" Russ asked.

"I will tell you as you need to know."

"Need-to-know basis. Great. You don't trust me or what?"

"No, I don't want to overwhelm you. We will go step by step."

"Even more great. I must be crazy, but I've got nothing else going for me at the moment." Russ meant it, every word of it. He had nothing—no family except his newfound nephew, Colton. Romantic prospects had grown slim to none at this stage. He didn't even have a real job waiting for him. He had always told himself he wanted to go out in a blaze of glory on a grand adventure. This might be the opportunity, so why not?

"First we must go into a side canyon. We will find a certain old mine shaft. The mine will take us into another ancient canyon. There I will point out what you need."

"Mine shaft? That sounds a little creepy. The bartender said they are dangerous, with vertical shafts. What do you say we head out at first light?"

"No, I will need to eat breakfast at the lodge. You can meet me there."

"Sure, that would be great."

"I'll buy this time." Chief grinned and walked off toward the trail that led to the lodge.

CHAPTER 13

Russ shook his head, shouldered his pack, and headed toward the campsite he had used last night in the hopes that it was available. It was not quite dinnertime, but a lot of the hikers had already started to settle in for the night. As he walked toward his old site, he saw that there were open sites available if his was taken, but he kind of liked his mascot. Goldie was sitting in the middle of the site waiting for him. Russ off-loaded his pack onto the picnic table, secure in the feeling that his claim was staked. With plenty of daylight left, he felt no need to rush to set up his tent. Instead, he broke off a piece of dead branch, teasing Goldie into a game of fetch, a game that the mutt did not tire of.

Russ set up his tent, then shared his dinner of crackers and jerky with the dog. He sat at his picnic table petting him and occasionally sharing a thought. They watched the sky turn as the sun set in the Arizona sky—blue-pink. One star appeared, then another, and finally the sky faded into black crystal, allowing for a burst of stars.

Russ had prayed last night when he witnessed the shooting stars, but tonight he had the urge to pray by the inspirations within his own heart. He felt blessed with the beauty he beheld in the valley and wondered what the next few days would offer. His prayers brought him peace. He shared them with Goldie, scratched the old mutt behind the ear, and soon crawled into his tent where he fell soundly asleep.

After a quiet night with no nocturnal visitors, Russ packed his gear and headed to the lodge where he met Chief for a hearty breakfast. After eating, they sat on the diner porch to allow their meals to settle. The whinny of horses could be heard, mixed with the occasional laughter of children. People attended to their business, but everyone who walked by offered a greeting. The Arizona sky was expectedly clear and bright, the morning air fresh with a light scent of warming.

Russ and Chief inventoried their supplies and tried to think of things they might have forgotten. Once they left the village, they would have only what they brought with them and their own resourcefulness.

"We will hike to a side canyon where we will find the old mine. The mine shaft grants us a shortcut, so to speak. The original trail of the ancient ones climbs many cliff faces and is dangerous. If you prefer, we can take the old trail."

"Hey, let's just keep doing everything your way. You say mine shaft—who am I to argue? Mine shaft it is. Lead the way!" Russ bowed and extended his arm for Chief to blaze the trail. As they stepped off the porch, Russ scanned the village and its visitors one last time. None of these visitors were aware of the adventure he and Chief were embarking on. They headed down the path through the campground and onto the trail that would lead them along the blue-green waters toward Mooney Falls.

Russ had read the story of Mooney Falls. It was named for a prospector, James Mooney, who fell to his death in an attempt to descend the falls by rope in 1882. He was part of a party made up of Alphonso Humphreys, H.J. Young, W.C. Beckman, Mat Humphreys, and W.W. Jones. Although there were several variations of the tale, it seemed Mr. Mooney went over the side on a rope that broke, plunging him to his death. He had removed his boots so that he could better feel for footholds before he attempted to descend. After he fell, his boots were tossed over the side of the cliff as a sort of funeral rite. His body rested on rocks at the bottom of the cliff for months before the party gained access to it. When his associates found him, he was encrusted in calcium. The group spotted an Indian wearing Mooney's boots long after they had thrown them over the cliff. As far as they knew, there was no way to get below the falls. The Indian then showed them a way down the wall alongside the falls through dangerous travertine ledges and tunnels.

Chief stopped at the top of Mooney Falls and pointed at a small opening in the travertine. Russ watched as several people emerged from the opening on their ascent from below the falls. The hikers were in good spirits and exchanged greetings with Chief. Russ removed his pack, for the opening was too small and the emerging hikers had suggested that it would be better to pull it along behind him as they had done. They assured Russ that the climb down had an element of risk but that it offered no grave danger if one observed the safety rules. Russ entered the tunnel followed by Chief. Chief had traveled the route many times in his youth, a time before the onslaught of tourists.

"This valley has changed greatly since I was a boy. Nothing is sacred anymore. There are many people now." Chief helped push Russ's pack along until they emerged on a ledge offering a view to the bottom. "We used to call this 'The Wall.'"

Russ lowered himself down on an old chain with his pack slung over one shoulder. Below him, several more people lowered themselves down on chains, and then disappeared into another travertine tunnel. It was a well-traveled path, but no less an adventure. One slip or misstep could send a person tumbling several hundred feet to the bottom. Russ cautiously set his feet firmly and held the chain until he rested on the next ledge, then watched as Chief did the same.

Chief had descended halfway down when both he and Russ heard the scream.

CHAPTER 14

Chief looked above him and saw only a small flash of skin and cloth tumbling toward him. He freed his right arm in an attempt to catch the bundle accelerating toward him. Russ stepped back too far and teetered on the edge of the precipice—quickly reaching out for the chain in front of him. He managed to avoid going over the edge and down to the canyon floor. Everything seemed to unravel in slow motion.

Russ braced for the worst. The tumbling bundle could knock Chief off the chain. Russ wondered if he would be able to stop Chief from falling to the rocks below. He prepared his mind and leveraged his body as best he could.

Chief snagged the bundle. Even with his feet wedged in fissures in the wall, the momentum of the object caused him to lose his footing. He rolled around, hanging by his left arm, his back to the cliff. Quickly, he caught his balance and faced the cliff. He kicked until his feet were once again firmly planted. His right arm wrapped about the bundle as he secured his grip on the chain. He caught his breath and looked at the prize pressed so tightly against his chest that he could only make out flowing blond hair, but he knew what he had. In his arm he held a little girl, the girl whose mother had asked him to pose for pictures in the village.

The little girl put her arms around Chief's neck, clinging tightly. Above him, the girl's mother sobbed while her father stared in stunned silence.

Chief concentrated on the task at hand. The girl's parents waited and watched Chief lower himself onto the ledge where Russ waited. Russ reached out to steady Chief and take the child into his arms. Chief gave her parents an "okay" sign. The three of them sat on the ledge as the girl's parents descended the chains. The weeping mother and father both hugged the girl before they turned to Chief.

"Thank you! Thank you! We don't know how you managed to catch our little girl. It was a miracle, an absolute miracle! Thank you!" The father shook Chief's hand. "I owe you big time. We came out of the tunnel and were watching the two of you when she slipped in some loose gravel. It happened in a split second."

"I didn't think you would catch her." The mother's voice quivered. "I thought she would knock you off the chains—oh, I don't want to think about it."

"Don't think about it. Think only that we are all safe. I only did what I had to do. Let's forget about this and enjoy the day." Chief patted the girl's hair and smiled at the parents.

"Forget about it? Are you serious? I won't forget about it! Look, I am a very wealthy man. I will reward you for this. Give me your name and address so I can send you something—whatever you want." The girl's father removed a note pad and a pen from his pack.

"Your wealth is right here beside me. I have no need of money or of any material things." Chief looked down and smiled at the girl.

"I have to do something to repay you." The father rubbed his head. The mother continued hugging her daughter.

"Reward me by raising this girl to be a beautiful woman, not in looks but in her values. Reward me by telling me that you will shift your focus toward your daughter. Live your life as if you gave me all your money so that you no longer have any. Then, I will be rewarded." Chief signaled Russ to enter the next cavity and continue their descent. Chief patted the father on the shoulder, hugged the mother, and kissed the little girl on top of her head. As he entered the tunnel, he turned to the family. "Be careful, God bless you, and enjoy this day and every day."

At the base of Mooney Falls, it was as if Chief could not move fast enough toward the trail that headed downstream. Something was on Chief's mind. Body language can speak loudly, and Russ was literate enough to read Chief's. He followed, knowing full well Chief did not want to face the family again. He had said his piece and wanted it left at that. Russ wondered if it was Chief's way of controlling some urge to lash out at the father for being so shallow. Chief definitely wanted to fade into the cottonwoods without further fuss. Russ's respect for him had reached yet a new pinnacle.

"Chief, I think you were wrong again." Russ put his hand on Chief's shoulder to slow him.

"Wrong?" Chief blinked and turned, gazing at Russ's hand until Russ stepped back.

"That girl is going to treasure her memory of you and that picture her mother took of the two of you."

Chief sported a small grin. "I helped a midwife birth my sons. Birth—that, my friend, is a true miracle—the gift of life. It is something that only a female can do. When it happens, all things change. The world becomes a different place, and no matter what, it will always be different. Some women kill their children before they give birth, but their world has still changed." He raised one eyebrow at Russ. "I would have nothing to do with a woman who would kill her child because I would always wonder what she might do to me, for I am not a part of her. Some deny the facts and believe that to not talk about it makes it all right, but it is not." He kicked at a rock. "Likewise, a man who abandons his children either physically or emotionally is all the fool. His life changed when his child was born. It is the focus of life now. To think that life is all about one's self is to live a selfish and therefore wasted life. I have seen all that life is. I have killed. I have been selfish. I have been loved and hated. Take it from me—a child is all the worth in the world, for in that child is the future. All else is nonsense. I end my rant; excuse my passion."

Chief turned, and Russ sensed that he did not want to hear any comments on his "rant."

Russ followed Chief at a slight distance and thought about his own life. He had done many adventurous things and been all over the world, but there had always been emptiness in it—a life unshared. He had never witnessed the birth of a child, let alone the birth of *his* child. He had always thought he could have been a great father, but so what?

He wasn't. He had always wondered about the son he never knew. He wondered what they could have added to each other's lives. He thought about the father of the little girl and how detached he seemed at the restaurant, how caught up he'd been in talking about himself. The trail wound through the cottonwoods, and Russ noticed that he had fallen far behind Chief. He quickened his pace until the distance was pared.

CHAPTER 15

They traversed the Havasupai, hiking into a side canyon beyond the range of tourists. Chief made deliberate strides and always stepped surefooted. The canyon walls cast shadows on its floor, and soon the verdure of the Havasupai dissipated among piles of rocks and boulders. Scattered along the trail were the skeletons of large mining machines, half buried in shifting sands blown by the winds of a hundred years. The machines were tilted at odd angles as if they had crashed to earth from somewhere in space. Russ wondered how in the world the old timers had brought them into the valley. Brought piece by piece on mules and then assembled, possibly. That in itself seemed amazing. He glanced up at the towering cliff that formed the side canyon. There were mine-shaft entrances cut into the sheer face of the cliffs. Rungs of iron ladders led to the mine openings, each rung hammered into the rock.

Chief paused and leaned against a boulder. Russ removed his pack and sat on a rock. A hot breeze drifted through the side canyon, and Russ could see that the vegetation would not be verdant as it was along the Havasupai. They were entering an arid environment with spare desert plants. Russ and Chief sipped water and stared up at the crimson and sallow bluffs.

"These are not the mine shafts we are looking for. We will walk halfway into the canyon before we find the ones we want." Chief took another sip of water.

"It amazes me that men came down here to mine. I can't imagine how they did it. They had to be some pretty hardened characters . . . what were they mining?"

"Lead and silver; there are large deposits of calcite. This area is rich in minerals, but fortunately it was not easily accessible back in the late 1800s and early 1900s, so no mass devastation occurred. The land is still scarred, though." Chief pointed toward a mine opening two hundred feet above the canyon floor.

A figure emerged from the shadow and clung to a vertical rod, lowering his body slowly down onto the first iron rung of an ancient ladder. He tested it before allowing it to take his full weight. Then he moved cautiously to the next rung and the next. Another dark figure emerged and knelt, peering over the edge of the precipice, anxiously observing the first person's descent. He waited until the first person reached the canyon floor before starting down the ladder. As the second person descended, a third appeared and watched as had the second—and when the second reached the canyon floor, he descended. Russ and Chief watched the three get safely onto the ground. The trio walked toward the trail and the point where Russ and Chief sat.

"Hello, what a beautiful day," one of the men offered as he approached.

"It is," Russ responded. "Great day."

They removed their packs and perched on separate rocks, water bottles in hand, two men—and a woman.

"My friend here"—the first man extended his hand toward the second—"is a geologist. He invited us to explore the wonders of the canyon. My name is Jim, this is John, and she is Helen. Helen and I, we're astrophysicists, and so we spend our nights looking up." He chuckled. "It is refreshing to go into the earth. We are witnesses to many spectacular sites thanks to John. He's given us a wonderful tour of the calcite crystals in the tunnels, and in return, we will show him the universe tonight."

If Jim hadn't mentioned they were astrophysicists, Russ would have guessed it by the intense, bookish look of them, their untraveled clothing and nerdy glasses, their disheveled appearance as if clothing and haircuts were forgotten trappings. *Just your stereotypical astrophysicists.* He chuckled to himself and wondered if he were being politically incorrect. Maybe astrophysicists are fair game. Russ soon realized no one else was in on his joke and caught himself long enough to acknowledge Jim.

"I'm Russ and this is Chief. Nice to meet you. We're just a couple of wanderers and wonderers."

"Are you planning to enter any of the mine shafts?" John asked.

"No." Chief quickly responded before Russ could open his mouth.

"Good, I really don't recommend it unless you are familiar with the tunnels. Maybe you are?" John scrutinized Chief, maybe only half believing his quick response. "I didn't mean to imply you weren't familiar, but there are a lot of vertical shafts that you can encounter without warning. You need to have a keen sense and good lighting."

"I am aware of these things," Chief replied.

"Oh, then you really should explore the mines if you get the opportunity. John would guide you, I'm sure. We will be in the canyon all week. How long will you be here?" Helen interjected.

"All week," Chief answered.

John spoke up. "If you decide you want to go, look for us in the campground in the evening. I would be glad to have you along. We usually get an early start, just before daybreak, and only spend a couple of hours in the mines. We like to be back at the lodge for lunch. We're getting a little too old to be making this a chore and pushing the envelope, so to speak. It's good to have a little afternoon siesta, too, so we're rested for Helen's tour of the universe."

Helen offered her enthusiasm. "Seriously, look us up. I'd love to share the stars with you two. The sky is so clear here. I have a couple of telescopes."

"It is nice of you to offer your hospitality." Chief nodded.

John beamed as he spoke about his passion. "Those red cliffs are known as Redwall Limestone. The color actually comes from a wash of the overlying red rocks. This region has been subjected to three transgressions and regressions of the Permian Sea during the Mississippian period. Near the rim in the uppermost formation you'll find a conspicuous cliff that is Esplanade Sandstone. Watch for the Sinyala Fault that crosses the canyon between Beaver and Mooney Falls.

The canyons expose millions of years of geological history. Sorry for rattling on, but I get very excited when I'm in these canyons."

"We understand. We don't know much about what we're looking at, but it still excites us, right Chief?" Russ looked at Chief for validation, but Chief was staring at the canyon walls.

John kicked at the dust at his feet. "It is said that there is a lost city of sorts in the canyon. A city that was underground with a population of as many as fifty thousand. It's just a legend, but it adds flavoring to the adventure. This land would have a hard time supporting such a population. It is surprising how many lives have been lost in search of it, though. There have been Native Americans living in this canyon for thousands of years. I suppose the climate must have been more hospitable at one time. The Hopi legends say that the Hopi came from inside the earth, maybe from the lost city. Their legend says that there were two peoples, those with one heart and the evil ones with two hearts. The people of one heart came to the surface to live in the light and tarried by *Paisisvai* to grow corn and grain." John removed his hat and wiped sweat from his brow. "*Paisisvai* is their word for the Colorado. I've wandered these mines for many years and haven't stumbled onto this legendary cavern."

Russ and Chief politely listened without interrupting while Helen and Jim rummaged through their packs. Russ was sure they had heard John's stories before.

"I won't say it doesn't exist, and way back in 1909 a fellow—I think his name was Kinkaid—claimed he found it, but he couldn't remember how to get back. He called it the 'Lost City of the Dead' and claimed he saw Egyptian artifacts in it. I think he was chewing too much peyote, but it did get a write-up in the *Arizona Gazette*. There is usually a base of truth in legends, though." John was a talker, and Chief waited for a pause long enough to inject his thoughts.

"This is why the *Diné* say these lands are sacred." Chief's lips tightened as John continued.

"Yes . . . yes, yes, I respect that, I really do. I hope these lands stay in the hands of the *Supai* forever. I feel privileged to be able to wander Beaver, Cataract, and Havasu canyons. There will always be those seeking *El Dorado* or the trinity of *Chiminigagua* with its energy contained in gold. *Chiminigagua* is said to constitute the creative power of all that exists. What a find that would be, eh? To me, it's nothing but a metaphor for true love, happiness, heaven, success—whatever one will never achieve, I suppose." John offered his hand to Chief. "Now you all be careful out here. You just never know what you'll stumble onto or into."

Some of John's words appeared to strike a nerve with Chief. Russ guessed that Chief was hoping to quickly part with their company.

"Well, that's awfully nice of you to offer to guide us through the tunnels and the stars. We'll see how our week plays out. Hopefully, there will be time for us to spelunk together," Russ said diplomatically, displaying sincere appreciation of their offer.

Helen sat on a rock beside a nice buffet of snacks all set out on a clean white linen napkin. "Well, sit with us a spell and share some of these fixings Jim and I put out. There are some fresh grapes and crackers with cheese. We have plenty. Let's share a little trail-side hospitality." It was a difficult offering to refuse, and Russ watched as Chief sat down without another word and helped himself to Helen's fixings.

The five of them chatted about what they had seen and experienced in Havasupai so far. Russ told a few short accounts of adventures gone wrong on other hikes, and after a half-hour rest, they parted company.

Obviously it was none too soon for Chief. The more time he spent with John, the more clearly irritated Chief became. The spelunkers headed back toward the campground. Russ and Chief started into the side canyon.

"White men, they must name everything and measure it. Why is that?" Chief looked at Russ with a knowing look. Russ didn't offer an answer.

"The need for names was a device used to pass along the knowledge of this place, and the measuring of things put a value on it. Both of these devices threaten to endanger the beauty of *Havasupai*." Chief looked back and watched the trio disappear into the cottonwoods.

"He is a man of too many words. I would never crawl into a tunnel with him for fear that I would emerge alone." Chief turned and strode up the trail leading into the side canyon, with Russ following close behind. The trail led them over a rise beyond where the trio had descended from the mine. A quarter-mile past that a sign posting read, "No Trespassing—Sacred Lands."

CHAPTER 16

"Really, a sign that says *Sacred Lands*; I didn't expect things to be labeled like that. Why don't they just say 'keep out' and let it go at that?" Russ looked to Chief for an answer. Chief grunted his disapproval. "In my youth there was no need for such things. The sacred areas were marked with symbols known to the native peoples, and that was all. This sign is a symbol of so-called civilization and an impediment to the nature of what is beyond. Still, it is necessary due to all the tourists. The tribe is conflicted; they like the tourist revenue, but there is a price to pay." Chief shrugged his shoulders. "No one will bother us. I am allowed to enter and take you with me. If we encounter anyone, just let me do all the talking."

Russ couldn't help himself. "Is this where El Dorado is?"

"There is no El Dorado here. That is in South America."

"I was just kidding, Chief. South America, huh?"

"Such things are stories for fools."

"Well, I can tell you, I hiked the Amazon Basin, and I wouldn't go back even if I knew exactly where El Dorado was. That was a nightmare hike if I ever took one, got sick as a dog with fever. It took me a year and a half to get over it. At one point I secured a guide who took me through some sacred temples, and I swear I received a curse. It was almost instantaneous."

"That's why my people lived in the desert; it is healthier here. I'll protect you from curses."

Their small talk was just a cover for Russ. He really felt as if he had ventured into an unforgiving zone, and his thoughts of the Amazon curse were real—Montezuma's revenge, dysentery, inflamed intestines, disentería amebiana, inflamatoria del intestino as his guide had called it, or just plain volcanic diarrhea. Russ knew that it had been a cursed thing. A curse isn't always executed by a mummy in the form of the living dead. There can be far worse things that just plain make one want to die and wish to be dealing with just a mummy. It had been an eighteen-month odyssey in search of a cure, trying special diets—dairy-free, gluten-free, wheat-free, meat-free, fat-free, but worst of all was the period of beer-free. The doctors all scratched their heads and offered drugs to alleviate the symptoms, but none offered hope for a cure. Eventually, the curse's grip loosened, and Russ found relief. Sometimes he wondered if it hadn't been through his pleading and prayers.

Looking around this sacred place, Russ saw himself once again as a violator of sorts, even though he was escorted by Chief. There was no immediate threat, just a vague, general sense of it. The trail was not worn, for it saw little recent traffic. Russ wondered if that was because of the effective signage or just good common sense. He doubted Native Americans even ventured here anymore.

A stick framework holding a small platform about head level stood not far up the trail from the no trespassing sign. The framework had feathers strung from the crosspieces and bleached bones from an unknown animal stacked on the platform. The skull of a buffalo rested on the ground below. Chief stopped, his hand rummaging about in his sack until it emerged holding an animal pelt strung from a piece of rawhide. He hung it from the stub of an old branch on one of the posts as he recited a chant and hummed. Russ stood quietly, watching and listening to a whistling wind and Chief's chant.

"No trespassing." Chief patted one of the uprights on the framework. "This is how you say it in my language. Come, let's go. My offering is our payment for safe passage."

"Now that's a proper 'no trespassing' sign. Does any part of it warn of a curse?" Russ queried, then offered a sheepish grin. Chief gave Russ a half smile on that bit of humor and moved on.

The terrain challenged Chief. The trail sloped up through tumbled and crumbled rock. They switchbacked around the larger pieces of debris, but in places they had to climb over boulders. Visibility was limited at ground level to the surfaces of the boulders surrounding them. Only when they climbed over a boulder could they see for any distance, but even then, all they could see were the tops of other boulders. Russ looked for the mine entrance but refrained from asking about their progress. Chief had informed Russ that trivial talk in a sacred place would offend the spirits, so they walked in silence.

Strange odors permeated the air—mineral spirits, a whiff of rotten egg, and then a little acetone. Odors Russ would never expect to experience mingling with the canyon's pristine air. Chief held a hand against Russ's chest to stop him. His other hand moved to his face with an index finger crossing his lips in a sign of silence. He pointed at a debris pile just off the trail, comprised of paint thinner and antifreeze cans, used rags, and broken lithium batteries. He signaled Russ to stay put, then climbed a boulder on the edge of the trail. Sliding back down beside Russ, the old Indian whispered in a barely audible voice, "Meth. Someone is cooking meth."

"Who would do drugs in a place this beautiful, Chief? Why?"

Chief once again signaled him to talk softly. Russ thought back to the kids he had given salve to at the edge of the village. It made sense now. This was the score they had been looking for. He had said nothing about the incident to Chief.

"It is a curse that has fallen even on the youth of Havasupai. Here is your curse, my friend. We must be careful; these people value only the drug. They are little more than zombies."

Chief continued. "Meth, it is bad. These men are molesters of the spirit. They make money turning brains to mush. Have you ever looked into the eyes of the living dead? This drug takes away a person's dignity. Our young women prostitute themselves to acquire their supply. I am not a prude. I have smoked my share of cannabis and have used peyote. This is different."

Russ had figured that Chief had partaken in a few ceremonial highs, so Chief's words came as no surprise. He was a little surprised, however, at the anger that seemed to be rising in Chief.

Russ knew all too well that drugs motivate men to take drastic measures. Doing the drugs to feel good is not the crime; it is the drive to get high and stay high. The money comes from somewhere—robbery, prostitution, lying, cheating, shoplifting, and whatever it takes to cover the tracks, even murder. The mind of the addict is not a normal mind. The men who had killed Russ's father, they didn't want the money. They wanted what the money could get them.

"If you stumbled upon a child being molested, would it enrage you?" Chief's voice took a terse tone.

Russ didn't answer; the thought of coming across something so unthinkable sickened his stomach. He didn't know what he'd do, but it wouldn't be pretty for the perpetrators.

"These men, I know of them. There has been talk in the Tribal Council. There have been those who have disappeared, and the talk is that it is connected to the meth trade. They are bad men. They have done many things that have caused much sorrow. They spit on the *Diné* spirit, just as they molest this sacred place. Their way is to snuff out life; if they see us, we are dead." There was a great anger in Chief's eyes, a fire.

"Chief, I think we just notched this whole thing up beyond my bounds. Maybe we should head back to the village and report this to the tribal police."

"Is that what you would do if you caught a man raping your wife?" Chief no longer restrained his voice.

Russ knew he had to find a way to calm down Chief, whose eyes had taken on a wild look.

"Chief, leave this to God; these men will get their due. Heck, the curse will get them. Let's just get out of here." Russ swore he felt heat coming from the old man, but it was probably just the sun. *Yes, that had to be it.*

"No, I will deal with this *my* way, the warrior way. You move slowly ahead. I will scout them out. It is best we find them before they find us. They will have a guard posted." Chief took on the intensity of a predator about to spring on its prey.

"Chief, let's just calm down and turn back . . ." Russ knew what they were up against. He was no stranger to the seedy side of life. He had been in some tight spots in South America and in Europe. In South America he just very gingerly slipped away into brush to avoid confrontations. The jungles were populated with cocaine farmers and drug cartels. Once caught in their territory, a person was dead, no questions asked. In a European seaport he got cornered in the men's room of a bar by a couple of crackheads. Luck got him out of that one. Russ saw no need to bother with these guys.

Chief wanted them, Russ could see it, but he wondered if Chief were in touch with his age. This was just like the bar fight the night they had met, only this time there were no cowboys to come to the rescue.

"No, we will be all right. I think," said Chief.

"You think? That's a little iffy, my friend. You already have a couple of bad calls going for you." Russ took a deep breath and gained his composure. *So what?* he thought. He had nobody waiting for him. If this is the way it ends, so be it. "Well, what are you planning to do to them?"

Chief's back was to Russ, but he quickly spun around. "Hide yourself—hide well!"

CHAPTER 17

Chief sprinted into the rumble of boulders that covered the canyon floor, and Russ—obeying his orders—sprinted as well, but up the trail. He stumbled, catching himself. *Why am I running away like a scared kid? Or some soldier obeying his officer? I can't leave that old man to fight a group of meth heads. Stupid, this is stupid! I should have insisted that we just go back, should have been more forceful.* Still, Russ knew that being careful and quiet was essential to survival at this point. One reckless move and who knows? *Shotgun? Crazy druggie coming after him in a delusion?* Moving on up the trail cautiously, quietly, Russ wrestled with continuing on and getting out of this alive or running toward Chief to talk him out of this insane idea, whatever it was. Fighting them? *Killing* them? All Russ wanted was to get through this canyon without detection and for Chief to come to his right mind. Then, the two of them could get out of here. *The meth lab was probably far enough off the trail that they wouldn't have encountered anyone. Who in their right mind would build their lab on this trail through sacred lands? But is any meth doper in his right mind?*

The trails led Russ beyond the scent of the lab up to higher ground. Scanning the terrain, he saw no sign of Chief or the dopers. The canyon looked at peace, and the long shadows hid details; he hoped they hid him as well. Distance, he wanted distance between him and the fouled air of meth. He spotted a recess in the rock wall and headed for that. Bits of human debris indicated that the meth heads had used this as a refuge at some point.

Suddenly, strange sounds—loud and horrible sounds—echoed

through the canyon. A weakness overtook Russ as he swung around and dropped spread-eagle on top of a large, flat rock. The rock outcropping above cast a secure shadow over him. The elevation gave him the advantage to catch a glimpse of anyone who might approach on the trail from the lower canyon. He raised up on his elbows and waited.

A voice of sheer terror echoed off the canyon walls. "My God, what is going on in the rocks below?" Russ muttered as he rolled onto his side and covered his head with one arm. Nothing could be seen but rock separated in shadow and a thin wisp of smoke a few hundred yards beyond the trail. Suddenly, all was quiet except for the wind whispering in the skeleton of a dead creosote bush. Russ flipped back onto his stomach and scoured the rocks below for movement.

The initial cries had faded before they fully registered in Russ's mind, but the echoes remained within him, reverberating several times. He recognized some as the sounds he had heard in the campground his first night in the canyon. Soon, those frightful sounds were replaced by the sound of his heartbeat and the wind. He strained to catch a glimpse of any movement among the rocks but saw nothing, only the breeze tussling at wispy sage. A whistling through nearby sparse bushes offered the only voice.

Minutes passed as Russ lay still on the rock. He watched for a sign of Chief or a meth head, whoever might have triumphed in battle. Finally, he sat up and took water from his pack to quench a dry throat. There was little point sitting here waiting to be taken out by some unhinged soul. He decided he should look for Chief. There was a chance he might need his help. What if he were a prisoner? What if they tortured him? Russ gathered his courage, grabbed his pack, and jumped to his feet. He took a step back down the trail.

CHAPTER 18

"It is over." A monotone voice sounded from behind him.

Russ jumped at the sudden sound and spun around. Instinctively, his fist clenched and his arm cocked, his backpack pulled tight against his chest. Then he relaxed. His muscles loosened. It was Chief. Somehow, the old man had maneuvered out ahead of him.

"It is over? Crap, man, you scared me."

"You scared yourself." Chief looked at Russ.

"How did you get ahead of me? Those horrible sounds down in the canyon, I thought they got you. I was just coming to help."

"I am fine. Now we can continue."

"Not so fast, old man. Did you kill those men? Did they try to kill you? What in the heck happened down there?"

"No questions, white man. A curse has been dispelled from the valley of the blue-green waters. That is all that needs an answer. We are safe to go about our business, and you may calm your nerves. These men trespassed on sacred land and paid the price."

"What? Just like that? If they are dead, won't the reservation police be looking for answers?"

"Just like that. They will be looking for a mountain lion, not an old Indian and his paleface sidekick. Come, enough talk."

The trail rose in elevation as they continued their journey toward the old mine. Russ's thoughts were swirling. *I should be thinking about how Chief just confronted death. Instead, I'm thinking about how quickly I obeyed when Chief told me to hide. I knew that Chief was going to be outnumbered, how he was an ancient, and I, a grown man, hid.*

Did Chief just scare the living daylights out of them? Did he send them packing out of here? Did he kill them somehow? Surely not . . .

The entrance to the mine was not a welcoming sight, though it was level with the trail. Dry-rotted timbers littered the foreground. The opening was slightly lower than the top of Chief's head. Chief moved some old boards that covered a large, dusty mirror, which he quickly polished with his sleeve. He placed the mirror against a rock to direct reflected sunlight into the opening of the mine shaft. The mirror illuminated several hundred feet of the mine shaft, but it would be insufficient to guide them through their entire journey.

"This will help," said Chief. "Inside, we should find more mirrors to reflect around corners, but we still need torches. There should be a stash of rags and oil hidden halfway down the shaft. They are neatly hidden, so I doubt that anyone has used them."

"Before we go any further, Chief, I want to say something." Russ sat down on a rock near the mine's entrance.

"What is it? What would you like to tell me?" Chief squatted as he cleaned a dead shrub branch of brittle twigs.

"I'm thinking about my actions, or lack thereof, back there. You had asked me about my personal stuff, and I put you off. I never really gave you a good perspective of my past."

"No, but there is no need; the present is all that we have. It is where we live. There is no need to look in the rearview mirror. We will live now and see what that brings in our future."

"No, Chief—I want to tell you a few things before we go on."

"I will listen." Chief continued to pick at the branch, breaking off dried stubs.

"You are the same age as my father, and like you, he was in World War II, in the Army Air Corp. He flew missions behind enemy lines in the dead of night and landed in mountain passes in the Balkans. His plane was unarmed. He flew supplies to freedom fighters in the mountains and brought back wounded fighters, women, and children." Russ's throat tightened, and he stopped talking.

Chief stopped picking at his stick and focused on Russ. "You are very proud of him."

"He was my hero, and I let him down. He deserved a better son. He saw me as a coward, and I have lived with that all these years."

"I do not see a coward, and I doubt your father thought of you as one. Did you speak to him about it?"

"No, when we had our falling out, I left home and we never spoke again."

"Has he passed?"

"Yes, he was killed. Murdered—" Russ caught his breath. He had never spoken of the event to anyone. To speak of certain things would be to cheapen them. It was the same as when Chief refused to speak of his scars. Russ took his time thinking about how to say it in a way that would be insightful but not burdened with too many words.

"You have no need to say more. Speak if you wish. I will listen, but I feel I do not deserve the honor of your memories of someone you loved as you did your father."

"No, I want you to know before you depend on me any further. You need to know more about me."

"There is no need. I can see into your heart."

"Yeah, but I'm going to say this anyway. My father owned a store, and I worked for him. My wife had worked for him also. When we got married, my father was not happy with us. My wife quit her job, and then I did. We moved near her parents, and I went to work for her father for a short time." Russ paused to gather his thoughts and clear the lump that was forming in his throat. He took a swig of water. "One night at closing time someone flattened my father's tire. His truck was parked behind the store. When he squatted down to change the tire, they attacked him from behind—drug addicts." Russ's eyes welled, and again his throat closed. He stood and walked away, leaving the chief silently squatting in the tailing of the old mine. Russ walked back down the trail from which they had come for several paces, then turned back toward Chief.

"This happened after you left?"

"I guess I got a little ahead of myself." Russ needed a better timeline, but his thoughts had jumped to events closest to his heart. "It was about three years after I left, but my father and I had never spoken to each other during that time. That is what makes it even worse—the silence. There is more, but I can't stomach saying it. Just be warned that I am not this pure-of-heart person that you think."

"This may be your second chance, I think. Few people are given a second chance. I am old. I do not have many options. I am willing to give you a second chance, if you are willing to give me my final one." Chief laid his right hand on Russ's shoulder. "When the time is right, there will be no secrets among men, and all will live in the light. First, we must trek in the dark. There is only one who has ever been pure of heart, perfect—so dread not. Come and help me fashion torches for the journey."

"Chief . . . when you're young you believe men like my father don't die."

Chief nodded knowingly without speaking. With torches quickly fashioned by Chief, the pair entered into the nadirs of the old mine, a burrow without light.

CHAPTER 19

Upon entering the mine, the men knew the terrain was going to be a challenge. Russ had no time to second-guess his confession to Chief, or worry about reservation police or meth heads. They must focus on the task at hand.

They squeezed through narrow passages impeded by cave-ins. Broken timbers littered the tunnel and snagged their feet. Vertical shafts rose above and dropped beneath them with little warning, as John and the bartender had warned. Chief led slowly and looked for gaps in the floor. The vertical shafts seemed to fall into an endless abyss; dropped rocks took moments to find the bottom. They traversed the pits on old planks that creaked and sagged under their weight. They dared not both be on them at the same time.

How Russ wished the old chief would work some magic and just turn them into a couple of bats so they could fly through this place.

At a large breach, Chief stopped, holding out his arm to signal Russ. No planks spanned the fissure. Two old bull ropes stretched across, one about four feet above the other. Years of dampness showed its work on them, even in the dim light of the torches. Chief grasped the ropes one by one and tugged, then shook them. It was not much of a test upon which to justify risking one's life, but what were the options? Russ took his turn to satisfy his doubts. He extinguished his torch and put it down so he could tug with both his hands and his back. The ropes held. Chief then put out his torch, leaving them in darkness.

Chief tucked the torch into his cloth belt, securing it for later use. The upper rope stretched and creaked under his weight as he tucked it under his arm and stepped onto the lower rope. Small rocks dislodged where the rope slipped off the precipice, and Russ listened in the dark as they bounced off the walls of the depths, but he never heard a definitive, robust plunk. Russ seized Chief's arm and pulled him back.

"Chief, I am heavier. I should go first. If it breaks on me then you can go back, but if you cross and I break it, you will be stuck on the far side."

"It does not matter either way. If something happens to you, I am finished."

"Let me go first." Chief obliged this time and stepped aside. Russ assumed Chief's position. With the upper rope tucked under his arm, he stepped off the edge, balancing on the lower rope. He hesitated just long enough to silently ask God to forgive him for all his sins, not as much out of a deep belief as to cover the bases. The ropes separated, not holding true above and below each other, and Russ felt most of his weight straining at the upper rope as he slid slowly along its length. Chief held the rope as best he could to steady it, but it quivered and oscillated out of his control until finally Russ heard and felt a sickening crack.

CHAPTER 20

The upper rope let loose far behind Chief, whipped instantly around him, and hooked under the shaft of the torch tucked into his belt. Chief's hands clasped firm on the rope as Russ's weight pulled him over the edge and into the black chasm. The two dropped blindly into the blackness of the vertical mine shaft. Their eyes strained wide in search of form and dimension, but they could see nothing.

Both Russ and Chief's grip tightened in the split second it took for them to swoop to the far wall of the pit. They struck hard enough to bounce. Even after striking, the blackness concealed the face of the wall. The wind knocked out of them, they struggled to catch a breath. Their feet kicked wildly, searching for a footing, but they found none. Russ knew his strength would fade fast, his grip would fail, and he would tumble to his death. He instinctively pulled up and reached higher with one hand, then repeatedly forced his torso up the invisible wall. His thoughts focused on reaching the crest of the wall. He closed his useless eyes to protect them from irritating falling debris. He spat bits of earth that fell into the gap of his lips, but still he moved steadily upward until his hand found the point where the rope rubbed on the rocky edge of the pit's rim.

Grasping the rope at this point was impossible. His feet searched for a hold and found a small ledge. Small but sufficient enough, the ledge allowed him to propel himself high enough for his chest to clear the rim. His outstretched arms and fingers searched until they found an iron railroad track to grip. He pulled up onto level ground and promptly rolled onto his back, giving thanks to the Lord for saving him. It was out of character, and it surprised him that he had the urge to pray, but he did.

Russ only allowed a second to rejoice, then took a deep breath before he began to tug on the rope in an effort to raise Chief to safety. He felt the weight of the old man on the rope and that was a good sign, but it was dead weight. Still, he pulled, and with each foot gained, he wrapped the rope around a large, protruding rock he had found by feel at the edge of the cliff. The action secured his gain. In the dark he could see neither the rope he held nor where his feet were planted; he proceeded by feel alone. He stopped to catch a breath, slowly feeling his way toward the fringe, and whispered over the edge to Chief.

"Old man, are you alright? Can you hear me?" Russ croaked weakly. He looked down but saw only more blackness—his eyes straining wide into a total absence of light. He forced himself to speak more loudly. "Chief, are you alright?"

There was no answer. Russ felt his way back along the rope to the securing rock. He stood and resumed pulling up on the rope. Occasionally, he stopped to reach over the edge to feel for the old man's hands. If Chief were holding onto the rope, his fingers would become pinched where the rope rubbed the rim of the pit. Russ feared it might cause the old man to lose his grip, and he began to realize that if Chief was not responding, how could he be holding on? Could the rope possibly have looped around Chief's head? The thought sickened Russ, but the truth was hidden from him in the dark until he reached over the edge and felt it.

Cold flesh like death, a cold fist locked around rope.

Startled, Russ pulled back his hand instinctively. Yet, just as quickly, he extended his reach to grasp a lifeless wrist below the hand and pulled. Russ lashed a bit of the rope around his own feet and solidly secured the rope to the iron railroad track. Then he reached with his other arm into the blackness in search of another point to clasp. He struggled to lift the body up over the edge. He felt Chief's hair, so slid his hand down to his neck. He didn't feel a rope wrapped around Chief there. A check of vital signs waited until Chief rested securely beside him, motionless. Russ was not hopeful. He sought to loosen the stony hands that clutched the rope, but they would not release. *Rigor mortis*, Russ thought. He discovered that the rope had entwined the shaft of Chief's torch and bore most of the body's weight as it had dangled.

Russ placed his hand on a cold chest to feel for a heartbeat or breathing and detected none. His hand slid toward the throat, up over the chin, and came to rest in a mass of coagulating blood around the nose. His hand cupped and dislodged the clotted material. Without the aid of sight it was hard to determine the extent of injury to the face, but Russ thought the worst.

He pulled the torch from the belt of the old man and lit it. The torchlight flickered and cast distorted shadows that danced on the walls. Russ held the torch high over Chief's face and illuminated a cold, drawn visage. Coagulated blood smeared across the forehead, nose, and chin, but the eyes were open, his lips parted.

Russ placed the old man's bag beneath his battered pate and moistened a cloth to gently clean the wounds. Before he began cleaning, he swiped his hands over the old man's face to close his eyelids. The grotto chilled, and the blackness beyond the light of the torch grew ever blacker. Russ's eyes watered and his throat tightened as he cleaned the blood from the death mask of a warrior. He rose to his feet, clutching his bag, then turned his back on the lifeless body. *What now?* Russ felt strange, as if he were watching from above; he also felt faint. With the bridge destroyed, there was no going back the way he had come, and he didn't know the trail of the ancient ones over the cliffs. Was this, then, the end?

CHAPTER 21

Russ tottered several paces, then hesitated. He had heard a sound—a strange resonance. He cocked his head and concentrated. He closed his eyes to avoid the distractions of the flickering torch, but the sound had already dissipated. Five more paces and again Russ stopped, hearing a vaguely familiar tone. He turned and held the torch high toward the old man. He saw only a carcass, lifeless and rigid. The reverberation had once more dispelled into the cracks of the stone walls, but Russ knew he had heard it. He crouched in wait for the next episode, staring out into the blackness beyond where the shadows flickered. All of his senses told him he was not alone. The silence wore on him, and an overactive imagination began to generate reasons to run, but he stood firm. Then he again heard a strange resonance, but this time it was gaining strength and direction. He turned toward the sound and watched stone-hard hands reanimate in the release of the rope. He lunged toward the old man whose arms stretched outward as the sounds grew into a chant. The dancing shadows cast on the walls reflected the image of spirits awakening the chief. He didn't know what else to call what he witnessed.

"Chief?" Russ whispered, not expecting a reply. The eyes blinked and the lips pursed to overcome a shortness of breath. The chest of the old man heaved and then took on a normal breathing rhythm. After moments of reflexive movement, fluidity returned, and Chief rolled onto his side, then to a sitting position on crossed legs.

Russ sat wide-eyed in speechless amazement.

"Trance, I invoked a trance as I fell through the dark void toward the wall. Strength alone would not support me, so I locked myself up in a rigid form."

"Yeah . . . right," Russ whispered under his breath. He realized that his adrenaline must have been pumping full speed, because he became aware of his own pounding heart and dry mouth. A chill ran down his spine.

"I am glad you were able to hold on and pull me to safety. I must sit for a while. Will you give me some water? It makes me weak to do these things." Chief struggled to settle with his back against the rock Russ had used to secure the rope.

Russ searched his pack and retrieved a bottle of water, handing it to the old man without a word. *Incredible*, Russ thought, *how controlled and clever is this guy?* They sat silently as the old man slowly sipped water and regained his strength. The chief closed his eyes and meditated.

"I am the father of two sons. When they were young, I taught them my ways. They were very bright, and we enjoyed many days walking the mesas. We spoke in our native tongue. Their mother taught them to be Christians and the way of the light . . . When you have little children, you also have big dreams. It is a very enjoyable part of life." The old man sipped another mouthful of water.

"When I was falling through the darkness, I had a vision of them. They gave me focus. My mind relived my past as I hung on the rope; I could see my two little boys laughing and running across the mesa toward me." Chief continued to sip his water.

"My sons eventually went off to the University to learn business and law. They married, but their wives did not approve of me and my ways. They did not want to hear my foolishness, and my sons turned their backs to me. My sons were who they were because of who I was and how I treated them, but now I am of no use." Chief's eyes searched far away and reached out as if still trying to understand.

"When a boy becomes a man, it is the natural course of things to rid himself of the things of his childhood. It is a painful time. My heart ached, but I knew the way of it. Still, I thought my grandchildren could learn from me." Chief's chest quivered as he took a deep breath. "One of my sons runs the tribal casino, and his wife cares only about the comfort of material things. Her children are spoiled and have learned the computer ways. My other son and his wife chose not to be burdened with children—I never saw my children as a burden. He is a tribal attorney and spends most of his time in Washington DC with politicians, probably leaving bags of casino money next to their desks. He has become very arrogant and sees himself as important, though he is really blind and lost. They all believe they are good Christians and that I am a heathen." Chief bowed his head and let out a sigh. "I am afraid I have become irrelevant to them. It happens with age."

"Sorry to hear that." Russ thought about how he departed from his father's life and knew Chief was responding to his story.

"My Rainbow Woman died of cancer while they were in college. I am sure she is not pleased with all of this. It has been lonely without her." Chief closed his eyes and rested silently for several moments.

"I only confide this to you because you spoke to me of your father. I thought you should know that I, too, believe that somehow I failed. It is the way of things that we judge harshly of ourselves. The truth is we do the best we can with what we are dealt."

"Thank you, Chief. You better rest." Russ lifted the canteen to Chief's lips.

"I will rest, but first I will finish my thoughts. When I was young I accepted the ways of the skinwalker and believed it was an honor. I believed I could use it for good, but my wife showed me that I was a tool of the darkness. What you have done here now proves that you are made of the stuff of your father and should no longer carry shame in your thoughts." Chief leaned his head back onto the rock.

"My sons are who they are, who they chose to be. I could blame their women, but they go along with it. None of my magic can work to change that. I will always be their father, and my love for them is always open should they seek me out. Your father was probably of the same heart, and one day you shall be with him. When we exercise our free will, people may take offense at it, but God gave us that right, and in the end all will be forgiven."

"Chief, I . . . well . . . thanks." Russ took a deep breath. "When you are ready, we better get out of here. We still have a lot ahead of us. I suppose we will have to find a different way back." Russ looked at Chief in the flickering light. The old man's dark eyes sparkled like the night sky with insight and wisdom. The wound on his forehead no longer seeped.

"I know the way, and we will be fine. Give me a few more moments to rest." Chief shut his eyes, then whispered as if some spirit might listen. "I thought that when I was in combat as a soldier that was the war. My wife explained to me that I fought in a *battle*. She said the *war* is ongoing with mankind and that it is a struggle between light and dark. She was a wise woman. I promised her I would shed myself of this burden called skinwalker and find her one day. I want to know the light. I want to bathe in it. I know the way; follow me." Chief stood and steadied himself with a hand pressed against the wall.

Russ plucked the torch from the wall and held it above their heads. The tunnel continued on without another vertical encounter. Although broken timbers and roof-collapse debris offered some obstruction, all were surmounted. Russ followed Chief down the tunnel, mulling over all the things that had been confided. It was easy to imagine Chief wandering the desert with his boys and teaching them the ways of their people. It was also easy for Russ to understand the old man's loneliness after the loss of Rainbow Woman.

Finally, they saw the proverbial light at the end of the tunnel. Chief stopped thirty feet short of the exit and sat on a large rock. Russ extinguished his torch and tossed it to the ground.

"This is as far as I can go. You must go from here alone," Chief said in an authoritative voice. He crossed his arms over his chest.

"What? What do you mean? You're alright, aren't you?" Russ hadn't yet recovered from the shock of Chief waking, and now Chief seemed to be changing the plan. *How am I going to get out of this mess without him?*

"This tunnel opens to what the old miners called the Canyon of the Dead. I cannot go there until you retrieve something for me. When you return, I will escort you to our return trail."

"Canyon of the Dead; I don't like the sound of that."

116

"You will be fine. The old miners had to call it something—now, I must tell you this. Within my heart I carry the souls of my victims. If I enter this canyon, their spirits will gain the strength to unchain themselves, and they will eat my flesh. Your heart is pure. So you have nothing to fear. You venture to the far side of the canyon. There you will locate the *Sipapu*."

"*Sipapu?*"

"It is a place of emergence from the underworld. It will be in the form of a spring. Cup the waters in your hands before you place it in this jar," Chief said as he produced a small glass jar from his bag.

"That's it, huh? It sounds an awful lot like a Canyon of the Dead to me." Russ took the jar in his hand and held it so the light from the end of the tunnel illuminated it.

"It would help if you sip a little and give thanks. Be sincerely grateful in your own words. When the water falls into your hands, do not be afraid, for you may have frightful visions. Know that they cannot hurt you."

"That's it?" Russ removed his backpack and placed it next to Chief.

"Yes, then return the jar to me. I must have this sacred water. In the canyon, look for signs that will lead the way. You will find skulls resting on poles in places where you should turn. Look carefully as there will be petroglyphs nearby that will signal the direction in which to turn. There is a petroglyph on the cliff above *Sipapu*. It is small, so be observant or you will miss it—wait!"

Barely listening, Russ walked toward the light of the opening. He squinted as his eyes tried to adjust. He raised his arms out at his sides as he teetered inches away from a sheer two hundred foot drop. Looking out on empty space, his head swirled in vertigo. His body swayed uncontrollably. Quickly, he dropped back into the shadows of the tunnel. Almost too late, he realized the exit did not lead out onto terra firma.

"You should listen." Chief stood with arms raised. "Step back, I must offer you a blessing."

"A blessing . . . ! You could have told me it opened onto a cliff ledge. I thought the exit was at ground level like where we came in. Make your blessing wings like a bird or something, can't you?"

Chief laughed at Russ's sarcasm. "Calm yourself. Come sit with me. There are iron pegs like those we watched the geologist descend, a ladder of sorts that will lower you to the ground. There is nothing to fear. When I was a boy I climbed down to gather water for Rearing Horse when he was turning me into a warrior. Sit with me. I will prepare you."

"I can climb down there. I'd rather not, but I can do it. That is probably as far down as the pit we fell into back there, but we had the advantage of darkness. I can see how far down this is. I'm not good with heights and especially right now after what happened in the tunnel. Give me a minute to gather myself." Russ wanted to overcome his fear, a fear he struggled with all his life.

"The Great Spirit is with you. He shall escort you down into the valley of the dead. Trust in the Lord," Chief preached.

The old Indian chanted as Russ sat by his side. Just like when they stopped in the car out in the desert, the chant relaxed and mesmerized Russ. He fell into a hypnotic state as Chief suggested that he picture himself leaving the tunnel, floating out over the edge of the precipice, drifting slowly along the vertical rock face, just lightly touching the rusty, old steel pegs of the miners' ladder.

It seemed easy just then.

CHAPTER 22

Russ looked up to see the hole in the cliff face that was the mine entrance. His boots sank into the soft soil on the canyon floor. He reached out to touch the rock wall in front of him and realized that it was not a dream. How it happened he couldn't explain; it reminded him of when old Doc Boggs used ether on him to take out his tonsils. Doc laid him on a cot, put the ether on him, and suddenly he was tonsil-free. Russ shook his head and turned to run across the open ground to the far side of the canyon.

Nothing about this canyon seemed different than any other. The broken rocks, sheer cliffs, and sparse vegetation were all he saw until he rounded a boulder, and there before him rested a human skull on a stick. He searched for a petroglyph, and above him on the boulder he saw a drawing of a bird in flight moving to the right, so he went right. The path led him through a maze of boulders. Each time he encountered a human skull, he found a petroglyph of an animal of some sort moving in a direction that he then followed. He walked quickly but watched for poisonous reptiles. He avoided outcroppings and shaded shelves.

Before long he reached the base of the distant canyon wall and searched for the mystic spring among broken rock and dust. He examined the cliff face for the sign Chief had described. The sound of trickling water caught his attention first, and then the light, sweet smell of moist air. On the cliff face he saw a symbol and approached it. He rounded a large boulder and there it was—the *Sipapu*.

Russ imagined the old-timers back in the day finding such a life-giving fountain. Wandering these canyons on the verge of death, they would see it in a spiritual light—sacred, *Sipapu*. The crevasse percolated volumes of cool, crystal-clear water into a small pool that overflowed and ran for only a few feet before disappearing back into the porous earth.

Russ plunged his hands into the cool flow that bubbled from the crevasse, the chill cramping his forearms. He splashed it over his face, then cupped his hands and dipped again. This time the water turned red, a deep blood red. Was it only an illusion? Nothing seemed to surprise him anymore. Then creatures surrounded him—animals he had hunted and killed in his youth. They looked at him with large, soulful eyes—deer, rabbits, squirrels, and grouse. His cupped hands shook as they moved over the neck of the jar and released the red liquid. Instantly, the visions dissipated. The water turned clear as he tightened the lid and deposited the jar into a leather pouch provided by Chief.

Russ sat for a moment to gather his thoughts. Then he sipped from the spring and asked for forgiveness for all he had done and failed to do in his life. When he finished, Russ felt an inner warmth and tranquility that he had never known. He muttered his thanks, then raced back toward the old ladder that would take him back up the cliff and into the mine where Chief waited. He ran between the boulders, switching direction when he caught sight of markings, but mostly he remembered which way he had come. There would be no magic to help in his ascent, just a newly found courage and inner peace.

Soon he stood at the base of the cliff and looked up at the ancient iron ladder. Slowly, he reached for the first rung and pulled himself up to grab the second rusted rung and then another. He inched his way up the sheer cliff face, stopping occasionally to gather his courage and his breath. How had he climbed down without a memory of it? When he reached a point about three-quarters of the way up, the rung his foot rested on sagged, then gave way. He dropped an arm's length. Russ's heart bounced in his throat, and his hands welded themselves to the rungs. He kicked at the cliff in search of a foothold as his biceps knotted in an attempt to raise his torso higher. He had to reach for the next rung above in order to raise his feet high enough to catch their next rung. He did a rapid pull-up, gaining the inertia needed to let go with one hand and reach for the next rung. He had one shot, only one shot, and Russ knew that if he missed, his body weight falling back through space would tear his one-handed grip free and plunge him to his death.

Three fingertips caught the rung. It was enough to prevent him from falling. He worked his fingers farther over the rung until his hand locked forefinger to thumb. He pulled higher, and his feet found a solid rung. He hurried the rest of the way up the ladder without hesitation, stumbling into the dark recesses of the mine.

CHAPTER 23

His eyes were slow to adjust to the tunnel's dim light, but soon Russ found Chief hunched over and braced against the cave wall, his form once again appearing to be lifeless. Chief's eyes were open, staring at the ground next to him. His hands rested open with palms up in the dust at his sides. Russ didn't speak until he noticed Chief's chest slightly rise then fall—at least he was breathing.

"Chief? The water you wanted!" Russ respectfully extended his hand, holding out the jar, but there was no response.

Dropping to one knee, Russ grabbed Chief's arm to steady him. He appeared ready to tumble over. Chief's head rolled and a blank, clammy, and skinned-up face stared back at Russ. Gently, Russ lowered him to the ground, where the chief stared sightlessly toward the ceiling and breathed shallow, irregular breaths.

"Oh, no! What's wrong? This doesn't look like one of your trances." Russ arranged Chief's arms and legs for comfort, watching for signs of life.

"Too much . . . you were right." Chief's lips barely parted as he spoke.

"I was right about what?"

"It has been too much for an old man. It is time for me. I will not succeed in my desires."

"No, we've come this far. Don't give up. Drink some water." Russ fumbled in search of his canteen.

"Not the sacred water."

"No, sip this." Russ tilted Chief's head and allowed him to sip from the canteen.

"Thank you, white man. Now I die without 'Anaa'jí. This was what I feared."

"'Anaa'jí?"

"The *Enemy Way*, an exorcism of the spirits of my kills. Now I shall spend eternity with their spirits taunting me. It is no good."

"Chief, just rest. It will be alright. Look, I've come this far with you, so don't you dare die on me. Hold on! I don't know the way out of here."

Russ lit the torch, sticking the stock in a fissure in the wall near them. He offered Chief more water, holding his canteen to Chief's stiffened lips with one hand and supporting his head with the other.

"No, I am going to die. I have something to confess."

"What?" Russ whispered.

"I'm not a chief." Chief formed a wry grin. "I only told the tourists that to boost my mystique. My sons, they are chiefs. My father died a drunk in New York City. That is why I was raised by Rearing Horse."

"No kidding."

"No kidding," Chief repeated in a whisper. "My mother and her husband never let me come back home after I became a skinwalker. They claimed they were too superstitious, but really her new husband had no use for me."

Chief's confession did not come as a shock, but it did stir in Russ an urge to come clean with his own past. A confession to a hero such as Chief was the hardest thing he could imagine doing. It had eaten at him all of his life, and finally he had to get it off his chest.

"Chief . . . I was an honest-to-goodness card-burning Vietnam draft-dodger." Russ watched for a change of expression or a verbal response from Chief, but he saw absolutely no visible reaction.

"That's a confession to beat yours, and you thought I had a warrior's heart." Russ couldn't believe he was saying what he was saying. "We're a couple of phonies, Chief, and we're going to die in this stinkin' hole in the middle of hell. Imagine you a war hero and me a coward—dying together. You can't let it happen."

"I—" Chief stopped. Moments passed as Russ waited for Chief to complete his words, but there was only silence.

"God will forgive you, Chief. Just ask . . . please ask. Whatever it is in your past that you are trying to redeem, just ask for forgiveness." Russ's voice trailed off as he watched the chief's face distort.

"Will you forgive yourself?" Chief coughed, and Russ did not respond.

The old Indian's eyes closed and his breathing slowed. Russ propped himself against the wall of the mine. He watched his companion until the light from the tunnel entrance faded. What was he going to do? How would he get out of this place? His mind mulled over the confession he had made to Chief. It was the first time he had voiced the words. The thought had gnawed at him all these years, but never once had he voiced them. It felt cleansing and hadn't hurt nearly as much as he had feared, although there was still shame in it all. Soon, night was upon them, and sleep overtook Russ in his struggle to monitor Chief.

A cool, silent breeze drifted from the back of the mine to kiss the departing light of day. A cloudless blue sky deepened into black, and the Milky Way appeared as long strings of dim but tightly packed speckles. A satellite streaked silently and swiftly beneath the stars, gone in minutes. Coyote yips and yowls echoed in the evening air as a wilderness rendezvous formulated in the shadows of rocky rubble scattered on the canyon floor. A long-drawn, reeling yowl was followed by a couple of yips, then another deep, long yowl as if a male offered a chilling death song.

"Song Dogs," Chief whispered. Russ opened one eye and looked toward the mine entrance, satisfied the vermin had no possible way to enter. He closed his eyes without as much worry, encouraged by the sound of Chief's voice.

Still, Russ couldn't sleep. He wondered what the morning would bring. Chief's injuries could be more extensive than he could determine, and he was not a trained medic. He second-guessed himself. Had he done the right thing, allowing Chief to move after the fall? He listened and heard Chief's labored breathing break into a snore. The coyotes continued to sing in tones that reverberated through the blackened Canyon of the Dead.

CHAPTER 24

A poke of a sharp stick in the side agitated Russ from an otherwise restful sleep. He crossed his arms without blinking and rolled onto his other side. Again he felt a poke. His eyes opened at floor level to the sight of a pair of hiking boots. He squinted in the glare of the bright light streaming in from the mine entrance and rolled his head to follow the lines of the legs protruding from the boots. The silhouette of the old Indian framed in the morning light stood over him.

"Sleep late is a habit for you. We must go. There is much to do." An impatient tone resounded in Chief's voice.

"I thought you died," Russ replied, half-jokingly. Nothing surprised him where Chief was concerned. He should be shocked to see Chief, apparently hale and hardy, but he wasn't. It was just easier to admit and accept that and go on.

"No, I was wrong. Sometimes that happens. Yesterday took much from me. I'm not ashkii—young boy—anymore. But I retrieved some granola from your pack, and that will do for now. I knew you would not mind. I owe you."

"Ha, you finally admit it. You also admitted that you are not a chief. I guess there's no lodge restaurant around, huh? You don't owe me."

"Did you hear the Song Dogs last night?" Chief asked, ignoring Russ's comments.

"Yes, it was a chilling sound."

"The male sang my death song. I decided that I would not let a coyote decide my fate. He taunted me. As I lay and listened, I decided it was not my time. When I made that decision, he stopped." Chief's face bore a sincere stare, and Russ didn't question him. What was the point?

"I also walked in a dream last night. There was a woman who looked very beautiful. She stood alone on the mesa, and her hair blew golden in the light of a setting sun. Then, I noticed she had a babe in her arms. An eagle circled above her with motionless wings. I saw a wild stallion with a flowing mane run toward her, but it stumbled. Its leg caught on a rope, a trap. The beast rolled in the dust but could not regain its footing. The woman tossed the infant into the air, and the eagle fetched it midair. The beautiful woman turned to dust and blew away. The stallion stood watching and then ran off toward the great wastelands to the north. I don't know what it meant." Chief's eyes shone as he slowly shook his head from side to side.

Russ stared at the old man, astounded. His jaw loosened, and his eyelids drooped. He stood silently, unable to gather words for a response. Chief was describing his life. The old man waited and watched Russ's spirit diminish as did the woman in his dream—dust in the wind.

"Uggh." Chief turned and disappeared into the darkness of the tunnel. Words echoed from the shadowed recesses. "Light your torch and follow me."

Lighting his torch, Russ recouped and scrambled to catch Chief, who had disappeared into a side shaft. Holding his torch high, Russ watched the tunnel floor for vertical shafts and tripping hazards, his thoughts consumed by Chief's "dream."

The tunnel was utter darkness, even embodied a smell of darkness, with a passageway floor that sloped upward. Yet Chief moved without the aid of a torch as if in the light of day.

Russ purposely lagged behind until he finally encountered the exit at a point high up on the canyon face. Chief sat on a rock waiting for him, looking off across the grand void. The bright sun hurt Russ's eyes as he held his hand over his forehead to block it. He dropped his torch on the dusty cavern floor.

"My words were painful? This was not my desire." Chief did not make eye contact.

"I'm fine, Chief. You do have great magic. Your dream has meaning, and I'm glad you shared it with me. I would like to sit and survey the timelessness of the canyon before we travel on. Sometimes I feel old too."

Russ felt ancient.

"That is an excellent idea. It is my wish also."

Russ lowered onto a rock near Chief. The canyon colors and shadows changed with the position of the sun. It made the red-and-yellow rock cliffs fluid and the blue sky pure. One rogue cloud wafted aimlessly high above the coulee where the Havasupai flowed. The cloud dissolved influence of the sun that ruled the sky and apparently deemed it a flaw. It was time to move again, and Russ stood ready to push on.

Chief hesitated. "We must collect earth from a sacred place along the Havasupai. At the bottom of the last waterfalls there is a cave; you will enter to find what I need."

"Beaver Falls?"

"If it must have a name, call it that." Chief's lips tightened in a straight, thin line. "We will travel the trail of the ancient ones. It is a good distance." Chief pointed toward a chiseled trail that was a mere ledge of eighteen inches wide. It was visible for a hundred feet and then disappeared around a sharp rock edge. Beyond, there was no way of knowing what obstacles they faced. Chief took a step onto the ledge and kicked a little loose debris off the edge with his foot. Dust drifted in the updraft from the falling rock that tumbled hundreds of feet to the desert below. He planted one foot in front of the other with a little shoveling of years of built-up rubble, for the path had not been used since the old man was last on it as a boy.

Russ hesitated, allowing Chief to show the way and reassuring himself that it was doable. "Chief, there's not much room for error. How do we know the trail is intact beyond this point? It's been a long time since you traveled this way." Russ felt like his shoulder, the one that rubbed the cliff face, was pushing him off balance.

Chief groaned. "Time is growing short. Come, we have no choice."

"What did you do for a living, I mean, in civilian life?" Russ asked.

"You want to talk?"

"Just curious . . ."

"Aren't all Indians ironworkers? That is your thought, isn't it?"

"That's a stereotype, Chief. I'm not allowed to think that, but the way you walk on this ledge, well . . ."

"Wait!" The old Indian stopped and raised his hand. "You want to talk? Then let us sit here."

Very gracefully, Chief lowered his frame down onto the ledge, his legs dangling in space. Russ froze, his right shoulder jammed into the cliff wall. He slowly slipped off his backpack and set it on the ledge. His fingers felt their way down the wall as he lowered to a sitting position on the ledge. He let out a sigh.

"My father was an ironworker in New York. He made good money but drank it away. I may have his agility. I may even have a touch of his drunkenness at times."

Russ appreciated Chief's candor and decided to let him do the talking.

"Actually, I worked in the oil fields when my children were young. I did climb rigs. I chose not to be like my father, and I sent home most of my pay. I did not drink when I was away from home. What do you do to feed yourself?"

Russ struggled with an anxious touch of vertigo. Strangely, he didn't have a fear of falling. His fear arose from a compulsion to jump. It made absolutely no logical sense, but his mind struggled to convince him that he really had no desire to jump or throw himself from the ledge. Still, the thought continued to arise. Each time, Russ put it to rest. He had always won the battle with such thoughts, but he feared the day he would not succeed.

The old man watched Russ struggle. "This is our only way out. I recommend that you gather yourself before we continue. I sense your anxiety, and it will give way to a mistake. The best way of it is to sit and talk to yourself. Defeat the demon."

"I think the best thing is to keep moving."

"No, I do not want you to get halfway and panic. Now just stay seated! There are two fears that paralyze a man. One, the fear of dying; the other, the fear of living." Chief looked out across the canyon and caught sight of an eagle riding the thermals.

Russ fidgeted with his pack and gently removed a sliver of beef jerky. Chief had once more struck a nerve that triggered a new perspective on his internal struggle, his compulsion to jump. Perhaps it *was* from a fear of living. Russ gnawed at the jerky.

"Chewing always helps me."

Russ pushed his back tighter against the wall, his feet dangling in nothingness. He ripped a bite of jerky and looked at the solidity of the rocks on which he sat and told himself that he was fine a minute ago, he was fine this moment, he would be fine two minutes from now, and that is all there is to it.

"What is it that makes us afraid? My life is over anyway, so it would mean nothing for me to slip. What is it that you do to feed yourself—that was my first question?" Chief glanced at Russ chewing his jerky.

"Instrumentation," Russ said as he ripped another bit of jerky. "I work with electronics and pneumatics in process controls. I've worked in power stations and refineries. I did a couple of paper mills in the south. It pays well, but I get laid off on a regular basis. I don't mind too much, though, because it's given me the opportunity to travel extensively. I do some freelance writing about my travels."

"Hmm, a writer . . . ? You have been published?" Chief gave Russ a quizzical look with one eye closed.

"No . . . not yet," Russ answered apologetically.

"So you write for your own entertainment? It would probably be best if you did not write about this, even for your own enjoyment. Can you promise me that you will never write about this journey?" Chief voiced legitimate concern.

"That's asking a lot . . . just kidding. I doubt anyone would believe it if I did write about it."

"Well, if you will not promise not to write about it, then will you at least use false names to protect the place I will take you?"

"I promise you that I'll do all I can to protect the sacred places.

And really Chief, I don't even think I will write about all this. I've become disillusioned with the craft itself. I started writing out of loneliness. I wanted to share my thoughts and experiences with someone, anyone. And then you find out that no one cares what you think or what you've done."

"It is my experience that only a few lucky people find someone that they can really share with."

"Well, writing didn't work out for me and neither did finding a mate."

"Maybe in both cases your focus was wrong. You need to set your focus on something other than yourself."

Ouch, Russ thought without a response. It hit home instantly because he had heard it before, but this time it made more sense than at any other time.

"Instrumentation, you said? The balancing of a process? That is what you must do here, bring everything into balance," Chief suggested thoughtfully.

"You're right, Chief—that's exactly what I need to do."

"It sounds like you have an interesting life, but has it made you happy? My own happiness came with my companion and my family."

"Happy—I've had my moments." Russ's silence spoke. He thought hard, as he had never allowed himself the question. He didn't have a ready answer, so he said nothing.

"When we are young we do things that set the tone for our lives. We are too young to know the way of it, but it is true, is it not?" The old man spat and leaned forward to watch it fall, as little boys do. It caught Russ off guard.

"Yes," Russ concurred.

"Yes, no matter what else you do, there are always those moments that we carry with us. There are people who fear sorting through these thoughts and letting go of them. They spend too much time looking back, and eventually, it causes them to trip. My wife said it is the way, for we are bound for greater things beyond this life and see this world with our eyes not our hearts, so we fail to appreciate God's gift. We only feel with our bodies, and that also ends in failure. She said there is more to life but because we are afraid, we lose opportunities to find the truth." The chief leaned forward, his shoulders out beyond the lip of the ledge.

Russ closed his eyes. "Don't do that."

"Does it matter to you? This old Indian will soon expire anyway."

Chief rummaged about in his pouch and eventually displayed a handful of fine downy feathers. He held out his hand, letting the wind lift them from his palm. The feathers floated above their heads, swirling in a dizzy display as they rose a hundred feet or more. Russ saw them as a flock of birds. They flapped their wings briefly to gain an advantage in the breeze and then glided in circles, catching thermals and going higher until out of view.

"If I fell or jumped, do you think I could turn myself into a bird?" the old man whispered.

"Yes, I'm thinking you could."

"You have become a believer. You know God granted man many options, options that remain our curse or our cure. Most men desire to walk in the way of the animal. He is lazy and shirks his responsibility of free will. This envy to walk without thought allows an opportunity for darkness to cause us to lose our way. You must engage in thought. Did you see the feathers until they disappeared, or did you see something else?"

"I watched as they turned into birds."

"Did they turn into birds?" Chief looked up toward where the feathers had last been seen.

"I saw them." Russ looked at Chief.

"I saw only feathers." The chief looked in his hand that had held the feathers. "Men have a fear of their own thoughts; it is human. Your eyes lied to you, and I will tell you that if I fell from this place, I would smash upon the rocks and be dead. Tell me, where we now sit, how is this any different from where you have spent your life?"

"Chief . . ." Russ lost his thought, or he choked on it.

"The truth is like these rocks. They have always been, and always will be. If you break a rock, all the pieces are rocks. That is the way of the truth. On this ledge of rock we are a lie. We live lies. If I break, I am no longer a human being. If I fall, my truth will come out of me, for my spirit is my rock and a spirit has the way of rock with each of its pieces. My flesh is the lie that does not hold up. Now, you have searched for happiness and know you will never find permanent joy. So why fear walking this edge? Look down, and look at where you are. You are not down there. You are only right here. Think about being right here; that is all there is."

"That makes it easier . . ." Russ looked down and took a deep breath, and he was prepared to follow the old man. The trail ledge perched hundreds of feet above the canyon floor, but it was a place of its own. It had nothing to do with the other place. There was now no feeling of fear in his heart. He regained the feeling he had at the spring of the underworld. Nothing mattered but to do what he had to do, and in the end, even that would have little meaning in the big scheme of things. He thought about his confession of dodging the draft and wondered if the old Indian had heard him or remembered. He hoped not. He was determined to show no fear.

CHAPTER 25

Driven with fond respect of this eighty-two-year-old fake chief and the knowledge that even he believed they both were living a lie, Russ stood. He prayed silently for protection from the myriad of dangers. His shoulder rubbed against the cliff and dislodged debris, bits of the rock that fell forever. Chief walked lightly, swiftly, without hesitation and disappeared around the edge. Russ followed. Much to his delight, they found themselves on an expansive plane that rose easily to the pinnacle of the mesa. The trail led them across the mesa and down a precarious switchback into the Havasupai river valley. There they would follow the river to the top of Beaver Falls.

Getting to the bottom of the canyon would require them to squeeze through a series of crevasses. In between these fissures, they descended a series of iron pegs staked into the rock face above the falls. The climb allowed intervals where Russ could actually see Beaver Falls. It was a low falls with smaller sisters above and below mixing blue-green with brilliant white froth. A treacherously built ladder marked the final descent as they slowly climbed down the last forty feet. From there they followed the trail toward the sound of the falling river until Chief stood on an outcropping near the top of the falls. Russ stepped onto the rock and looked down on the cascade.

"There!" Chief shouted, barely audible over the roar.

Russ's gaze followed the line from Chief's pointing forefinger across the mist-soaked boulders to a spot at the base of the falls. The chief then held out another jar for Russ to collect a sample in.

"Jump in right there. You must drop all the way to the bottom.

You will find a crevasse under the rock. You must squeeze through it. You will feel like you are trapped. It should be fine."

Russ stared at Chief's lips and tilted his head, trying to absorb, over the river's roar, every spoken syllable, every utterance from the old Indian's mouth.

"It *should* be fine?" Russ shouted back over the liquid thunder. "What does that mean, Chief?"

"It has been a long time since I went in. The river changes with floods. But it should take you into a cave under the falls. Scoop up the red clay where the light beam shines."

"If it's a sacred place, shouldn't it be a little more stable than that?" Russ shouted.

"You'll see. The clay is sacred. I will offer a prayer to the spirits. You will be fine." Chief pronounced, patting him on the back.

"You'll see? You'll say a prayer? I'll be fine?" Russ repeated as he stripped to his shorts, clutched the sample jar, and with only the slightest hesitation dropped off the edge of the boulder into the frothy discharge of the falls. Reemerging for a last look up at Chief, he sought some reassurance before the dive. His lips felt numb and his teeth chattered as he bobbed in a black portion of the river of blue-green water and white froth.

"Be careful of the current. If you get caught in it, it can hold you down," Chief shouted with his hands cupped around his mouth.

The words were almost lost in the sound of thundering water. Russ shook his head yes in an insincere gesture and faded beneath the surface. Fortunately, the water was crystalline, allowing good visibility to the bottom. The rays of an Arizona sun proved to be his best friend as laser-like streaks cut brightly in the water around him. Russ felt along the boulder and found the crevasse, scarcely sufficient enough for a man to pinch through. A mere crack in the boulder offered only blackness. Possibly a nonentity, for it offered not a clue as to what was beyond. It could culminate in a trap, so with a hard thrust of his feet on the river bottom, Russ surged toward the surface, lungs exhausted.

"I found a crevasse! It's like you said!" Russ shouted.

Chief looked down without expression. He gave him a hand

gesture to dive.

"I can't see if there's an air pocket in it!" Russ shouted.

"It'll be there." Chief nodded an approval.

Again, Chief gave the signal to dive. Taking in a deep breath, Russ dropped to the bottom and squeezed into the crack in the rock, shifting his shoulders and sucking in his already-flat abs. Stuck halfway in, halfway out, an overwhelming anxiety grabbed him, clouded his judgment, and threatened to take his life. *There was no way to free himself!* Russ struggled to dismiss the thought born in panic. He grappled to find something in the cave to push against to dislodge him back out into the river. But his arms failed as the oxygen in his burning lungs was expended. Unknown in his panic was the fact that he had rotated his body ninety degrees and made his shoulders too wide to fit back through the passage. He pushed, twisted, flexed, and squirmed to no avail.

His legs kicked as he twisted his body, bringing his arms back along the side of him as he made a final commitment to enter. He pushed back against solid rock and projected headlong into open space. *In!* Swimming upward, he prayed and searched for the air pocket—his only hope of survival.

Air! His arms upstretched, he broke the surface in a small, black cave. Coughing, gasping, he clung to a rock, sucking in moist air. Chief had been a boy when he entered this space, and Russ thought, *I'm probably twice the size he was.*

Allowing his eyes to adjust, he saw a faint light in the distance, down an earthen tunnel. He paddled to the edge of the black pool. At first, the tunnel was large enough to only allow crawling, but it widened to allow standing as he approached the light source. The air was heavy in moisture with droplets falling like rain. There in the enlarged cavern shone a penetrating beam of sunlight. Russ looked up for the source and saw a small hole in the rocks above. The light beam illuminated a square-foot of red clay on the cave floor as Chief had predicted. Russ gathered the sample and then paused to gather his wits for an exit. He leaned back on his elbows, mesmerized by the light above and a tiny patch of blue sky. Russ felt no need to hurry back into the tiny fissure that had threatened to strangle him on the way in.

Finally, he made his way back to the watery exit. He entered into the water, sucked in a deep breath, then submerged. The crevasse didn't seem as tight on the way out; perhaps it was because he knew what was waiting in that direction, not like when he was entering the unknown. His exit was a flawless movement, and he returned to the top without anxiety.

He broke the surface of the water, sucked air, and with his eyes closed let the sunlight warm his face. He held up the clay sample and gave out a war cry to Chief. He swam toward the shore. Chief squatted at the water's edge, and Russ handed him his clay. It drew a smile of grand satisfaction on the old man's face. Russ felt great pleasure in the satisfaction of risking all.

"How's that?" Russ shouted with cupped hand near his mouth.

"It is good! Very, very good. It is the basics from which the red man came. You are a warrior, my friend. I do not believe you when you call yourself a draft dodger. There is more to it."

Russ rose from the water close to Chief, spun around, and sat basking in the sun.

"There is, and thanks for having faith in me. When I was a kid we used to jump off a dam into the river. It kind of reminds me of that." Russ drifted off into a mumble that was obliterated by the background noise of the river.

"What was that; what did you say? The roar of the falls is too loud." Chief pointed to his ear.

"Nothing, nothing at all; what's next?" Russ spoke in a normal tone; he didn't feel like shouting.

"Come, follow me to where we can talk quietly." Chief motioned.

The old Indian moved over the wet boulders without missing a step as Russ scrambled close behind, slipping on the wet moss. Chief's every movement was deliberate and sure, his bag slung over his broad shoulders. Russ snatched up his backpack and slung it over one shoulder. Chief didn't look like an old man from the back. They didn't make people like him anymore. They stopped in a small, shaded stand of trees and sat on a comfortable rock.

"I am grateful to you for what you have done," the old Indian offered.

"You have no idea what it has done for me." Russ looked off toward the river.

"Do you believe in what we are doing?"

"Yeah, we've come far. I wouldn't have believed any of this if someone had just told me. So I believe a lot that I didn't believe before."

"It is very important to be a believer. The last thing I need you to do will take all the faith that you can muster." Chief looked very serious.

"Chief, I have done a lot of things and have been a lot of places in this world, but I have never felt it as spiritually as I have on this trip."

"It is growing late in the day. It is best that we make camp near here. We will rest so that we are fresh tomorrow. You can pitch your tent, and I will sleep beneath the stars."

They walked off the trail into a group of boulders that had an area of soft, flat sand with no underbrush. Russ rolled out his tent and Chief his bedroll. It was two hours until nightfall, so they walked back to the Havasu to watch the water flow. The sun felt warm but not blistering as in midday. The sound of the river sufficed, and neither man tried to engage in conversation. With all of the tourists safely back at the official campground, the valley was at peace as it had been when Chief was a boy.

A pair of coyotes played at the edge of the water downstream. The breeze was with the two men, and their stillness offered the Song Dogs no trepidation. The animals looked well fed and groomed, not mangy vermin as they're often described. Russ and Chief watched the larger male climb onto a bluff above the stream, the fur about his neck roughed in a breeze. A silhouette against the pink of a setting sun, he stood with chest puffed out and head pointed high, singing an evening song as his mate paced below. Yips followed by long, drawn-out yodels that echoed from the distant canyon walls had a different pattern than the ones outside the mine last night.

Chief lit a pipe, and smoke drifted about his crown. He too had become just a silhouette in the fading light. "This is a love song, unlike the death song."

The day departed and evening settled in. Stars appeared one by one, and soon a milky haze of stars dusted the sky from horizon to horizon. With no moon, the canyon turned black and melted into a single mass. The Song Dogs had moved on. The flow of the Havasu echoed from somewhere in the dark, and only an occasional glow of Chief's pipe marked his position. Russ fiddled with a piece of tree branch, picking off its bark and thinking about the magic of the night. Chief finally announced that he was turning in.

Russ said good night but stayed on to enjoy the peace. He mulled over the meaning of old songs from his youth about deserts and rivers and horses and death. It struck him how some songs at a certain time in one's life can touch the soul.

Russ kicked the loose earth at his feet as his mind wandered. He was a long way from the beginnings of his journey, in terms of years and miles. —Dewey Bunnell's "A Horse With No Name" ran through his mind, and Russ thought back on memories long suppressed. That was when the crack had happened in the looking glass. He had fallen through. Actually, the whole nation had fallen through.

Times of change, upheaval, chaos, and confusion, when right became wrong, and wrong became right. A culture evolved that might someday elect the Mad Hatter president. When killing the unborn became a right, and executing the wicked became a wrong. A time when the thoughts of the old became disrespected, and the young expanded their thoughts not by reading but with chemicals. Pop culture had packaged up the whole deal, glorified it, and distributed it to a generation.

Russ took a deep breath of clear desert air and looked at the stars. At the moment he saw no confusion; everything seemed simple and good. Did anyone remember the truth anymore? Was every generation left feeling as conflicted as he did? His thoughts turned more specific, to the day his journey began . . .

CHAPTER 26

The date high above the entrance of the salvage building read, *Erected 1880*. The brownish-red brick wore a coat of soot from the surrounding steel mills and ninety years of industrial activity in the Monongahela River Valley. While providing good jobs and a good work ethic, industry had tainted and poisoned the entire region. Now, with new government regulations on pollution, the energy of the area waned, and once-massive steel mills were closing, their frames silently mirrored in the muddy face of the polluted river.

Nineteen-year-old Russ felt lucky to have found this job in the salvage building, a scrapyard that processed the disemboweled internals of the once-productive mills and mines of the region. It wasn't pleasant or challenging or even lucrative, and there would be no opportunity for advancement, but it was a job, and he had a wife and a baby on the way.

In the locker room—not really a room but an area sectioned off by a ring of lockers, three toilet stalls without doors, a couple of old wooden benches, and a round washup sink—Russ removed his street clothes. The men, twelve in all, stood shoulder to shoulder as they undressed. They were a group of hardened men—all but Russ, the only kid. Most of the men were recent returnees from hell.

Vietnam.

To Russ, they all appeared damaged, even when they joked, but the damage hadn't all been done in Nam. They were a racial and ethnic mix who tolerated, and even enjoyed, making fun of each other's stereotypical images. They donned their filthy oil-soaked work clothes,

clothes that were worn for months without a wash and eventually thrown away. Russ never confided in any of them about his draft status, and to his relief, no one asked.

At eight a.m. a sudden silence befell the crew as Jack issued work assignments. Jack Brown was the foreman and common enemy who united the workers through their shared hatred of him. Jack's office had a single light that dangled by a wire from the ceiling. The light's position rested directly above his head, and since Jack wore a broad-brimmed hat that shaded his eyes, no one could tell if he was watching them or sleeping. The building was one cavernous room totally visible from Jack's office. Jack deducted nonproductive time on a regular basis, but a docked employee would not find out until he opened his paycheck to find he was not paid for the entire forty-hour workweek. There was no disputing Jack's call on these matters.

The day his journey began, Russ walked into the locker room at the lunch break. As the men circled the wash sink and pulled up their sleeves to wash away the morning grime, Russ noted taints on the arms of his two favorite characters, Bobby and Mark. Bobby was summer help, a black man who had a full scholarship to the University of Pittsburgh. Mark was a longhaired, bearded hippie-type who always smiled and had an unchained energy about him. Russ was shocked but not totally surprised and maintained his cool. He recognized them as needle marks, and he knew the whole crew smoked joints whenever Jack stepped out or his attention was otherwise diverted. Most believed Jack really didn't care as long as what they smoked didn't cost him his bonus. It was here that Russ chose to confront Mark about his needle tracks.

Russ pulled his work friend aside and asked him if he was doing hard drugs, but Mark assured him that he had everything under control. He shrugged it off. He said that Russ's concerns were misguided; it was no big deal. Even at nineteen, Russ knew he was now talking to the drug and that Mark offered answers that only another druggie would accept. Russ looked around the salvage building that afternoon, and it all looked different somehow. Mark looked different. It dawned on him that everything and everybody in the place were damaged goods. Russ knew that a lot of guys were getting hooked in Nam and wondered who else in salvage was a user. Salvage had always exuded an atmosphere of gloom from day one. It had a stench that followed you home.

As Russ walked to his car that afternoon, he didn't realize that he had finished his last day in the salvage building. Bobby didn't report for work the next day and was found dead from an overdose—alone in his apartment. Mark used for another two years and went to rehab after destroying his life, but still died in a relapse ten years later. The rest of the guys faded away just as Russ did. This was the fateful night Russ went home already depressed, only to be greeted by his mother-in-law instead of his wife. When he had left for work that morning, he had no idea it would be the last time he kissed his wife . . .

Russ shivered in the chilling night air of Havasupai. With the stars twinkling above, it seemed so far away from that place, that time, but was it really? How defining that day had been, and Russ now realized he had spent *his whole life* in salvage.

His thoughts switched to his earlier confession to Chief about being a draft dodger; originally he had hoped the chief had forgotten or not heard him. Now, he had an overwhelming desire to purge his heart. He wanted the old man to know into whom he had placed his faith.

Russ looked up at the stars and felt insignificant. Did anything he said or did ever matter? Tonight it felt like an easy answer for the night was faceless. In the morning light he would be facing Chief, and he would bring it up. He walked slowly toward camp and crawled into his tent. Sleep did not settle easy on him. His mother always said it was a guilty conscience that kept people awake. He concentrated on his breathing until he finally drifted off.

CHAPTER 27

Russ awoke to the morning bake, his tent smelling of hot nylon. He knew he had slept late by the direction and intensity of the shine invading his shelter. He lay gathering his thoughts, then sat up quickly as if a slow movement at this point would matter. Stretching and letting out a low groan, he unzipped the tent and crawled out onto the sand. He saw no signs of Chief or his bedroll. He knew Chief would be disapproving of his late sleep. Quickly, he packed his gear and flung it onto his shoulders. He looked at the tracks in the sand and followed them to the edge of the stream where Chief sat perched on a rock.

Russ offered a smile. "I slept well; how about you?"

"It was a good night. I feel rested. We should sit, drink, and eat. Today will be a challenge, but the coyote's song was a good omen."

Chief reached into his pouch and stuffed his mouth with granola he had earlier pilfered from Russ's pack. Russ raised an eyebrow and chewed on a piece of jerky. Chief showed no sign of remorse or guilt.

"I could go for some fast food, Chief. That isn't like me, but this morning I'd be fine with it."

"Yes, it is human nature to always want what we can't have."

Silently they sat and satisfied their hunger with the food at hand and hydrated with water. Chief seemed in no hurry to get started, and Russ followed his lead. Russ thought back on the promise he'd silently made the night before, to come clean about being a draft dodger, but in the morning light it didn't seem necessary. He argued with himself and finally surrendered.

"Chief, I told you I didn't go to Vietnam." Russ forced a

confident tone.

"I remember," Chief responded, but without any particular interest.

"I was a draft dodger . . ."

"Hmmm, what does that mean?"

"You tell me; what does it mean to you?" Russ actually had hoped Chief would show aggression and somehow take the lead in the conversation.

"It depends on what it means to you. Tell me the whole story if it will help you, but I am in no need to know. I trust you." Chief reassured.

Russ gathered his thoughts. "I told you I had to get married."

"Yes. That is not the best way to start married life."

"Well, my father-in-law was a man of means, very wealthy, and he had friends. I was classified 1-A, draft bait, and he did not want me to go off and leave his daughter." Russ paused once again to gather his thoughts and speak with caution.

"I can understand his thinking," Chief interjected.

"He was also a wounded World War II veteran and hated war. He said it always ended too political, after so many young men die. I was young and really hadn't given it much deep thought. I was willing to go. It didn't go against my politics because I didn't know enough to have any."

"I can understand this man. He was thinking of his grandchild, not so much you."

Russ shook his head; he had never thought of it in those terms. The old man was probably right.

"Well, whatever his reasons, he sent me to meet a very old and powerful man, a man who knew how to manipulate things. I had tea in the old man's mansion, and we talked for a couple of hours. I think he wanted to know where my heart was. When I was ready to leave, he walked me to the door and told me not to worry. He said it very matter-of-factly with no sign of doubt. I would not be drafted, and I would receive a letter in the mail stating that I would be classified 1-H, on hold. He said I would be on hold until I was a very old man."

"I told him I was willing to go. I told him I thought it might be good for me. He just smiled at me and patted my shoulder. He said nothing more."

"I see. Then you weren't actually a draft dodger in your heart; others were interfering for you."

"I was sick about it. The system seemed so unfair. I had friends who were going and I wasn't. In my mind, I was a disgrace. I told my father and he didn't respond; he never said a word. In about a week I received my new draft status, 1-H."

"Your wife and child needed you more than Vietnam did."

"You served and you can say that?"

"It was a different war, and I had no one. No, I take that back; it was no different." Chief poked the ground with a stick. He watched a white-lined sphinx moth drying its wings in the morning sun. Chief raised his stick in the direction of the moth.

"The moth knows all he needs to know. He has spent three weeks in the warm earth transforming from a crawling caterpillar into a winged insect that will swiftly search this valley for a mate. In the process, it will feed on the flowers of the very plants it ravaged as a caterpillar, and in the process, it will pollinate them. That is a miraculous thing, don't you think?" Chief sighed. "It will only live long enough to mate, and then it will die."

Russ watched as the moth lifted from the mesquite branch and hovered like a hummingbird before it swiftly darted out of sight.

"Miraculous . . . ," Russ whispered.

"It does what a moth does, that's all, and for millions of years moths do what moths do. Millions of years. Now look at this valley of rock, dust, and sands. It too has been doing what it does for millions of years. Now, how long do we live, and how long has man been doing what he does? Human arrogance, the curse of it all. Man thinks he knows so much. That moth lives quickly; to him we move like the turtle. He is too busy to be bothered by such a sloth-like creature; from his point of view, we are guilty of one of the seven deadly sins, and yet in our time frame, we move quite swiftly. We tend to view ourselves in our own frame of reference, don't we?"

"I suppose we do." Russ stared at the blue-green water flowing past in the stream. It cascaded over small dams of mineral deposit that had leeched out of the water itself.

"It is one of the most difficult concepts for a man to come to terms with. We are finite and short-lived creatures, we pass in the blink of an eye, and yet we view our lives as significant and important. Do you know much of your grandfather's life? What about your father? Do you think that in general people of today know or care about what I did in the Great War or how your generation suffered in Vietnam? Chief etched symbols in the sand with the stick. These boys who are being sacrificed right now, their history may be written by men who will declare them oil thieves. Good and evil are long-lived, and men fail at every turn to recognize it—just as that moth failed to recognize us, and yet we both had the power to smite it from existence on a whim. These wars, all of them, are orchestrated by the hand of evil that we do not see. We are all blinded by our arrogance, and so it shall continue. Mankind is being messed with."

"Chief . . ." Russ looked at him in reverence.

"No, let me finish. Forgive yourself. You have punished yourself too long, and I don't think your father held it against you. It is written in the Bible that all that we do is for naught. Looking back, I regret a lot of what I did, for although we thought a war was won, it was but only a battle and probably a manipulation at that. The war rages on and has since the beginning of human history. Did the Vietnam War make any difference? The politicians undermine everything for their own self-interest. They even had a hand in creating Hitler, and now a lot of the things Hitler sought have come to pass anyway." Chief stood and stretched. "What I did, I did with a good heart, and I am proud of it. In the eyes of God though, I think I have been a fool and Satan's tool. Rainbow taught me this. Remember? I spoke of this before."

"I remember."

"I defended our country's founding words, words from God, and the hypocrites in Washington laughed at me. What you have done for me on this hike proves who you are. What you speak of happened a long time ago and is now meaningless. What I will ask next of you, well .

. ."

"What could be worse than what we have already done?"

"Always, there can be something worse. This will tax your imagination. Your own heart is what will make things worse or better. It will be as if I were asking you to enter our capital and seek truth." Chief once again poked at the ground with a stick as if putting a period at the end of his sentence.

"All I can say is that I'm willing to give it a try."

"Very well. You have captured the water from the spring of souls; you have retrieved the earth from which the 'human being' is made. Now we must find the plant that breathes life into our air. It is a very special plant that opens the mind to seeing the other side."

"I don't know. You said I'll need a lot of faith but . . ."

"Have you ever heard of Diviner's Sage?" Chief asked.

"No."

"*Salvia divinorum?*" The chief spoke in a foreign tongue.

"I don't know, Comanche. Chief." Russ made a feeble attempt at humor.

"These are white man's words. Never mind; I know what we need and where to find it."

"I'm with you, man."

"What we seek is a flower that is native to the Sierra Madre of Mexico. It lives on the edge of a grass-covered field lower in the canyon. It was brought there by my shaman many years ago. It is a special place that will require much of you."

Russ contemplated all the danger and effort being required of him. He was also growing a little apprehensive about participating in some sort of pagan ritual. He had never been a deeply religious person by any stretch, but he was aware of the basic tenets of Christianity. They walked a long way without speaking, but finally Russ could no longer contain himself.

"Chief, you spoke of the Bible, so I know you are aware of its teaching. Did you ever think to just ask God for forgiveness?"

"That was the way of my wife. She kept me on the good path and taught me love. She said God is love, for He offers forgiveness with only the condition that we love Him. She was a wise woman, but did not understand the scope of my failings. It must also be done my way, the warrior way. We are all warriors in this fight, and I must release the souls I have imprisoned in my heart. That is what this is about. I know God will forgive me, but there are others involved in this. Just as I have used and imprisoned the animal spirit, so I have done with other men. I captured the spirits of those that I have slain. It gives the skinwalker more power to possess the spirits of other warriors. It is also a dangerous thing. There is only one way to set it right, at least only one way I know of. My wife searched for an answer, but it all goes back to the teachings of Rearing Horse."

Chief rose and signaled Russ to follow him deeper into the canyon, and they continued on. They crisscrossed the river several times, the water offering instant refreshment from the scorching heat. In several places, the trail led up the canyon wall and offered a view of tumbling blue-green water capped in brilliant white riffles. The river cut through the rocky, red belly of the canyon floor and offered a vivid contrast of hues. The old man stepped at a rapid pace, for there was much ground to cover, and they needed to find the area of the sage before the sun faded.

CHAPTER 28

Chief stood near the edge of the river, reading the canyon walls as if he had memorized the words to a poem. The lines on its face, the outcroppings, each bend and turn spoke to him. He read the words chiseled in the stone, words that had not changed their meaning in a million years. Finally, Chief pointed to a point far off across the canyon.

"Come down to the river. You must prep for this," the chief commanded.

"Prep?" Russ quizzed. They walked down to the river's edge. Chief sat down on the bank and removed his tote. He pointed to a calm pool of water near him.

"You must enter the water up to your chest to cool the flesh. I will mix the clay of the bank into paint. When you leave the river, you will paint all your exposed skin with it and then cake it onto your clothing. You must put a heavy coat on yourself."

A loud crack, two echoes, and a zip broke the tranquility of the morning. Chief shoved Russ into the cold, shallow water, Chief's arms grasping him as they flattened themselves into the gravely bottom. Gasping for breath as his face emerged, Russ managed, "What is going on?"

"Stay down in the water—only expose enough to breathe. We need to reach the far bank of the river. That was a shot." Chief whispered.

"A shot?"

"Yes . . ." was all Chief was able to say as two more cracks echoed through the canyon. This time the zip sound came from the parting of close air, as water splashed within inches of their heads.

"He's zeroed in on us. Move quickly. He's in the hoodoos on the opposite side of the river. If we make it to that bank, he won't be able to hit us. We must swim under the water. Go!"

The old man pushed on Russ's shoulders, forcing his head under just as he secured a final breath. They swam swiftly as they watched bits of lead silently and harmlessly expel energy in the clear water and sink to the bottom. They emerged on the opposite shore and scurried across a short beach to the safety of an eroded high bank. It offered them cover from the angle of the shots.

"What is all this about?" Russ whispered.

"Probably a meth head."

"I thought they had gone, one way or the other."

Chief lay on his back, his chest heaving as he caught his breath. He looked at Russ with a guilt-ridden look.

"I missed one at the meth lab. I only saw two. I wasn't sure if there was a third one."

"What do we do now?"

"Wait," Chief replied.

"Wait? Wait for what? Wait for him to walk down here and kill us?"

"Wait—the best thing is to wait. He can't get us from where he is. He will grow impatient and come to us. The rest will take care of itself. We will count on his fear. Hopefully, he will wait for nightfall."

"You seem awfully confident for a guy who's had some missed calls. This could be the last one."

"At my age it has finally occurred to me that sometimes your best action is none. Patience is our ally, and time is our friend. Now we must be quiet and listen for his approach. It may take a while; listen." Chief held his forefinger to his lips and settled into a comfortable, prone position; Russ followed his lead.

The pair lay in wait, silently and occasionally batting a fly away from their faces. The old man eventually dozed off, and Russ wondered how he could possibly be so at ease. Russ resisted the urge to peer over the bank toward the hoodoos, for he envisioned the loss of his scalp to a well-placed sharpshooter's projectile. The day dragged on, and Russ watched the sun move across the crown of the coulee, casting long shadows from the far rim. The sky turned sky-blue pink in an Arizona-style sunset that brought shame on any Russ had previously seen, and he wondered if it was because it was setting on his life. If not for the threat of imminent death, he would have relished such a sight, but as he watched, he knew night would follow, offering the predator a cloak. He wished the elegant spectacle might never end, but as with most wishes, the darkness swelled, and Russ's hope faded.

"I must have fallen asleep," Chief whispered. "Ah, our friend of darkness has covered us well."

"Our friend is also that guy's friend. We have no idea where he is, and he has a gun. We have only rocks."

"No, we have the canyon on our side, with this riverbank, the rugged terrain, the sage that lies between us and the hoodoos. The sage and all that lives within it. This night is on our side. Now wait and listen." Chief spoke with a renewed confidence. "Our advantage is that he does not know what we have."

Russ waited and listened, but only heard the eerie and mournful whistle of the wind through the mesquite, like sirens calling sailors to a rocky shore, enchanting them and inviting them to their deaths. There was no moon. A trillion stars twinkled above, and a bright streak occasionally crossed the heavens. Each time, Russ silently made the same wish. Dreamy and warm, the night air embraced Russ, and his eyes became too heavy, then closed. Chief had been very alert since his nap, and Russ showed his confidence by dozing. He knew Chief would keep watch.

Terror—shrill screams of terror—woke Russ to the pounding of his heart. He woke in time to hear a crack that echoed in the night. Missing was the familiar zip of lead passing near his head. Another crack, and shrill screams were followed by loud moaning. The moaning continued until it finally broke in desperate cries for help, haunting cries, and sobbing. Russ looked in the dark for the old man's face, but it was too dark to define an expression. A cold hand reached for Russ's arm to comfort him.

"We cannot help him. He will die very slowly, and we will have to listen to it. He will be silenced as the sun comes full circle. Tomorrow belongs to only us and will find him still. We will be able to proceed. If we sleep, we will not hear his agony."

"That won't be easy," Russ spoke into the faceless night.

"He wanted to kill us, and he would have." Chief let go of Russ's forearm.

Chief lay on his back staring at the stars, at the Milky Way that flowed across the heavens. "The moans of that poor devil remind me of other nights long ago, in the Philippines and Korea. A man is dying; even if he is the enemy, he is dying. There is a legend that I often told my sons when they were young and we camped out on the mesa. It was a more pleasant time; I will tell you that."

Chief cleared his throat and began in the unique cadence of the Native American . . . "The Havasupai tell of the beginnings of mankind after the great destruction. It is a story much like the white man's Noah. It is said that before the great flood, when the earth opened up to the waters of the deep that gushed forth upon the land, there were two gods. *Tochopa* was the god of all life and living things. *Hokomata* was like the white man's devil. It was *Hokomata* that brought forth the flood to kill all living things, but before the flood, *Tochopa* hollowed out a pinion tree and sealed his daughter, *Pukeheh*, in it."

Chief shifted, seeking a more comfortable rest. "The pinion tree floated for many days with *Pukeheh* safely inside. As the waters began to recede, the great mountains began to appear, *Hue-han-a-patch-a*, *Hue-ga-woo-la*, and all the other mountains of the world. The waters surged and cut through the plateau, forming the *Chic-a-mi-mi*, this canyon. During this time there was only darkness. When the flood was over, *Pukeheh* saw the sun and gave birth to a son named *In-ya-a*, son of the sun. The following year she gave birth to a daughter. That child's father was the falling waters of Havasupai, *Wa-ha-hath-peek-ha-ha*. To this day, the girls of Havasu are proud to be known as the 'daughters of the water.' From these two children came forth all the peoples of the earth—first the Havasupais and then the Apaches, the Hualapais, the

Hopis, the Paiutes, and the Navajos. *Tochopa* told them all where to live, and that is where you will find them today." Chief rolled onto his side and closed his eyes.

"Hey Chief?" Russ whispered.

"Ah." Chief closed his eyes. "Good night, my friend; in the light we will talk about our would-be killer's death, and I assure you that those responsible will be given their credit due."

Moaning from the field continued, accompanied by the snores of the old man. Russ was amazed at how quickly Chief's snoring had commenced. One or the other prevented Russ from slipping into immediate sleep, but eventually both sounds faded and sleep began to claim him. He looked up at the stars and tried to picture Helen rattling on about the constellations the way that John had about the canyon. It took his mind off the weakening moans. Russ gave in and drifted into a sound sleep.

CHAPTER 29

The warmth of the morning sun and a pesky fly woke Russ. Without moving a muscle, he gazed across the blue-green water to the opposite shore. Chief emerged on the far side and walked up onto the beach. Russ listened; there was no sound. The wind had died. He sat up and brushed sand from the side of his face. Chief waved to him. Russ plunged into the river and swam toward the opposite shore.

"Last night was like a bad dream; now that the sun is out I feel like it didn't happen." Russ looked toward the hoodoos with wonderment, for they had a mysterious look to them, almost ghostly. Depending on the position of the sun and the angle of light, the character of the canyon constantly morphed.

"Oh, it happened alright. That poor devil walked into the sage over there when the demons are most active. I suppose he didn't know this part of the canyon." Chief held a cupped hand over his brow as he looked toward the hoodoos. He saw nothing of last night's predator.

"What do you mean? What about this part of the canyon? Last night you said credit would be given where it was due. Now, let's hear who took out our shooter." Russ scrunched his eyes to block out the intense light.

"The cries last night brought back many bad memories. We must never forget that we are all warriors, whether we want to be or not. The battle between good and evil is not a fairy tale and does not take place somewhere far away. It takes place in each of us."

Chief waved his hand toward the sky, then brought it in, placing it firmly against his chest. "It is here in our hearts that God resides.

Heaven is down deep within us, at a molecular level. We started out at the molecular level, did we not? When we die we retreat to where we came from. We were given eyes to search the horizon for food and threats, but this gift has also diverted our understanding of the truth. We fail to see the magic and miracles that surround us. We call God and Satan supernatural beings, instead of realizing that they are as natural as all we see."

With a thoughtful nod, Russ picked up a flat stone and skipped it across the water.

Chief let out a sigh and retired to sit on a rock. "When men make their great wars, don't they start in the heart? Isn't that where the first battle is lost? I could stand here for eternity, and no war would spontaneously occur out there." Chief pointed across the canyon.

"It is only when other men's hearts lose their battle and join forces with evil that war happens. What is so supernatural about it? Hell, war is truly hell on earth. You didn't go to Vietnam, and for that you feel guilty, but ever since, you have been fighting battles in your heart and winning.

Chief took out his pipe and fussed with it for a moment; as he lit it, a ring of smoke circled his head. Russ took a drink from his canteen and a deep breath of morning air. He looked around and took notice of the river, the plants, and the insects. A dragonfly skimmed the water. Butterflies dried their wings in slow rhythms as they rested on mesquite bushes.

"I would like to know who or what killed him, Chief."

Chief just stared out at the hoodoos. It was obvious he was in no rush to give an answer. As Russ pondered Chief's ideas of good and evil, he watched a large bird, larger than an eagle, catch a thermal. Wings fixed, it rose higher and higher in the clear blue sky, its grace unparalleled.

Chief was also watching as he fussed with his pipe. He looked at Russ to see if he had noticed the bird. "That's a California condor, very rare. It is a good sign," he declared, but Russ figured he was just avoiding the question.

"I've never seen one before. Good omen, you say?"

"Yes. We will begin where we were when the shooter interrupted us. I will tell you as we go. Now, enter the river again. We will get an early start. You must lower your body temperature."

"Lower my body temperature . . . yeah . . . right . . ."

Russ waded back into the river up to his chest in the cool, gushing water. The chief mixed handfuls of clay with river water using a large stick. The mixing bowl was just a pit in the slimy clay bank. Chief mumbled to himself as he proceeded.

"Can I get out now? I'm starting to shrivel."

Chief kept at his task of mixing mud. "You must stay in the water to drop your body temperature. I will tell you when to come out. Then, you will cover yourself with this clay. It will make you invisible to your enemy." Chief pointed his mixing stick at Russ.

"Invisible? Like when that cowboy couldn't see you?"

"No, this is different. Trust me. You will be invisible to those who would do harm to you, the ones who saved us last night."

"Can I come out now? I'm numb. My temperature is ambient, about fifty-five."

"Wait. Be patient. Listen to me. You will be moving across the grassy field to the far edge of the canyon. There you will find a plant with strange-looking small flowers. You will pick these flowers."

"I'm going to pick flowers? That's it?" Russ asked as he emerged from the water.

"This grassland has the densest population of rattlesnakes of anywhere in the country. There are diamondbacks—the worst—but there are not so many of them. The most plentiful and hardest to see are the pink Grand Canyon rattlers. They all see body heat. That is the trick. The coating of clay will disguise you. You must walk very deliberately; keep moving but always know where you place your foot. The ones you can see won't hurt you. The one you don't see is the one you must fear. Be *chotacine*."

"Be what?"

"*Chotacine* . . ."

"Right! Come on, no way! That's what happened to the shooter last night? He got snakebit?"

"He didn't take precautions. It works. I've done it. *Chotacine* is one who knows. I would guess he was bitten several times. It was a painful death. But you will be alright."

"Then you do it. You're the skinwalker. All I know is that snakes bite. I've seen you handle them. You're a natural. Those moans are still fresh in my mind; that guy did die a painful death."

"It is not possible for me to go. It must be done *for* me, or the curse will not be broken. You will be fine. This will prove that you truly are a great warrior."

"Warrior? What makes you think I care about being a warrior? All of a sudden I'm feeling kind of proud of my draft-dodger self." Russ felt the need to offer some sort of resistance.

"Here, just cover yourself with the clay," the old man spoke, bluntly.

Russ, numb from the cold water, covered himself with the goop. It actually felt very soothing, and although he took sport in conflicting with the chief, he really had confidence that the old sage knew what he was doing. That perhaps they were engaged in something profound— spiritual . . .

After he dabbed on the last of the clay, Russ didn't feel very warrior-like, but he looked down at himself and didn't think he looked like snakebite material, either. *Whatever*, he thought; *let's just do it!*

"Hurry, before the clay starts to dry. If it dries it will crack and fall off. That will let them sense your body heat. That is what they target."

Russ started off across the sage- and grass-covered field toward a point where Chief indicated he would find the potent posies. The distance looked to be a hundred deadly yards. The grass to his right moved opposite the wind, an unnatural direction that peaked Russ's senses. The movement in the tall, dry grass made his heart rock in his chest. Sweat bled down his forehead as his shifting eyes scrutinized movements in the endless field between him and the flowers. Russ jumped, and a roadrunner darted from the grass with a small reptile dangling from his beak. The grass waved gently, a breeze swirled softly in front of him, and again his senses intensified. His eyes tricked his mind with patterns of false snakeskins visible with each placement of a foot. Step after step he brushed back tall strands of grass before securing a foothold, sometimes exposing a thick, rotting twig that he was sure was poised to strike. More than once his knee would jerk, disrupting his balance, in reaction to a startling glimpse. False patterns they were, the ones snakes evolved to mimic. He listened to the deadly silence until an awful sound chilled him cold—a high-speed buzz to his right—no!—to his left. A warning sound offered by a deadly foe, it was a sickening sound and caused him to stop dead in his tracks.

"Don't stop!" the old Indian shouted.

Momentarily, Russ turned to look at him and then refocused on the task at hand. He looked skyward; the sky was clear, a contrast to the field, and he closed his eyes with a sigh. He placed his right foot slowly and then picked up his left; he continued by repeating the motion. The buzzing never stopped; only the direction from which it originated changed. The ophidians of sound remained out of sight, dangerous. *Only fear the ones you can't see*, Chief had said. Well, he hadn't seen one yet.

The flowers looked farther and farther away as the grass thickened. His progress slowed. The sward was so thick he could no longer see the placement of his feet. Slowly, he moved his feet high above the field, twirling the grass before he stepped down, his arms held at shoulder height for fear of a strike to his hands. His movements made him think of some sort of Native American ritual dance.

Finally, he reached a place where he could grab two huge bouquets of the flower. He secured them in a pouch, turned—heart pounding—and headed back toward the old Indian as cautiously as he had come. Russ soon stood on the high riverbank, smiling in satisfaction. His focus had been in a downward direction, which left him unaware and vulnerable to other dangers lurking in the canyon.

"You have done well, my son. You could be a skinwalker." Chief held his arms skyward in praise of Russ's accomplishment.

"Thanks, but I thought being a skinwalker was what got you into all this trouble?"

"Not trouble—no, it is something else, and I joke at you being a skinwalker, white man." Chief lowered his arms down to his sides, letting out a chuckle.

"I know," Russ muttered under his breath, unheard by Chief.

—*Ka-rack!*

The sound didn't register at first. Even as it reverberated in Russ's ears and in his bones, even as the echoes bounced around on the canyon walls, the vision of blood and flesh ripping from the old Indian's body finally sank it home. An explosion like a tomato could be seen coming from behind Chief's back, juice and red bits in the bright Arizona sun.

Russ's lungs expelled every molecule of air within them. "Nooooo!" he yelled as he jumped into the river and rushed toward the human being who had become his friend, his companion, so much more.

The old man tumbled from the rock upon which he had perched to observe Russ's fetching of the flowers. He tumbled into the stream, his bright-red blood mingling with the blue-green waters. He floated face down, his motionless arms straight out at his sides. Russ reached him in an instant, rolled him faceup, and held him with never a thought that he might be the next target. There was no sign of life in Chief. Russ looked up at the far bank of the river, catching a flash of reflection on a piece of steel, but the sun washed other details out. He heard the whinny of a horse.

"Is he dead?" A voice sounded from an area washed in the sun's glow.

CHAPTER 30

Russ squinted, his hand shading his brow, but still he could not make out the antagonist, only the legs of a horse and part of its torso.

"Is he dead?" The voice sounded weaker this time, and again Russ heard a whinny followed by the snort of a horse. Russ pulled the old man toward the shore, his movement offering him a different line of sight so that now he could make out a man sitting on a horse on the far bank. The man slowly raised his rifle to his shoulder, drawing a bead on Russ. Russ stood firm, holding the chief's head out of the water, and waited for his fate. There was nothing he could do.

The horseman wobbled but caught himself and then *Ka-rack!* Russ winced, his shoulders shuddered and his eyes shut, but he felt no pain as the air near his ear parted in a zip. The Ka-racking sound echoed up and down the canyon, and Russ opened his eyes in time to see the shooter slide off the side of his horse, thumping on the ground in a puff of dust. He lay spread-eagle and motionless. The horse stomped its foot next to the man's head.

Russ dragged Chief onto the beach and made him comfortable, then checked his vitals again. His breathing was labored and he had a weak pulse as blood oozed from his right shoulder. Russ ripped the old man's shirt and removed his own, which he tore into pieces, and packed the wound to stop the bleeding. Russ felt for protruding bone and looked for bone fragments. It appeared to be a meat shot, clean and smooth, and bleeding did not appear to be arterial.

The bleeding finally eased. He stood and walked toward the stream. He paused to survey the shooter and then waded across through the water. The shooter lay where he had fallen, and Russ grabbed the horse's reins to steady him. He stood over the shooter and looked down on him in anger and disgust. Reaching down, he retrieved the man's rifle without a struggle. The man's legs were bloated and discolored. Russ could see fang marks on his shins.

"I'm snakebit," the man whispered in a parched voice, "been bit several times."

"I can see that, mister. You had a bad night." Suddenly, he felt no remorse, and the sounds of last night no longer bothered him.

"I need help," the man mouthed.

"You shot at us yesterday; guess that was you screaming last night." Russ pulled the rifle to his shoulder and pointed it right between the man's eyes.

"Go ahead. Finish me!" the shooter hissed in a shallow voice. Russ lifted the gun away from the man. He looked over at Chief who lay motionless. He knew Chief had picked him because he had never killed anyone, but if Chief wasn't going to make it, what did it matter now? What did anything matter?

Russ pulled back the hammer on the old Marlin 32 Special and renewed his bead on a spot between the man's eyes. A rage boiled in him, demanding release. The snakebit man closed his eyes and gritted his teeth in anticipation of the energy about to be discharged into his skull by a rapidly moving projectile of lead. Russ took a deep breath; he was in control and savored the moment. His hesitation was not from doubt.

"No, don't shoot him . . . let the poison take him."

Russ didn't turn.

"Russ, it's not over. I still need you clean."

Finally, Russ lowered the rifle, turned toward Chief, and saw him raised up on his elbows. Maybe the old man still had a little life left in him after all. Maybe they would finish their journey, their quest. A dark shadow moved across the water and engulfed Chief for only a moment, then continued up the bank, disappearing in the grass. Russ looked up. It was the condor, an omen. It floated on thermals a hundred feet above the canyon floor. Chief also looked up in time to catch sight of him.

"Is that an omen, Chief?" Russ asked.

"Ha, I would like to think it's an omen, but more likely he just smells death, mine or our friend there."

"I'd say it's this guy."

The man at his feet moaned and writhed in pain. His arms moved without focus, and his legs twitched. He no longer seemed aware of Russ. The poison had entered the man's brain.

"Just let him die," Chief instructed.

Russ looked at the man, his face contorted with pain. "You know what, mister? You died the first time you hooked meth. You've been dead, and you just didn't know it."

The man showed no response. Russ looked up and down the man's body. The man's hands clawed at the bites on his legs, bites that were swollen and black. Russ led the horse away from the dying man, across the river toward the chief. He tied the horse to a driftwood log and knelt beside his friend, whose bleeding had stopped and whose breathing had eased. Russ checked his pulse. It was stronger. There didn't appear to be any signs of shock. Russ looked back toward the other man who lay completely motionless and silent now.

"How far do we have to go?"

"My friend, I am done. He killed me. I have lost too much blood. It is a good way for an old warrior to die."

"I thought you stopped me from killing because you still needed me."

"I lied. I wanted to protect you from your anger. It would have been enjoyable, but eventually, because of who you are, you would have been tormented by remorse. It was better to just let him die. You are a good man, Russ."

"You're not dead yet. We should keep going on until you are dead; that is how a warrior should die. I don't think he hit anything vital. We'll use this horse to carry you."

"That's because it's not *your* shoulder. You make it sound easy." Chief managed a slight smile.

"There is no other choice. This is the way we must go. How is this any different from the way you have lived your life? Isn't that what you said to me?" Russ felt the sun burning the bare skin on his shoulders and reached into his pack to retrieve his other shirt, draping it over his shoulders.

"My words haunt me . . . that was why I gave up on speaking before you came along. We shall keep going, then. It is only a couple of miles to the sacred place. On the way I shall tell you things you will need to know in case I fade before we arrive."

Russ opened the pouch containing the flowers. "Are these the right blossoms?"

Holding the florets to his nose, the old Indian breathed deeply, sighed, and wrapped them in a cloth before stuffing them into his bag.

"The flowers are important; the flowers are the essence of the spiritual experience."

"What now?"

"Now? Now we have all we need. Now we will go to a very sacred place. Now you will see things that no other living person has seen except me. Go into the Havasupai and wash. I must rest." Chief closed his eyes and sighed.

Without further encouragement, Russ jumped into the Havasupai and watched the red clay dissolve from his clothes and skin. It looked much like the blood he had seen when Chief fell into the water. Russ watched the old man sprawled on the shore and prayed he would have the strength to see the mission through. Chief turned on his side and covered his exposed skin with a blanket from his bag. Russ took his time washing off. He removed his clothing and scrubbed at the dirt with a palm-sized rock. The snakebite victim made no noise.

CHAPTER 31

Russ dried in the sun and wondered if Chief could complete the journey, his condition had deteriorated so much. He watched as Chief twitched beneath the blanket that sheltered him from the sun. He looked as if he were dreaming. Russ was just glad that he was resting. He knew there would be demanding times ahead, and so he sat quietly, watching without disturbing him. Several rabbits, a couple of lizards, a roadrunner, and a deer all walked casually by without the slightest flinch. The condor circled high on the thermals. Russ felt eerily at peace and looked forward to doing whatever else Chief needed to complete his journey.

It had been hours since the snake bit man had made even the slightest movement or noise, so Russ figured him for done. Chief had been right. Russ was already having regrets for the way he treated the man before he died. Russ looked at the dead meth head and wondered if he should bury him or at least cover him with something to protect his remains from scavengers. Feeding scavengers would probably amount to the most worthwhile thing the man would ever accomplish in his selfish life. He decided to just let nature take its course with the scumbag who had gunned Chief down. He had regrets about the anger that had motivated him to want to shoot him, but he would leave it at that and let the canyon feed on his remains. The canyon had killed him—the canyon could feed on him.

After a long stretch of time, Chief rolled toward Russ and related his dream from his nap. It was Chief's own story from long ago.

In his dream he had seen a war-weary Native American, freshly arrived in the oil fields of Beaumont, Texas, in 1951. The oil derricks sprouted like a skeletal forest across the otherwise barren landscape. He was a newly discharged warrior, no kid by any stretch but a proven veteran with a belly full of war. A job waited for him on the recommendation of his commanding officer whose family was in the oil business. The crew he had been assigned to was made up of tough, hardworking, and hard-drinking roughnecks. The foreman was the toughest and more than willing to resolve labor disputes with his fists, but overall, the men formed a well-honed machine. Chief fit the team perfectly.

They had been in the process of drilling the current well long before Chief had arrived, and any day it should produce a gusher. The expectations were mounting, and the whole crew listened and watched for signs. Chief watched the others closely. This would be a first gusher for him, while they all laid claim to having brought in dozens of wells.

Once it blew and they capped it, it would be party time with a trip into town. Chief was on the wellhead when he heard the rumble and saw the others scatter to gather tools. The high-pressure oil blew violently sky-high and showered down unmercifully on the men, soaking their clothes, their hair, and the ground as they struggled to place the cap valve. The threat of a fire was immediate and the men worked at great risk, but their task was achieved and the valve cranked shut. They cheered and danced about more like greased pixies than roughnecks.

The crew stripped down, hosed off, wiped down, and donned semi-clean duds before climbing into and onto a pickup headed for town. It was an era when men with pride worked hard and a profitable well was deemed patriotic. The men realized that when the company did well, so did they and the country. This afternoon would be the reward for their hard work and dedication. Chief sat in the bed of the pickup with five others. The foreman drove, and two of the more senior roughnecks rode in the cab with him. Chief liked the bed of the truck anyway. It was less confining.

The wind blew their long hair, and the air smelled of crude. To the roughnecks, the smell of crude was like the smell of roses to a lady. The weather was perfect and the mood festive. One of the crew, another Native American named Tom Canyon, invited Chief to come to his house for dinner instead of running the bars with the rest of the crew. Chief accepted.

The pickup pulled up in front of a little bungalow on the very edge of town, and Chief hopped out with Tom. The pickup pulled away as Tom and Chief paused at the gate of a white picket fence. Chief thought to himself that this was a long way from Korea and the Battle of Chosin. It had been many years since he had actually had dinner prepared in a home by someone's wife. He wasn't quite sure how to act and was feeling a little apprehensive. Tom clapped him on the shoulder to assure him that it would be alright. There had been no way for Tom to forewarn his wife that he was bringing home a dinner guest. But Tom's wife was a kind and giving soul, and she always made more than enough food.

"Really, my wife won't mind." Tom gave Chief a gentle little nudge as he swung open the gate.

"I've been in the military so long I'm not sure how to act around family people."

"Just don't cuss. My wife has a very low tolerance of such things. Oh, and say please and thank you. That's about all that she fusses about. You do those things and she'll be happy with you. Come on, let's get in there."

Before Tom pushed open the front door, the aroma of home cooking overwhelmed the smell of crude. Tom and Chief stepped inside to be greeted by Tom's wife, Mary, and her visiting sister, Anita.

Tom was as surprised to see Anita as Mary was to see Chief. Anita looked like a desert flower to Chief, and he was instantly smitten. She had long, straight black hair and dark eyes set above classic cheekbones. Her figure was athletic, and she had an intelligent air about her. Either of the two sisters could be beauty queens, and yet there seemed to be so much more to them than just physical beauty. Chief felt totally lost in Anita's presence. He had no idea that his life had just changed, for this woman would become his loving wife and give him two sons.

"This is my wife, Mary. This lovely creature is her sister, Anita.

Anita, how and when did you get into town?" Tom asked in a loving tone.

"Tom Canyon, you save your questions until we have all been properly introduced," Mary jokingly scolded her husband, lightly slapping his arm. Anita laughed, her eyes shining. Both women's eyes were on Chief.

"Oh, right, I'm sorry. This is Charlie Hawk. He joined the crew a couple of weeks ago and has fit in perfectly. The boys in the crew just call him Chief." Tom smiled and shook Chief's shoulder gently.

"Well Chief, in this home we will refer to you as Charlie, or Mr. Hawk if you prefer that, but I think we'll leave 'Chief' for the boys—if that's alright with you?" Mary smiled and offered her hand, which Charlie shook. Then Anita reached out. The warm touch of her hand shot the proverbial tingle through his fingers and up his arm—a vibration of awareness. Charlie had a little trouble letting Anita's hand go, and she certainly didn't seem in a hurry to have him let it go.

"Charlie. Charlie will be fine." Charlie spoke to Mary, but his gaze was locked with Anita's.

Tom broke the lingering pause. "We have a lot to celebrate, Mary. The well came in today."

"I thought you two smelled like it. I've got a roast in the oven and home-baked bread; we'll eat in about an hour if you two want to wash up and relax. Anita, I think I can manage the kitchen myself. Why don't you take Charlie out to the back porch to enjoy the fresh air?"

"Charlie, the bathroom is right through there. You wash up first and then go with Anita. There's a real nice porch swing out back." Tom pointed down the hallway and winked at Anita.

Charlie headed down the hall toward the bathroom as Anita grabbed Tom's arm. "I got here this morning, Tom. I came on a bus from Flagstaff. I just needed to get away from the Rez, to see Mary. She is my best friend, you know."

"I know, and you are always welcome here, little sister. Are there problems at home?"

"No, I just needed a change. We didn't know you were bringing a guest home. What do you know about this guy? His eyes are so calm and trusting. I don't think I have ever seen a man so—" Anita caught herself. "What I mean is, he reminds me of you, Tom."

"I've only known him a couple of weeks. He just drifted in and doesn't talk much about his past. He just got out of the military. He said he was in for twelve years. I know this, he could have gone drinking with the boys and instead he chose to come here for a home-cooked meal. I also know he has a lot of pride in his work. He's probably the strongest man on the crew. I've seen him pick up pieces of equipment that usually take two men to tote. The foreman said if he had three men like Chief he could get rid of the rest of us. I don't think he would ever throw the first punch, but God help the man who does. When we changed clothes at the well, I noticed that he has a lot of scars. I think he has endured a lot. That's about all I know. You'll have to do your own research."

"The crew calls him Chief?" Anita asked Tom in a way that sounded like she sought clarification.

"Oh, I know what you're getting at, and by no means was it meant in a derogatory way. It came about with the utmost respect and admiration of Charlie. Anita, this man is the smartest guy in the crew. He just seems to know things. He has shown guys that have been drilling twelve years better ways to do things. Even the foreman has commented on Charlie's raw natural abilities." He paused and glanced up at the ceiling as if thinking of things to add to his laundry list of Chief's attributes. "I'm telling you, it's downright spooky. A couple of the guys said it seems like he can read our minds. He keeps everybody laughing with his wit."

"Tom, stop. Please don't tell me anymore," Anita said with a laugh. "Leave something for me to discover on my own."

Tom walked into the kitchen to check on Mary and left Anita to wait for Charlie. She looked into the hallway, then perched on the couch to practice her disinterested look. Charlie returned to the room and pretended to look at some of the pictures of Tom and Mary that were on the wall. Anita turned the pages of a magazine without acknowledging Charlie's return.

"They're a good-looking couple." Charlie nodded his head toward the pictures as he looked at Anita.

"Yes, they are. They've been together since they were fourteen. Tom was one of the most sought-after boys on the Rez. But no one could turn his head from my Mary."

"Your sister is a beautiful woman."

"My sister is also very intelligent and completely dedicated to Tom. She's my best friend."

Charlie looked at Anita and her rapidly fading look of disinterest. He walked over to the couch, offering his hand to help her up.

"Would you like to go out back on the swing for some fresh air?"

"Yes, I would love to."

Six months later, Charlie and Anita were married. Tom was best man, and the crew of roughnecks all attended, as did Anita and Mary's large family. It was the happiest day of Charlie's life, and Anita's parents and family immediately fell in love with Charlie. For the first time in his life he had a family, a real family. Charlie and Anita were lucky enough to rent the bungalow right next door to Tom and Mary, and so there Charlie Hawk's new life began.

It was about a year after the wedding that Anita first experienced the other side of Charlie, the part of him that he carefully concealed from everybody. She awoke in the middle of the night, awakened by a noise or movement or maybe by the damp feel of the sweat-soaked sheets. She was alone in bed. Charlie had gone to the back porch to sit on the porch swing. Anita stumbled down the dark hallway, whispering Charlie's name. She heard the squeak and jingle of swing chains from the porch and opened the screen door, stepping through and letting it slam shut behind her. The Texas night was stifling hot, with only a whisper of a breeze.

"Charlie?" Anita whispered. "Are you alright?"

Charlie didn't answer. He was hunched forward, his head resting in his cupped hands. He never looked up. Anita sat next to him and put her arm around him. His T-shirt was soaked in cold sweat, and his skin felt clammy as her other hand gently glided over his forearm. Anita felt a surge of fear like none she had ever known. This was not the man she had known, the happy, sensitive, and loving man that she had just this evening greeted on his return from work. She feared he might even be having a heart attack. She reached up and touched his hair. It was wet, as if he had just stepped from a cold shower, and then she felt Charlie shiver.

"Charlie, look at me, honey. Do you want me to take you to the hospital or call a doctor?"

"No, I'll be fine in a little while," Charlie spoke, his head still cupped in his hands.

"Can I do anything for you? Do you need some water?"

At that point Charlie began to shake. She very quickly realized Charlie was sobbing. Her strong, intelligent man was breaking down. She had no choice. She joined him.

Their first year together had been joyous and fun; now she wept in empathy with no understanding of what had brought all this on. She pressed tight against her husband's body and clung to him for dear life. She closed her eyes, and without another word, moved with Charlie to the rug on the wooden floor beneath the swing. They slept in each other's arms until the morning light and a songbird awakened them.

CHAPTER 32

Russ lifted Chief onto the horse, patted the horse's neck gently, and reached for the reins. He led the horse down the trail toward where the Havasupai met the Colorado River. There were about two miles between them and the Colorado, and Russ wanted to make it as quickly as possible. The chief held the saddle horn tightly.

A cool breeze moved up the canyon, carrying the scent of the Colorado's turbulent water, and the old Indian's head fell forward, his eyes shut. An occasional cottonwood offered shade from an unforgiving sun.

"You have helped me much," Chief whispered without opening his eyes.

"I'm trying, but God knows why." Russ watched straight ahead for obstacles that might spook the horse.

"You have been like a son, I think, and I do believe God knows why. When I rested back there I remembered God and my wife, Rainbow Woman. The dream gives me strength and hope. I have good memories of my sons and my wife." He coughed and wiped a small bit of blood from the corner of his mouth. "There was a time many years ago when my sons would have died for me, and me for them."

"Well, you've been pretty pushy. You aren't giving me many options."

"We have free will and you are of your own mind; you create your options, not me. You have a need you are trying to fulfill." The old man slouched in the saddle and struggled for a breath.

Russ had to agree. "You're probably right."

"Not just in what you have done for me. Why did you climb Mt. Humphreys and do the things you told the man from Europe you have done? All your life you have been driven to prove something."

"The girl at the check-in asked me why I am hiking into the canyon, too. What's it matter? When I told her, she called me a liar." Russ waited for a response and heard none. He turned in time to see the chief fall forward onto the horse's neck and grab its mane. Russ lunged for his arm as he pulled on the reins to halt the horse. The old man slid from the saddle into Russ's arms. "Chief?"

"Called . . . you . . . a liar?" The old man's voice was weak and raspy. Russ saw dried blood around his mouth—not a good sign.

"Well, she said she was marking my answer as a lie." Russ lowered the chief to the ground, dragged him to the side of the trail, and leaned him back against a rock.

"You know the truth and it does matter, but only to you. Enough said! I am spent. I shall not enter the Kingdom of God, for the spirits shall drag me down. It was our dream. My wife and I prayed to God to help fight against spirits. I think they have won."

"Hush, old man. We aren't giving up." Russ removed the lid from his canteen and put it to the chief's lips. "Now, I have been thinking about it. You remind me of my father in a lot of ways. He didn't look like you, talk like you, or physically resemble you in the least little bit, but there is something remarkable about it. It's your . . . your spirit. You have kindred spirits."

"How does this matter?"

"I wasn't with him when he died."

"This you have said."

"He died, but when it happened, I had run away. That's what I'm always trying to make up for. Well, this time I'm not running away. This time I am with you, and I'm staying on until this thing gets done. Whatever it takes, we're going to do it."

"You have courage. The things you have done for me took courage. It was selfless. Nothing can change what you did in the past . . ." The old man writhed in pain, then sighed and relaxed. Russ offered him another sip of water and then stood to secure the horse to a

171

mesquite shrub. He looked at Chief who sat with his eyes closed and his arms limp at his sides. There didn't appear to be any fresh blood seeping from his bandage. Russ knelt and felt Chief's forehead. There was no fever.

"There's more to it." Russ again held the canteen to Chief's parched lips.

"There is no need for me to know anything except what you have done for me. You must forgive yourself." The old man was at rest, and his bleeding had stopped. The horse stomped his feet and shook his head, then, almost as if approving, let out a whinny.

Russ was insistent. "We have time to rest; there is no hurry. We have been traveling too fast, and that is pointless. We should pray. We need to ask God for help and strength."

"It is a good thing that you say. You are right. I will pray and rest. Since the death of Anita, I have used alcohol more than prayer to contain my demons."

"So Anita was your wife's name?" Russ spoke in a low, reverent voice, yet wanted to keep Chief alert.

"Yes, that was Rainbow Woman's Christian name."

Chief silently prayed, his eyes clenched. Russ watched for a moment before he began his own prayer. Chief recited a prayer that Anita always said, and it made him feel better. Russ made up a prayer asking for forgiveness for both himself and Chief. He asked for strength to get them through their journey. They sat side by side without speaking. Chief slipped off into a sleep as Russ thought about the confession he wanted to deliver when Chief awoke.

They had been resting for about an hour when Chief began to stir. Russ awoke to the sound of Chief coughing. He checked but found no new blood in or around Chief's mouth—a good sign. Chief drank a little more water.

"Chief, listen," Russ offered a preamble of sorts. "You know that I had to get married, and it didn't work out. I wanted to be a father and a husband, but my wife was too young. All her friends were off to college. She had been a bright student and was well prepared for college. She wanted to be off with her friends, not married to me."

"Yes, it is the way of youth. Your values are different when you are young." Chief opened his eyes as he spoke, then closed them again.

"I had quit working for my father and had only worked for her father a couple of weeks. It wasn't good, working for him, so I quit and took a job in a scrapyard. It wasn't well received. It was dirty work with long hours, but I wanted to prove I was my own man. When I came home at night I didn't look preppy, and my smell came through the door before I did. My new bride wanted none of it. One day I came home and her mother was there. There was no sign of my wife. Her mother told me there had been a miscarriage, but she had a mischievous grin. Who smiles at a time like that? I was in a panic, worried about my wife, and when I asked where she was, I was told I couldn't see her. Her mother walked out the door without another word. I never saw my wife again. I searched for several months and went to her parents' house several times, but they told me she had moved away. They warned me that I was guilty of harassing them and that my wife didn't want me to know where she was." The memories rushed at him now. "I felt I had lost face with my own family. I had dodged the draft; then I failed as a husband. I was overwhelmed with shame. One day I started walking and never went back. I hitchhiked clear across the country. My mother died shortly after my father was murdered. She had a heart attack they said, but it was heartbreak. I didn't make it back for either one of their funerals. I haven't been back to that part of the country since I left."

Chief's hand gripped Russ's arm. Even in his weakened state, his grip was firm. "It's time for you to heal. When I am gone . . ."

"When you are gone?"

"I am not long here."

"Yes, but not until we find your sacred place; it is not far, I think." Russ leaned back against a boulder and told the old man to rest.

"We are close," Chief whispered with his eyes shut.

"Chief, I don't know how this is going to end up, but I want you to know that you have changed me. I hope the changes stick. I'm not the same guy I was when we started this journey. I promise you I am going to do all I can to help you. Chief?"

Chief was asleep again. Russ closed his own eyes. He could hear the faint sound of the river as they sat in the shade of the boulder. Soon, they were both asleep.

The moving shadow of the rock allowed the sun to touch Russ's face, bringing him back to awareness. Chief still rested in the shadow, so he decided to climb the boulder to gain a view of the trail ahead. The Havasupai rushed over boulders to meet the Colorado, the sound telling Russ they were indeed close. The trail ahead had few trees and was littered with uprooted debris.

The Colorado's thundering chocolate waters washed out the blue-green of the Havasupai where they met, and its pungent odor of disturbed mud, dead fish, and violent froth overpowered Havasupai's sweet smell. The Colorado was a raging serpent that rumbled in the canyon, grabbing at the shore and tossing debris. In one jealous moment, the beauty of the Havasupai was devoured. The trail ahead offered only more difficulty. It narrowed and climbed, then disappeared around a sharp precipice. Russ thought the journey looked impossible, even for a healthy octogenarian.

He sat on the stone above Chief and looked down. He wondered how in the world he could fulfill his promise to Chief. The sun sat at midafternoon; there would be several more hours of light. Chief twitched slightly and then a little more violently. Startled, Russ reached out to steady him, then realized he was just out of reach. Chief began to convulse.

Russ scrambled down the boulder to his side. He tried desperately to awaken Chief but could not. The old Indian's movements seemed not to be involuntary physical gyrations but deliberately executed interchanges. Russ supported Chief with all his strength in an attempt to protect him from injury, but in no other way did he restrict his motion. The seizures continued for several minutes as sweat rained from Chief, his jaw tightly clenched on a strap of rawhide that Russ provided.

Prayer, Russ thought. *I believed prayer would protect him.* Chief's face contorted, and his eyes moved rapidly under his lids. The strength in his arms was not that of an old man but even more powerful than most young men's. Russ held on for dear life and prayed by himself. Chief's breathing was deep, and strange noises sounded from his throat, like those of a distant wolf, growling. He didn't have time to ponder what Chief might be dreaming or its significance. He just wanted it to end. The trauma of it all had to be taking a toll on the old man. Russ had an eerie feeling of being watched.

CHAPTER 33

The horse snorted then whinnied as it reared up, suddenly spooked. Twenty feet away stood a grey wolf, *Paseo del Lobo*. A luxurious coat feathered in the slight breeze; its eyes gleamed an intense yellow. A Mexican grey wolf, a creature not known in these parts for at least eighty years, though Russ had read about a possible reintroduction project.

The wolf stood still, its head low, its stare nonthreatening. Still, its presence left Russ feeling uneasy. Its nostrils flared as it tested the breeze for a scent. Chief's seizures calmed. He rested in Russ's arms, and the wolf stepped slowly toward Russ, taking three steps forward, then one back.

There existed no doubt. It was a wolf, not a large dog or coyote. It showed intelligence with a sort of sagacity about it. It cautiously resumed its approach. Russ sat motionless, holding a calmed Chief. Russ held his breath as the wolf advanced toward them. It sniffed at Chief's feet, then his shin, working its way up his body. Then it stopped and looked directly into Russ's eyes. *Never make eye contact with a canine? Was that the rule? Was he making a threatening mistake?* The wolf continued to stare and Russ looked back, into eyes that knew the wild, eyes that looked on the world from the top of the food chain, eyes that calculated every move so as not to waste effort. Russ's face was within snapping distance of its powerful jaws and razor-sharp fangs, yet the animal showed only the covering of moist lips. It turned to sniff Chief's wound.

Russ thought it best to maintain his composure and wait to see what the wolf's next move might be. They were known predators as well as scavengers. Russ slid his hand slowly into his pack and felt for his knife. He looked up and saw the rifle holstered in the saddle on the horse. His hand found the knife and he gripped it tight, prepared to plunge it deep into the wolf's neck.

As if it sensed Russ's thoughts, the wolf turned back to again stare into Russ's eyes. It cocked its head to the side, sniffed Chief's wound again, and then gently licked the bandage again and again. It whimpered softly, then licked Chief's face. Its large foot pawed ever so lightly at Chief's chest. There seemed a kinship between the two.

Thoughts of aggression disappeared as Russ released the knife. Finally, the wolf backed away, always facing Russ and Chief. When it reached the position in which Russ had first seen it, it emitted a couple of muffled barks before it let out a blood-curdling howl. Its head started out low to the ground, and as it expelled its woeful moan, it turned its head straight up.

Goose bumps peppered Russ's spine as fur rose on the wolf's back. Three times the wolf howled, and on the third time, Chief's moan distracted Russ from the wolf. When Russ looked back again, the wolf was gone. Russ saw no sign of the wolf, yet he knew no animal could have moved out of the range of sight that swiftly, at least not by conventional means. Chief began to stir.

"Chief—can you hear me?"

Chief did not respond, other than another moan, his eyes still shut. Russ leaned Chief back against the boulder and poured water onto a cloth. He wiped the sweat from the old man's face and neck, then held the damp cloth on Chief's forehead. He watched for the wolf to return, but there was no sign of it. The sun's position indicated that the day was fading, and he wondered if they should wait out the night in this unlikely spot. Chief blinked and gave an encouraging grunt, stronger than his moans.

"Chief, can you speak? Chief, it's Russ."

"Russ, yes, I had a dream . . ." Chief's voice was just above a whisper.

"Easy, Chief, just take it easy."

"No, I must tell you."

"I guess our prayers didn't work for you; I guess God wasn't listening."

"God is always listening. You have to be willing to accept His answer, even if it wasn't the one you sought. He always answers, but we don't always listen."

"I guess you're right."

Chief's voice grew stronger as he became more alert. He pushed up into a more comfortable sitting position, and winced at the pain it caused in his shoulder. "My dream was not like others I have had. It was not about the spirits from the wars. It was a battle between God and the Dark One. Evil is trying to stop us, Russ. That is why I was shot. In my dream I could not transform myself; God stopped me. It is difficult to find words, but when I took out the meth makers, I interfered with the work of the Dark One; I brought attention to myself. Now he wants to stop me from achieving my goal. It had been many years since I had conjured up my powers. It was a mistake."

"Well, I watched you go through some agonizing moments."

"In my dream I gained strength. God gave me strength. I believe that I am stronger now." Chief's voice did sound stronger, Russ admitted to himself.

"We had a visitor while you were out."

"A visitor . . . ?"

"Yes, a wolf came up the trail. It walked right up to us and sniffed your wound. It licked it several times and then left."

"A Mexican grey wolf?" Chief appeared to be deep in thought, a slight grin crossing his face. "Anything is possible, but the wolf is my symbol. It is the one that the shaman assigned to me when I was twelve years old. There are no Mexican wolves left in the canyon. They were all killed by the park service, but when I was twelve, they still roamed these canyons.

"The shaman left me alone for several days to test me. He sat on the cliffs to watch over me, but I did not know it. A lone grey wolf also watched me, but I did not know that, either. The wolf never attacked me, nor did it enter my campsite. The shaman eventually came to me and told me how the wolf was my sign. I have never seen this wolf myself, but others like you have seen it throughout my life. It is a good sign. It makes me happy to hear that he was here."

"It scared the heck out of me."

"Our people tell of a grandfather who tells his grandson that we have two wolves that live inside us. The first is the wolf of peace, of love and kindness. The other is the wolf of fear, of greed and hatred. These two wolves struggle with each other. The grandson asks his grandfather which wolf will win the struggle. The grandfather tells him the one that is fed. The wolf that visited us is the first wolf, and so you had nothing to fear. I have been feeding him for a long time."

Russ could not bring himself to utter a response. Anything he could say would cheapen the thought. "It is getting late. Should we just camp here for the night?" he asked softly.

"No, it is not far to where we are going. Daylight will not matter there as long as we have light while we travel."

Chief looked at the sun and held up his fist. Each fist between the sun and the horizon marked an hour of daylight.

"We still have a couple of hours. We should go."

"I'll ready the horse." Russ stood and walked to the mount.

"You know some tribes never adopted the horse when the Spanish first brought them. The Comanche, though, were great horsemen. I am no Comanche, but this horse will be a great help."

"Yes it will; it'll be a lot better than me trying to carry you."

"The whites slaughtered the Comanche horses in 1874 and 1875. It's figured that the US Calvary shot thousands of horses in Palo Duro Canyon after they raided a Comanche village as they slept. The horses' carcasses were left to rot, and their bones piled high became a monument to the end of the horse tribes."

Russ walked the horse closer to Chief who had straightened to a standing position. With Russ's help, Chief mounted the horse.

"Quanah Parker would be proud of me," Chief muttered as he settled into the saddle. "Quanah Parker was a great Comanche warrior chief at the time of the massacre. It is said that he walked 200 miles to surrender and to ask for mercy for his people. He lived two lives—one on the warpath, fiercely defiant, and one in peace, walking the white man's road after his surrender. Before he surrendered he went out into the desert seeking a sign. It is said that he spoke to a wolf and watched an eagle glide toward Fort Sill, and it was then that he knew he must surrender for the sake of his people. We have had our signs; now I ride to my own surrender."

Chief motioned for Russ to follow a high trail that led up the canyon face, upstream of the confluence, on a trail barely as wide as the horse's flank. It was the trail Russ had observed from the rock as Chief slept, and it was as brutal as he had imagined. Rocks broke free under the hooves and tumbled hundreds of feet to the river below. Russ's hand touched the rock wall on the high side as his other hand clenched the reins and led the horse. Chief sat high and had a vantage point with which to see the trail ahead.

"Stop!"

"What is it, Chief?"

"The trail has fallen away. There is a thirty-foot gap ahead. It looks like a fairly fresh slide."

"Really?"

"No use." The chief grumbled.

"Look up at that outcropping. The rocks form footholds. I think I can ascend to the outcropping. I'll tie off a rope, and then you swing across the gap. You should be able to make it, and with your good arm, grab onto that side. I'll use the rope to descend to the other side of the gap. What do you think about that, Chief?"

"Good plan. You got rope?" Chief looked smug.

"Ah . . . no."

"You have another idea then?"

"We'll have to drop down to the river and hope we can manage to work our way along the edge. You'll have to walk; the horse will be useless."

"It will be difficult, but it's our only chance. We must back up so I can dismount and turn this horse around."

"Horses have a reverse?" Russ coaxed the horse by whispering to it as he held the reins tight and placed his hand on the horse's outbound shoulder.

"Just go slow, be gentle, and keep whispering to him. We need to get back to that wide spot." Chief showed no signs of fear or concern as the horse kicked loose rocks and bounced its head in protest.

Russ nuzzled alongside the horse's head, rubbing its neck with one hand and holding shortened reins in the other. He whispered soothing commands to back up as he watched the placement of its hooves. The horse took a few reluctant back-steps and then halted, letting out a whinny with a headshake. The old Indian leaned toward the cliff, readied for an inward slide should the horse stumble. As they slowly backed up, the animal's rear hoof misplaced a couple of times, so close to the edge that it sent debris tumbling to the canyon floor a hundred feet below. Instinctively, the horse would balance and reposition itself. Each time it happened Russ stopped, and everybody, including the horse, regrouped. Finally, they reached the wide spot, and the chief dismounted. Russ removed the saddle and bridle, then tossed them over the edge of the cliff. After a swat on its rump, the horse raced down the trail toward the canyon floor.

"I guess I will walk to my surrender."

"How do you feel?"

"I have been better, but I still feel strong. We will make it."

CHAPTER 34

Backtracking a short distance along their route, they dropped to an area where a narrow, loose-gravel trail split off in a rapid descent to the Colorado's edge. Like roller bearings, it made their footing treacherous. Slipping, they grabbed at whatever they could find—small shrubs, roots, rocks—anything to save them from a tumble down the steep embankment. At the river's edge they climbed over and around boulders, helping each other by boosting or pulling. It was a strenuous endeavor even for a healthy man, and it took an obvious toll on Chief. They took breaks and sat on boulders to watch the torrent of silt-laden water gush only a few feet from them. The hot sun dehydrated them, and the river mocked them with its abundance, its thundering tumult taunting already frayed nerves.

"Nothing worth doing is easy."

"That's what I've been told, Chief."

"It might be better not to do anything worthwhile."

"I won't argue with that; people live their whole lives that way."

"Ugh, we better keep moving. This is the wrong place to change our ways."

"Gotcha, Chief."

They peered up and saw where the high trail had slid away. They had finally reached the point beneath where they had turned around. Far up on the cliff wall, Russ could barely make out a structure in the shadows beneath a huge overhang of rock. It looked to be an adobe cliff dwelling, and he wondered if it was their destination. He didn't question Chief though. If he was right, they had their work cut out for them. Climbing, crawling, hopping, and inching back up the hillside, they moved on for a laborious mile and finally came onto the trail they had originally sought.

After the torturous detour, the old trail seemed easy. The chief began to chant. The boulders along the trail were covered with petroglyphs that depicted animals, humans, and spirits.

"I ask forgiveness for entering this sacred area," Chief whispered.

"Ask for me, too," Russ whispered.

"We are close. Let me study the writings. It has been over sixty years since I have been here. We can walk while I chant and read. You be silent."

"If it there is anything about a curse, just keep it to yourself. It will be better if I don't know."

They had walked a few hundred yards when the old Indian finally dropped to his knees. He let out a shrill cry and grabbed fists full of dirt, which he tossed into the air. He bowed down and kissed the earth, then, turning his head, he rested his ear on the ground. Minutes passed as the old Indian rested motionlessly and listened to the earth. Eventually, he stood up and pointed toward the cliffs a hundred feet above, to the adobe dwellings that Russ had seen from below. The cliff had a slight angle and footholds that would assist them in the climb. Chief started up without hesitation, followed quickly by Russ. When they reached the dwelling, Chief looked around briefly without entering, instead easing along a precarious ledge for about thirty feet.

"There, the entrance to the underworld is there!" The old man pointed toward a solid stone wall.

Cautiously walking toward Chief, Russ looked for a gap in the stone and then suddenly stopped.

"This is the one. See here. That is a drawing done by me. I drew that when I became a skinwalker." Chief stood by a very small petroglyph on the wall.

The petroglyph depicted seven men, each dressed in a different animal pelt. There was another larger figure with his arms outstretched toward the seven men.

"These are pictures of the seven animals that I can transmute into. This figure here was my shaman. This is where my training took place. These images are still here after all these years. If I sit, I will see the whole ceremony as it was. We sit. Let me concentrate."

"Chief, I don't see an entrance. The rock is solid."

"Wait, I will show you, and I ask that as you follow me, you restore the entrance behind you. This is something you must do. As you enter, slide the stone back, and then work it until no light shows around its edges." Chief used his hand to brush at the dirt and debris that had accumulated on the ledge beside him. As the debris fell away, it exposed a flat rock with the head of a wolf faintly painted on it. The rock was barely the width of a man's shoulders. Chief used his hunting knife to pry up one edge. He slid the rock across his lap and onto the ledge on his other side. He had exposed a small hole barely large enough to allow a man to squeeze into. Apparently, no man had entered since Chief had placed the stone years ago.

Chanting, Chief swung his legs into the hole and faded into a trance. His eyes followed movements that Russ couldn't see. His head moved about as if there were other people with them. Russ sat with his back pressed tightly against the cliff face, his eyes straining to see what the chief saw, to no avail. Nothing was visible to him. Then Chief rose with a blank gaze and slipped down the hole in the rock ledge. Russ jumped up and followed close behind, sliding the capstone partially over the hole.

The hole opened into a large room, a room that appeared to have been excavated by men. It was dim, lit only by the light that leaked in through the entrance. They stood at a large, flat rock in the center of the room. Chief rolled three round rocks off its edge and then knelt in the dirt to slide the flat rock aside until a fissure appeared in the underlying rock. If anyone had found the hole beneath the first rock, it would be unlikely that they would have thought to venture beyond this room. The crack was barely wide enough for Chief to squeeze into.

"Now, you must replace the first stone above you and then follow me to replace this stone." Only Chief's face was visible in the crevasse.

He disappeared like a jackrabbit into its burrow, dragging his satchel along behind him. Russ peered into the black hole and saw nothing but darkness. He reached up and worked the stone the rest of the way over the first entrance until he was in complete darkness. He crouched down, felt the edge of the second hole, and squeezed in. Pulling the second rock over him in such cramped and dark quarters left him feeling claustrophobic. Like Alice following the rabbit, Russ followed Chief, crawling along a narrow, suffocating passageway. He tracked nothing but the scraping sounds and strained breathing of Chief—all there was in the complete darkness.

Like crawling down the throat of some ancient beast, they continued as groundwater oozed in from all sides. They continued through a natural spring laced with carbonic acid from decaying surface plants of the type known to dissolve limestone and create caverns. The trickle grew into a wash that lapped beneath their bellies with a dispiriting chill, soaking their clothes. The rocks became slippery, easing the physical challenge and yet heightening the psychological trial. Russ could not help but think he was being ingested. He wondered how he would ever be expelled. Suddenly, they launched into a slide.

Without encouragement, they slid down the ogre's gullet, greased by layers of ancient, glowing slime, fungi that had evolved into offering an eerie, blue glow. Headfirst they traveled and futilely struggled to slow down. Then, without warning, they dropped into a wider black void, a free fall that ended in a splash of deep, frigid water. The cold took Russ's breath away; his muscles knotted, and his diaphragm arrested. Bobbing up and down, he finally caught his breath and grabbed out into the darkness for a handhold on any solid object.

Finally, Russ found an ancient, calcified stalagmite, its roughened surface a godsend. He shinnied up quickly and soon found a secure seat on a ledge at the water's edge, his feet still dangling in the cold subterranean water. He listened for Chief, but heard only the sound of softly lapping water. He hugged the stalagmite with one arm and reached out with the other. He shivered and his teeth chattered as he strained to listen for any sound from Chief.

"Chief, here, I'm here. Is that you?"

"Yes, here I am."

Russ felt the firm grip of a human hand on his own that pulled him forward. Their hands locked, pulling Russ into the water, but he maintained his grip on the rocks. Onto the rough rock, he lifted Chief. Coughing and gasping for air, he strained his eyes, but he could not see Chief. Russ looked up toward a faint blue glow of fungi where they had fallen out of the spring. He guessed it to be fifteen feet above them. The ceiling of the cavern appeared as a star-studded sky—the Milky Way. There were no other lights, just spooky speckles and the blue glow in an otherwise absolute darkness. In all directions he could hear falling water splash. There was no way to determine the size of the room where he sat, though the sound of the water varied greatly, and he believed the tomb to be grand.

"This is the way it was in the beginning. There was no light, only the stars." The familiar voice of Chief rang out.

"Where are we?"

"This is the underworld. This is the entrance to the lost city that legends talk about," Chief said softly.

"What are those speckles across the ceiling?"

"Those are the silk strings of Waitomo Glowworms. They are the larvae of cave gnats. They exist here and in the caves of New Zealand. You must speak softly. If they sense a threat, they will turn off their illumination. They are trying to catch other cave bugs with their lights."

"It's spooky, and I'm cold."

"This is a place that only the two of us know about. We must sit here in the dark and pray forgiveness for violating this place. When we receive a sign, we may light a torch," Chief whispered.

"Light a torch? I'm soaked. I'm sure you are too. We don't have materials to make torches," Russ argued.

"Speak softly; there is a stack of torches behind us. I made them when the shaman brought me here. They are of paraffin-soaked rags made to last forever. Now, pray silently that I may be granted entrance to this place," Chief whispered.

"I'm going to pray for a way out of here. I know we can't go back the way we came." Russ stared at the blue glow above them.

"You are right, but there is another way, and I will show it to you. You will be alright. This cavern is ancient. At one time the Havasu flowed through here instead of on the surface. That was well before the days of men. It hollowed out the earth and made this place. When the earth shifted and formed what the geologist we met called the Sinyala Fault, the river began to flow on the surface," Chief whispered. "The old route in this underworld still exists. When we complete what we came to do, we will exit that way. It will bring us out near Mooney Falls. It is better than the way we came, you will see. Now, we must pray." They sat, prayed, and waited for a sign. *What sign can take place in a hole like this?* Russ wondered. He was full of doubt, and after an hour their eyes had still not adjusted to the void of light. Sitting in the dark, they might sit forever waiting for a sign that they could not see . . .

Then Russ felt some*one*, some*thing* touch his shoulder, or was it a twitch? A muscle spasm from the cold in his right shoulder? Then he felt it in his other shoulder.

"Chief! Is that you? Or is it just my imagination? Maybe a muscle spasm?" Russ whispered, turning his head in the direction where Chief had last spoken.

"Shhh! No, my hands are here. This is what we have been waiting for," Chief said, taking Russ's hands in his to acknowledge that it was not he who was touching Russ's shoulders.

"Someone is kneading my shoulders, I think," Russ whispered in a quivering voice, chills crawling up his spine. Still, he could not discern whether the feeling was generated internally or externally. He wanted to believe it was just a twitching muscle, an involuntary spasm of sorts.

"And mine. It is the sign we are accepted by the *dighin Diné* into *Sipapu*. When it stops, we will wait a little longer to show respect and that we are not too anxious. Quiet now, this place is most sacred. The spirits ask respect. Listen now to Nightway *[Tł'éé'jí].*"

"Chief, the stars have gone dim. Look—the glowworms must sense danger."

"No, there is no danger. Wait, you will see them return. When they do, it is time for us to move."

Sitting in unmitigated blackness, Russ heard a melodious chant that stimulated his senses. Visions, mysterious sensations, crept into his mind, inspiring him to prayer. The voice was not that of Chief. His mind drifted into contemplations that he had no knowledge of, Native American visualizations of a past foreign to him. It was a continuation of the dream he had had in the campground. His eyes closed, useless in the dark, and yet he saw entities and domiciles. He sensed smoke from cooking fires, rocky foundations, brightly hued clothing, and soft buckskin. The laughter of children mingled happily with the chanting. He felt the emotions of a people he had never known. Sensory deprived but for the melodious chant and gurgling water, Russ joined in the chant. It seemed familiar, and it joined his prayer. He heard Chief begin to chant. His breathing slowed to a minimal rhythm, as did his heart rate. Time passed without a mark. Then he saw the stars, the glowworms.

"It is time," Chief said softly, reverently. "I will light a torch. Keep your eyes closed, for the torch will hurt them until you adjust. We must move slowly."

CHAPTER 35

Chief lit his torch and held it high above his head. The cavern walls glistened as if coated by a fresh fall of crystal snow. Huge columns of quartz stalactites mated to stalagmites. Row after row, the columns faded into the dark reaches of the cavernous room, a hundred times larger than Russ had imagined while sitting in the dark.

Chief and Russ stood on a causeway that stretched across a lake of crystal-clear water. Small waterfalls flowed from tunnels near the ceiling. The upper reaches of the main ceiling were beyond the illumination of the torch. The port that Russ and Chief had entered through was in the lowest section of roof, a mere overhang.

Chief handed Russ the torch and took up another. He lit four in all so they would have a torch in each hand. As each torch was lit, more wonder appeared. Huge, clear crystals with hues of gold, silver, and blue shot out from the walls, the floor, and the ceiling, as large as trees—the soft, white light of Selenite, said to have metaphysical and healing benefits in abundance.

Russ felt their effects. "I've never experienced anything like this," he whispered. "I read about *Cueva de los Cristales*, Cave of Crystals, just south of Chihuahua, Mexico. The pictures I have seen were spectacular—but nothing like this."

"Not many have, and hopefully not many will. We have left the Fourth World and entered the Third. This is the *Sipapu*. Nothing else is like this place. You must be pure to enter beyond here, or you will be consumed by your own evil. Slowly open your eyes. Keep your focus beyond yourself; be selfless. This is what God offers us, a focus beyond our own being. These crystals alter mental focus and can soothe emotions," Chief said in a reverent tone.

"I feel it Chief; I do."

"These crystals formed from vapors seeping out of fissures in the bedrock. Below us is a pocket of magma that acted as a giant smelter many years ago. It has cooled now, but still, do you feel the warmth of the air, the humidity? At one time, probably a hundred thousand years ago, these chambers would have been too hot for a man to be in."

"My chill has been relieved." Russ walked the causeway absorbing the wonders, breathlessly following Chief. They walked upon solid ground into a tunnel in which the walls glittered from veins of gold. The ground was littered with shiny golden stones that Chief kicked.

"These are just pyrite—fool's gold they call it—but then, doesn't gold make fools of us all? Some of it is an arsenian pyrite that does contain real gold, but that is not why we are here. Pyrite breaks down and makes the waters acidic; it was a great contributor to the erosion that created this place."

Russ jammed one of his torches into the ground and bent down to retrieve a fist-sized chunk of pyrite to examine. He pitched it aside, retrieved his torch, and caught up to Chief as he entered a chamber larger than the first.

"Chief! That's—"

"That's what? Gold? It is just a different rock. It is nothing. You must look beyond it to see what is of value here. We see different things. Here you envision all the temptations of man. You must maintain self-control. I don't see what you see."

"El Dorado," Russ whispered. "This must be El Dorado, the city of gold."

Chief stopped in his tracks and Russ bumped into him; it felt as if he had hit a wall.

"No! This place has no name!" Chief spoke with firm authority. "This place has no name. It will have no name. That is the word of the ancient ones. It must never be spoken of; therefore, it needs no name.

You see why this place is sacred and why it is believed that we came from this place. It is a spiritual place. If it were known, the wicked would deface it and plunder it."

"I've never been a regular churchgoer, Chief, but I have toured some of the great cathedrals of Europe, and this place would make them blush." The effects of the surroundings aroused a spiritual feeling in Russ unlike any he had felt in a cathedral.

The reflections of the torches' glow mirrored from every angle. The walls and pillars, naturally gilded in gold, rose beyond the torchlight. But the strangest sight to fathom were the everyday items, like eating utensils, made entirely of gold. The very rock upon which they stood streaked gold. The room went on, Russ guessed, for hundreds of feet beyond the light of the torch. The cavern's size surpassed imagination. Russ studied the chief, amazed that he showed no sign of being affected by all that Russ saw, by the wonder.

"The people of the surface once worshiped here. At first they worshiped the purity, the inner peace that the crystals evoked. All men were welcomed. But in time, man turned his worship toward the rock and began to carry it to the surface. It was used to influence and purchase the spirits of others, and it caused great suffering. Much evil began to be done to acquire it. Lust and greed ate at the hearts of men. Then a wise shaman decided to give it back to the earth so his people could return to the gentle way of the ancients. He ordered all the gold of the Nations be brought back here and hidden forever in this place. He sealed the cavern, and all people were forbidden to speak of it or give it a name. Only a few shamans were granted access for the sake of meditation and purification of thought. It is said the great shaman offered all of humankind's temptation to be brought here. Knowledge of this place has been passed from one shaman to the next. You are the first man, not a shaman, to enter in a thousand years. I have placed my trust in you. I am the last shaman to know of this place."

"Do you have any idea what all this is worth?" Russ looked about, wild-eyed, but Chief soon caught on to the fact that he was just kidding.

"You are a funny guy, but this is serious." Chief gave Russ a hard look.

"Seriously, Chief, I have never looked for the big easy or quick score. All this is overwhelming, though. I have to admit; it makes me a little giddy."

"Your words did disappoint me at first. Remember, these things have worth, but nothing here is worth one human life, not one minute of time. It only causes men pain and suffering if their hearts are not as pure as the crystals. You must believe this, for this is why we are here, for the purification. If you don't put aside temptation and your materialistic thoughts, then the reason we came here will be lost. This is your first test in the 'City of the Dead.' Make peace with your greedy thoughts or die."

"You're asking a lot. More than anything else you've asked of me," Russ replied.

"You are right; to ask a man to be pure of heart is asking the impossible, but that is what I ask. I ask it, but expect you to fall short. We are all mortal."

"I will try my best."

"You can never leave here if you covet the gold; if you do, you will die here, becoming the property of the rock. A skinwalker will see to it. You may think I am asking a lot, but in fact I am giving even more. Your inner peace is worth more than all these rocks."

Russ saw that the threat was more of a promise. He didn't need to be threatened. He knew his own resolve. He knew he would be true to the test. The thoughts of compromising this place would never become a path he would take.

"Please, you must struggle against your desires. Walk with me. I'll show you the city. Think about what you have said. This city is a temple, a shrine to inner peace and love. It was meant to be a place where men worshiped God. God offers His love selflessly to man, and man uses Him to seek power, to control others, to endorse their words and become false prophets. What you see here are tools of evil if in the wrong hands, or an offering of peace to those who understand. It is like being in the presence of a beautiful woman, appreciating her without seeing her as the target of a conquest. It is not easy."

They held their torches high as they walked along an avenue of adobe structures, a street in the "City of the Dead." The canopy of the cavern edged hundreds of feet above with glowworms that caused the effect of a cloudless night sky studded with stars. Chief held his torch toward the ground as he stepped over the litter of human bones. Several skeletons hugged assorted golden objects. They appeared to have died struggling to carry the objects, perhaps refusing to put them down. Adobe buildings clung to the walls of the cavern, like those of the cliff-dweller buildings on the surface near the entrance. The windows, like dark, deep-set eyes, offered haunting stares. The doorways, mysterious voids, offered no sense of welcome.

"These skeletons have been here since the earliest days," said Chief. "They were robbers who foolishly intruded, and the shaman struck them dead and let them lie. It is a warning to others. Rainbow Woman said to me once that human beings like to say 'God moves in mysterious ways.' She said that God's ways are mysterious only to those who are not familiar with God. Human beings don't say that Satan moves in mysterious ways. She said that is because humans are more familiar with the ways of Satan. After all, we live in his world."

"We could be in hell," Russ whispered.

"These are tortured souls who thought that these rocks were of value rather than this place and the peace it offers. We are here to release souls attached to mine so that I might enter the spirit world. I want to be with Rainbow Woman. Love is all that matters. What you lust for is nothing. It is fleeting. This is not hell, and the dark one is not here; the ancient ones hid these tools from him. I want the souls imprisoned in me to go in peace and love, but that is not possible for me to do alone."

Chief grimaced, and his voice shrank in a surge of pain obviously radiating from his shoulder. "My skinwalker magic can be of the darkness, much like these rocks. The magic was entrusted to me, and I used it for my vision of good. Most skinwalkers end like the fools you see lying about, destroyed by selfish conquests. They misuse their gift, which causes them to die a horrible death. Fortunately I did not, and here in this sacred place you will help me break the skinwalker spell. I have spoken to you about my ways, but never have I let it be known to others except my wife and the elders of my tribe, who have all passed." Chief winced again and clutched his shoulder.

Russ lifted his torch near Chief's shoulder to take a look at his bandages. The warm air rising from fissures in the floor had dried their clothes, but Russ could see that Chief's bandages were moist. Chief stuck his torches into the ground to free his hands and removed his bandage. His flesh was swollen. It oozed, and the light of the torch accentuated the redness around the wound.

"What do we do now?" Russ looked about at the dried and contorted bones on the street, convinced that the old chief spoke with wisdom and truth.

"You sit here and make friends. Meditate and search your heart. I will return, but first I need to make preparations without you. You will be here for quite a while. Your mind may play tricks on you, but you will hopefully find your spirit. Remember to feed the right wolf, for if you feed the wrong one, it will grow strong and eventually feed on your flesh." Chief took the torches from Russ's hands and held them high before pulling two more from the ground. "I am taking all the torches with me. Look around now, and be mindful of what you see. While I am gone, all you see will be with your mind's eye. There will be nothing to mark the time."

"I don't like this. What if your wound makes you too sick to return? What if you fall and can't get back?" Russ looked at Chief and saw no concern in his face.

"These are your thoughts? I suggest you feed the other wolf." Chief walked away, taking with him the light.

Russ lowered himself to the ground and worked on his thoughts. He looked up at the glowworms. They reminded him of the stars that first night in the campground, of the skinwalker puma. *Feed the other wolf,* he told himself. His thoughts turned to youth and good times, family times. Warm summers spent in the mountains of Pennsylvania, exploring shady hemlock forests with his grandfather. Lessons of life learned by hard knocks. He wouldn't have wished to grow up any other way. He had worked for his father since he had been twelve, a father he admired. He ran with a wild crowd, but instinctively knew where misadventures end and what the price of stupidity was. He prided himself for turning his back on the stupidity that his so-called friends tried to entice him into.

This is who I am, Russ told himself. With his mind's eye, he took inventory of himself. I am not selfish nor a fool. In the complete blackness he thought of times he had worked shifts for family men so they could be off for holidays, tossed money to panhandlers even though he disapproved of their lot, and the times that he struggled to not judge others. Everyone had a story and a reason for why they sank into obscurity. He had never accomplished anything grand in his lifetime, but he had never intentionally done anything abysmal either.

With the darkness came a conflict though, a suppressed honesty that he quickly attempted to block. A question haunted him: Had he led a selfish life? It wasn't my doing, Russ argued. He started off wanting to be a family man and to live a shared life with his wife and children. His lot had been cast by others, and he had only made the best of it. He strained his eyes in the darkness to distract from his thoughts, but only his mind's eye had vision. This is my lot now, he thought. This is nothingness, sensory deprivation. The only thing that exists now is my inner self. He saw nothing; he heard nothing. He reached down and grabbed two fists of powdered terra firma. It flowed out of his hands and smelled of the earth.

CHAPTER 36

An appreciation of the solitude grew in Russ even as he struggled with his inner self. The last images before Chief took the torches still flashed in his mind. The purity of the crystal, the comfort and serenity they brought to him, their impact he still sensed. If he died right now, right here, it would be fine. He had lived a salvaged life the best he could, and so found no shame in it. Sifting through his life's debris, he detected no guilt of an intentional hurt or lessening anyone's life experience. Some women might argue that, he laughed silently.

"I'm not perfect," he whispered. "God, please forgive me. I know that you loved us so much that you provided the perfect plan for our salvation through your son, Jesus Christ. I remember that the book of Romans tells me that your word is near me, in my heart. Now I want to confess that I know you are the Lord, and that only you can save me. I will protect this place and time with all my heart." He breathed in and out, slowly feeling his own existence. He wasn't trying to control anything. He wasn't running. He wasn't even really thinking. He was just . . . being. He felt open—open to love, open to peace, peace with himself, peace with the universe. As he opened his eyes, he saw in the distance reflected light on a tunnel wall and heard a muffled cough.

It was then that Chief approached, carrying only two torches. Russ stood and accepted the one that Chief offered. Chief looked hard at Russ's face. Russ looked at Chief's wound. It had grown even more inflamed, but there was nothing he could do. He said nothing, though his heart ached.

"I have done all that is needed to prepare for the moment."

Chief's voice was weakened and weary.

"Would you like to rest awhile?" Russ asked.

"No."

"Then where do we go from here?"

"We will go into a space where I have taken the flowers. I soaked them in the water you collected. We will need to build a fire to burn the rest and paint our faces with the red-earth mud from the bottom of the river. Follow me." Chief turned and walked toward the tunnel from which he had come.

"This tunnel has no branches. It circles around to the main tunnel, the original flow path of the Havasu. Turn left and just walk the tunnel until you come to an abrupt shift in the bedrock. That is the fault. There are petroglyphs that will show the way from there. You will be near the campground. Do not let anyone see you or where you emerge from the cavern."

"You will be with me, won't you?"

"Maybe, but it is not our decision. I tell these things in advance just in case. You are not to look for me if I am not with you when this ends. Each of us will be on our own. You will know when it is done. So just go."

They walked the tunnel in silence now, their torches casting flickering shadows on the walls. There were no stalagmites or stalactites in the tunnel. The walls were marked, hand-hewn in ancient times. There was no longer glitter of crystals or gold. They entered a room, a purple-crusted geode.

"We will breathe smoke and drink an aqueous solution. Then we will perform 'Anaa'jí to exorcise the ghosts of violence and ugliness, a purification ceremony. The red clay will protect us from spirits like the mud protected you from the snakes. You will subdue the spirits as they are released from me."

Russ studied Chief, his surroundings, and Chief's words. There was a fear in him, he had to admit. A fear of the unknown, yet not a fear for his own safety. He had resolved that his life had been spent in an endless cycle of repetitive endeavors, adventures in exotic places, but each basically the same as the last. For once he had embarked on this new adventure. To succeed, he would have to cast aside all inhibitions and fears.

"It sounds like we're going to get high. How is this any different than what dopers do?" Russ was never comfortable taking substances, even those prescribed by doctors. Now he was being offered something by a skinwalker. He had to question it.

"They get high for the sake of getting high; theirs is a selfish endeavor. What we are about to do is selfless. We are embarking on a demanding journey that will benefit those that we have hurt. It is necessary to achieve this altered state of mind. There will be no long-term result or addiction." Chief fussed with the contents of his pack.

"I'll do battle with them, and they will benefit? How many will there be?" Russ questioned.

"All. The count will be quite involved; there will also be influences from battles you have fought that I cannot know about. It's ceremonial. It will be frightening, but the only physical harm that can be done to you is by your own terror. The spirits cannot hurt you as long as you hold onto that thought. This shall be a battle in the Great War between our creator and His fallen angel; we are just soldiers."

"You said yourself that I wasn't much of a fighter."

"Your battle will be one of spirit, not of flesh. You have a strong will. Never let your fear be known or even perceived. If you let that happen, all will be lost. Let love be your shield and truth be your sword, and let it be sharp. The truth of your own being will be known to you, for your efforts. Your heart will heal and be purified."

"It all sounds so easy," Russ muttered sarcastically.

"Easy it is not, but always keep in your mind that they cannot hurt you. You can only hurt yourself. Tell me, what is the opposite of love?"

"Love? Hate I guess."

"No. Selfishness. Think, my son, I know it is not what you have lived. It is why I chose you. Love and selflessness are the only things that can free me, any of us. These are the warrior powers that you possess. These are the powers that will provide a shield of love and a sword of truth."

"I possess these?"

"Yes. You possess these. It is what will free me and protect you. You will be triumphant over the hatred of those I have slain. Their poison will be sucked from them. They will move beyond the grip of the darkness. Then, I will be prepared to enter the next world. You must focus beyond yourself; remember this."

Chief pulled his hand from his pack. He held a small, folded piece of rawhide. He held it out to Russ.

"Put this in your pack in a secure place, and do not open it until you are alone and safe. I want you to have this." Chief put his other hand under Russ's and pressed the rawhide firmly into Russ's palm. Russ secured it in an inner pocket in his backpack.

Chief chanted as he entered a chamber carved into the grit of the cavern wall connected to the geode room. Prepared for the ceremony, he lit a flame to a stack of ancient wood. In the dim luminosity of a smoky, smoldering fire, the two men smeared red clay on their faces, limbs, and upper torsos. Chief reached in his bag and pulled out a fistful of powder that he tossed into the flames; the odor was pungent as the dust flared.

"What's that, Chief?" Russ whispered.

"Purple sage. It will hold the spirits at bay until we are ready." Chief sat his pack near the doorway that led back into the geode room.

"You will remain in this room as we proceed, but I will be out in the geode room. The effects of the crystal are an important part of this ceremony."

Russ's mind spun trying to make sense of it all. *Science asks us to accept that there are Black Holes in space that suck matter into oblivion and that all life on earth came about by morphing from some other form. We are told that we are made up of tiny, invisible particles that resemble planetary systems. And yet, as all of these things are to be considered natural, to believe in a spirit and God and Satan is designated as supernatural. Man struggles merely because he demands proof, an instrument that will detect and show him that life-force is real, and yet the evidence is all around him.* Russ breathed deeply and accepted his thoughts as truth.

Held out over the fire, Chief's elixir became blessed, shaken, and swirled. Chief chanted as his hands articulated an ancient story. Finally, Chief drank half, then passed the jar to Russ. Russ hesitated, and then took a swig of the bitter concoction. The remaining flowers were tossed onto the fire to give off a thick smoke that they inhaled. Chief continued to chant as their distorted, flickering shadows projected onto the walls, or perhaps it was the walls themselves that undulated and flickered. Russ, eyes wide, sat in anxiety and anticipation.

The smoldering fire burst high with hideous orange flames for a moment of visual revelation. Russ muttered the Lord's Prayer under his breath, wanting to set himself apart if this was a ritual of witchcraft. A vision of a sunset and then of the moon shimmered on the cave ceiling. The moon turned blood red. Chief raised his arms, chanted, tilted back his head, and closed his eyes. The shadows on the walls swirled wilder, swifter, faster, until Russ fell backward onto the floor of the cave, nauseous and dizzy, as the thought of being poisoned repeated over and over in his head. He saw himself from outside his body drinking the potion and looked down on the room. Was the experience an actual astral projection or an illusion? A sensation gripped him that he wished to expel if only to regain his wits. Struggling, he reclaimed a sitting position although he still observed as if from above.

Chief had withdrawn either into the shadows or into the very walls themselves. A specter fired from the shadows to engulf Russ, ripping at his body with steel claws and teeth. Russ could see his own torn flesh bleeding. The sight of the blood threw Russ into a panic although he felt no pain, for he watched it all at a distance. Fear embraced him. These things were not supposed to be able to hurt him! Then he realized that his body was not his spirit. It was flesh.

"No!" he shouted in defiance and shifted his focus beyond himself. He drew the demons toward his spirit, away from his flesh. The bleeding was no more; it had never been. The wounds of the flesh dissipated. Russ turned toward the fire in time to catch the sight of a Japanese soldier, his feet kicking the embers of the fire in a release of sparks. Eyes wild and clutching a bayonet, he lunged at Russ's spirit. Russ knocked the knife from the phantom's hand and wrapped his arms about him. The soldier struggled to break free.

Russ didn't speak the words, yet a voice flowed from a power beyond him. *The war is over! Peace, find peace in your heart. God is salvation.* Russ's thoughts were in a soothing tone, and the words repeated over and over until it started to have an effect. His attacker was young, a mere man-child. Russ sensed the soldier's terror. Hatred had been replaced by fear, and the attacker's anger became terror. Russ realized that the man's soul had been captured in the conditions of war—kill or be killed—and in all the psychosis generated to survive the hostilities. These qualities in others' spirits were what the skinwalker fed on to create the fiercest of warriors. The youth of these soldiers had been used by an evil force. Even the chief had been used.

The apparition struggled violently to break free and caused Russ's footing to slip. They tumbled in a free fall but never landed, caught in a vortex of sorts. At last the soldier peacefully faded, but Russ was left with little time to rest. Within seconds, the first was replaced by a second apparition, only to be replaced by another, then another, then a Chinese soldier, then three at one time. Each time, Russ struggled face-to-face, hand to hand, and a voice sounded in his head that was not his—soothing tones, words of peace and love. At times his arms would bleed, his clothes would shred, and he would feel pain, but it was only when he focused on the struggle instead of the goal. Mustering his focus made the wounds and damage to his clothes disappear. Still, his energy was taxed and his arms ached; every muscle in his body ached.

Swirling in a maelstrom of sorts, his feet never touched down. The battle continued to present new spirits, many varied, not all soldiers. One common factor was the violence, the anger, and the hatred in their eyes. Every one of them was someone's son, some were fathers, and some were someone's brother, but they were all blood on politicians' hands. All had been used to do the work of a government. As naïve youths for a perceived worthy cause, their hearts were sincere yet misguided.

Russ absorbed the hatred cast off by these victims released from the skinwalker. It was the way it worked, and something that the chief had failed to mention: the poison. The process was toxic, and the poison took its toll on Russ. Russ's spirit, though strong, needed to dissipate the hate to the ether, but this process was slower than the accumulation. The result was a noxious buildup in Russ.

"My God, what evil do men do?" Russ agonized, his strength nearly gone.

Finally, the meth heads from the canyon appeared in all their insane glory, still bearing the effects of meth. Their poison caused the most pain of all, the poison of selfishness. Reasoning was out of the question. Physically, Russ was no match. They scratched, bit, and gouged at him. Dopers, their endurance lacked, their focus faded, and so their insanity was also their weakness. Their drug-induced high wore off, and as their images faded, Russ spun ever faster until he bounced off the stone walls of the cave. The "City of the Dead" spun beneath as he rose above it all. The glitter of gold filled his eyes like sirens in a Greek tale, the skeletons of dead gold-seekers fleshed out.

Phantasms beckoned him back, enticing him with treasure, clutching fists full of jewels and chunks of gold to lure him. Their female forms of great perfection and voices sweetly comforting tempted him. Russ closed his eyes, but their appearance his eyelids could not block. They reached for him, and although they were not near, he felt their tender touch. All of his senses were engaged as their fragrance offered visions of fields of wild flowers. He knew he weakened. His desires overpowered his reason, and he floated toward them. Only once before had he felt what he now sensed, and his lifelong struggle to eschew that feeling saved him now.

"In Jesus' name, I command these demons away from Chief, and away from me." Suddenly, there were new visions, and the sirens crumbled to dust.

A vision welled deep in his heart and stood at a doorway, more powerful and seductive than the sirens. Russ's heart raced. A face hidden for twenty-five years, beauty not faded. He hungered for her touch. He stretched out, emotions out of control, and the door opened. A woman took her hand and the apparition, his love, turned, and his heart ached as her face—so sweet and inviting—vanished. He rushed toward her, hands outstretched, reaching.

She was but a child. Russ winced as a tear opened his heart. His great love had been but a child still, not the beautiful woman of his memory. A Daddy's girl, his young wife had been, the pride of a father's heart. Russ, being lost in his lust, had defiled her. He had led her on her path to destruction, no one else. She had been part of her parents' dream, their child. In his self-centered youth, he had only seen his desires. Chief had been right. Russ sobbed as his spirit shriveled.

Above the door where his love stood, he saw a portion of the sign "Clinic," and suddenly he knew the fate of his unborn son. He convulsed, and his mother-in-law's face contorted into the smile she had worn the last time he saw her. A mother who wore the look of a woman believing it was right, a mother unwilling to take a risk on the unknown. Russ watched his young wife fade in anguished regret, and now that he knew, he wept. Chief's dream of the baby thrown to an eagle and a young woman turned to dust made complete sense.

Two children, two mothers never to know peace or happiness ripped at his heart—long suspected, now verified. He shot like lightning away from the revelations only to be caught by another vision, his lost wife aged beyond her years, stabbing at her veins with a steely knife laden with smack. Mortified, Russ looked away, and saw a young man wandering a lonely country road with thumb out to passing vehicles in a vision of the day he left home—the stallion in Chief's dream. His hurt, his pain had been his only focus all these years, but no more. He realized that many had suffered at his hands.

Russ closed his eyes to retain his tears. It was then that his father's voice whispered to him: "Be your own man. Don't let others make your choices for you. What you have done is not the business of man. I love you, son . . . it was never about courage . . . just choices." Russ stared, yet couldn't perceive his father's face. "Forgive yourself. You punished yourself long enough. The Lord forgives, so why not you?"

A wave of sentiment encompassed Russ's being. Visions of all his days spent with his father, then his lonely days of wandering appeared in split-second flashes, and Russ spun faster until he shrank into a vapor. His consciousness was lost. The body of flesh that had been him crumbled to the ground next to the fire . . .

WRIGHT & EDMISTON

WRIGHT & EDMISTON

WRIGHT & EDMISTON

WRIGHT & EDMISTON

WRIGHT & EDMISTON

WRIGHT & EDMISTON

WRIGHT & EDMISTON

WRIGHT & EDMISTON

WRIGHT & EDMISTON

CHAPTER 37

He covered his head at the deafening reverberation of chopper blades. Dust kicked up by the blades blasted his face. Russ turned his head and saw the whirling wings flicker as they cut the sun's rays, like a dragonfly hovering close to the ground. Squinting, he tried to focus on the silhouettes of the men who dashed toward him. His head turned again until his face was planted into the sand on which he lay. The smell of the earth refreshed his senses, a homey smell after enduring the death scents of the underworld. His swollen legs throbbed with heated pain.

"Hey Chief, can you hear me?" a voice coaxed.

Russ tried to form a word, but he couldn't speak. He struggled to make out a face. His skin felt taut, raw, and burned. His lips were cracked, and he tasted blood. The battle had taken a toll, but even so, he somehow felt new.

"You're going to be all right. You've been snakebit. It looks like you've been lying here a couple of days. The poison got a good hold on you. I'm a paramedic, do you understand? Just nod if you do; don't talk." The man opened a leather bag that had been placed next to Russ's head and removed a blood pressure cuff. Another man cut away the pant legs of Russ's trousers. Russ looked down at his blackened legs and nodded a confirmation as the figure injected a serum into his arm.

The paramedic turned to his partner. "This one is luckier than that poor stiff we picked up in the lower canyon a couple of days ago. He had been bit half a dozen times." They went about the business of checking Russ's vitals and setting out their equipment. They placed a stretcher next to him.

"Wha . . . hap . . . ?" His throat—dry, swollen tight—refused to release his words.

"Looks like you took a nasty hit from a rattler. You're full of poison." The medic looked over the damaged flesh of Russ's legs.

"Hate!" Russ whispered.

"Hate, what?" The medic looked puzzled by the remark. The other medic offered Russ water to relieve his dry throat.

Russ swallowed; the tightness eased. "The poison, it is hate!"

"Yeah, whatever. It's snake venom. You take it easy, mister. You've been through a lot. I can't seem to locate the bite though."

"No . . . hate." Russ shook his head, but the medics ignored his words.

The rescue crew secured him onto the stretcher, their deliberate movements improving Russ's confidence that he might be alright. The medics started to carry Russ toward the chopper, but stopped when Russ grabbed one's arm. Russ nodded toward a stray dog sitting on a rock.

"Strangest thing . . . if it weren't for that old mutt over there leading some hikers to you, you'd probably be dead. These canyon strays are opportunists for the most part. There are hundreds of them in this ravine. They follow hikers, looking for scraps of food. This one actually led some hikers to you. He has a nasty festered wound on his shoulder. We're going to have to put him down. It's a shame to do it to a hero, but he's suffering," the medic said, as he paused to let Russ look at the panting dog, who looked like it was almost smiling.

"No stray . . . it's Chief." Russ managed a few words and raised his hand to protest the plan. The dog stopped panting, licked its chops, and with soulful eyes took on a stoic look.

"I called you Chief when I woke you; sorry about that," the paramedic said. "You're a little foggy about things." The medics continued to walk toward the chopper. Russ struggled to lift his head and keep the dog in sight.

"No . . ." Russ struggled to rise off the stretcher.

"Lay back now; relax." A firm hand pushed him down, and he was too weak to resist.

Russ looked at the stray, sitting next to a mottled old satchel. It was Chief—he knew it was. The mutt stood with the satchel strap gripped in his teeth and golden tail wagging as the helicopter pilot approached it. The medic slid the stretcher into the chopper at an angle that gave Russ a full view of the dog. The pilot pulled out his pistol, and without hesitation, a sickening crack echoed. Deprived of even a whimper, the stray fell lifeless on the trail to Havasupai. Tears rolled down Russ's cheeks as they strapped his stretcher to the floor of the chopper. The pilot walked back to the controls, and soon they were soaring high, fast, and furious out of the canyon in a surreal moment that seemed but an extension of Russ's exit from the underworld. Russ closed his eyes and listened to the flutter of the blades and the crackling voice on the radio repeat back the team's reported ETA and patient's condition.

CHAPTER 38

Russ woke in a Flagstaff hospital, his first sight that of the IV bag hanging next to the bed. He followed a tube down to his arm where tape covered the needle that entered his vein. He looked toward the window and saw only the reflection of his room. It was dark outside, and Russ wondered what time it might be, what day. The room was sterile, devoid of cards from any well-wishers or even a suggested sign of a visit from a concerned relative or friend. He couldn't remember anything about his arrival. He could hear voices and laughter out in the hallways and sounds of moving equipment. A minute later a face peered around the door, a pleasant face that broke into a warm smile when she saw Russ's eyes were open.

"Hey sleepyhead, did you finally wake up?" She pushed back the door and stood in front of him. He didn't respond right away, trying to figure out who she was. A nurse, he finally told himself. His mind felt like it was on pause.

"Yeah, I guess so. How long . . . how long have I been out?" Russ's words formed more slowly than his thoughts.

"Oh, they brought you in three days ago. You've had the doctors scratching their heads." The nurse checked the IV bag and looked at Russ's chart.

"Why's that?"

"Well, first reports were that you were snake bit, but they couldn't locate a bite. All the blood work has been negative, but you showed all the symptoms of a snakebite or some sort of poison." The nurse checked the IV in his arm and then took his wrist, feeling for his pulse. Russ chose not to offer any insight or explanation of his condition. His mouth felt too dry to talk. He looked up at her as she counted his pulse and took his blood pressure. She confirmed her results to those on a monitor, marked his chart, and then returned his look with a smile.

"My name is Andrea. I'm your night nurse. Here, let me moisten your mouth." She dipped a small sponge attached to a stick into a glass of ice water, rubbing it between Russ's lips. "Suck on it, and I'll dip it again. I've been doing this for three days for you. They put the IV in to hydrate you, but your mouth still dries out."

Russ nodded his head in agreement as she retrieved another swab of water. Her eyes revealed a deep compassion.

"Do you have any idea what caused your condition?"

Russ shook his head. She pulled down the sheet to expose his chest. She listened to his heart with a stethoscope.

"Take a deep breath and hold it. Good. Once more."

"Vitals all seems pretty normal; you're just very weak. Let me look at the coloration of your legs." She covered his chest and exposed his legs. Her hands felt cool as they gently examined his inflamed skin. The flesh was swollen, and the skin appeared stretched. She compressed her lips and shuddered almost imperceptibly.

"Better. Your color seems to be clearing, and the swelling has gone down a little—all good signs. There had been an awful thickening in your skin—hard to the touch—but it has softened a bit." She covered his legs and gave one of his knees a squeeze. Then she dampened a washcloth in cool water, blotting his face.

"When do you think I can get out of here?" Russ scooted higher on his pillow with a silent wince.

"Slow down, cowboy. If you're going to sit up, then let me adjust your bed. As far as you leaving, that's above my pay grade. The doctors will be making their rounds in the morning. You can ask them."

"You know, we almost lost you twice. You flat lined."

"I flat lined? Were you here?" His voice strained.

"It happened on my shift."

"Did you save me?" Russ whispered with a slight smile.

"This is a team effort. We're not here for the glory." She winked at him. My quick responses may have stabilized you before the emergency room doctor arrived."

Had she had been giving him special consideration? On some level he was aware, even though he had been unconscious. *Sympathy. Maybe because I haven't had any visitors or cards, or maybe because I'm just so ruggedly handsome.* He chuckled.

"What? What are you laughing at? Andrea paused.

"Nothing. Just an inside joke. When you've been knocked out for three days, you have to wonder what you missed and what people were doing when they thought you weren't home."

"You need to rest, not concern yourself with that. Here, take a sip." She put a straw between his lips, and Russ sucked in ice water. Cool, refreshing ice water, which he held in his mouth until it warmed. He closed his eyes in ecstasy.

"My guess is that you'll be out within three days, but that's based strictly on my observations of the way your symptoms are fading. The doctors might have more insight. They want to determine a cause for your condition, so please don't say I told you that."

"The doctors will never figure out the cause of my ailment."

"Is that so? We have some very good doctors on staff."

"Maybe a pastor would be better qualified than a doctor—no reflection on their ability." He looked toward the window, where he could see her reflection. He wondered if she were single. *I must be feeling better to think about that.*

"A pastor might, but not a doctor? I don't get it." She saw Russ contemplating her reflection in the window and gave him a perplexed look.

"It's a long story. Maybe when I feel a little stronger we can talk." The tone of Russ's voice resonated with an inner peace. She wasn't a kid. Maybe she would be able to relate to him. She was probably just a couple of years younger than him and had probably had a full life.

"I have to finish my rounds. I'll check back in a little while. You better rest." She walked toward the door. She paused as she grabbed the handle.

Russ waited, perhaps with a little too much anticipation, to hear what Andrea was going to say.

"Hey cowboy, if you need me, pull that string."

Russ exhaled. *Let it go*, he told himself. Still, he was surprised that he was even thinking of this nurse taking a liking to him. He shook his head. She intrigued him—but he knew he would never call her for anything.

In the morning, the doctors came into Russ's room early. They were pleased with his progress but still concerned. He had suffered severe sun poisoning along with a strange, unidentified toxin in his blood. Their biggest concern was the blackened tissue in his legs. Like Andrea had said, the doctors were dumbfounded by the lack of fang marks. The symptoms were textbook snakebite, but none of their tests came back positive.

"Hi, doc," Russ offered when the first doctor peeked into the room.

"Well, it's good to see you awake. I read the night nurse's report. It all sounds good."

"Andrea has been taking good care of me; she's a true professional."

"Yes, yes she is. She's been on staff a long time."

"I heard I flat lined, doc. That's bad, huh?"

"Yes, that's bad."

"Are you the one who saved me?"

"No, the night staff saved you. I hear they lost you twice."

"The night staff—that would be Andrea, right?"

"I don't know. I would imagine Andrea had a hand in it."

Just then, another doctor entered the room, and Russ listened as the doctors discussed his prognosis. They made Russ comfortable while questioning him, looking for insight as to what had caused his condition. Russ barely spoke, offering them no help. *It doesn't matter,* he thought. There was nothing they could do for him. It would all just take time and prayer.

CHAPTER 39

Russ had been awake most of the night, and rain pelted the window of his hospital room. Drops slowly collected until heavily swollen and then ran down the glass. He hadn't seen rain in a month and wished he could walk out into it. He would love the cool feel of the water on his face after spending so much time in the desert. His thoughts were on Chief, and the rain seemed appropriate.

His eyes closed as the door to his room slowly opened. He knew it was Andrea. He didn't open his eyes, wanting her to think he was asleep. He could feel her presence in the room. She stood, watching him breathe, and said nothing for the longest time. Finally, Russ couldn't contain himself and rolled over, his gaze meeting hers. Neither one of them smiled.

"Hey, how's it going?" she whispered.

"Swell. I'm getting out of this dump in the morning. The doctors are finally releasing me. Said I was a medical mystery, but there really wasn't anything more they could do." He had been hoping that she would have called off tonight; then he wouldn't have to say good-bye to her. He wanted to know everything about her. Instead, he settled for a little bit.

"I always wonder why people do what they do. What in the world made you want to be a nurse?"

"Well," she paused. "My older brother developed cancer when I was teenager. He never complained, even with the excruciating pain I know he felt. His only concern was for me. We had always been close. When they brought him home I cared for him, even though we had hospice. He eventually passed away. I thought I could save him. I think I blamed myself for not doing enough. I made the decision to be a nurse, so I could try to help save other people."

"I'm so sorry. I shouldn't have asked."

"Oh no, it's fine. He was wonderful."

"An old Indian taught me about the blessing way. There is a God, Andrea. I believe. Someday we will all be together, but you have to believe. I've run all my life. I always felt like a coward . . . I'm not so wonderful, Andrea. But I met someone in that canyon who set me straight. The world is at war, and it is our choice to not give in to the enemy. We all have our battles to fight. Our greatest weapon is love—true, honest love. That is what God wants from us."

"Is that Chief? Is he the one who set you straight?"

Russ smiled. "I mentioned him, did I?"

"Yes, you were worried about him."

"Ha, worried about *him*? He was the instrument. He held the mirror for me to see my reflection. Chief walked with one foot in darkness and the other in the light. That's where I am now. I am just stepping into the light. It feels good. I think you feel that, but let it grow in your own heart. It's in you—your brother is letting you know it's time. Your life will change if you let go of the need to control things and just focus on love, on goodness, on God, Andrea.

"Is Chief dead?"

Russ looked at the raindrops gathering on the window. They hit the window individually but soon found each other, collected, and streamed down the glass. The drops hadn't died—they had lost their singularity, but their essence was still there in the pool at the base of the window.

"No, Chief isn't dead."

"I'm so glad. Well, Mr. Philosopher, I need to leave to make my rounds, but I'll be back to check on you."

"Hey, do you think you can give me a ride out to old Route 66 in the morning? If not, I understand." The minute the words left his lips, he regretted them. He had spent most of the nights lying awake and slept during the day so he could be alert for Andrea's shift; he was guilty of that. There was a long pause as a flash of something—some type of mind tussle—wrinkled Andrea's forehead before she finally said, "Sure, that shouldn't be a problem."

Although inviting her to stop somewhere for breakfast crossed his mind, he didn't push it.

CHAPTER 40

Soon after the sun rose, Andrea rolled a wheelchair into his room. "You know this is just part of the protocol," she said. She wheeled him down to the exit as policy required and then pushed the wheelchair off to the side of the lobby. Steam rose from the macadam outside the hospital door as the morning sun scorched away the night's rain. The air smelled washed and pure, offering relief from the stagnant, tense air of the hallway. Andrea briefly searched her purse for her keys as Russ waited by the passenger's door. She unlocked her door and turned to Russ. Her eyes widened.

"Look, look behind you!"

Russ turned, and there, in the distance, was a rainbow. Just above it arched a less striking rainbow but a rainbow all the same. It truly was a double rainbow. Russ dropped back against the car to stare. A sign—it could be taken as a sign or just a coincidence. Given the choice, why shouldn't it be a sign? Russ felt the warmth of the ten o'clock sun and grinned. He raised one arm and gave a slight, hesitant wave, an acknowledgement to an old friend.

"Did you just wave at that rainbow?" Andrea softly asked. "Is it Rainbow Woman?"

Russ rolled around and put his arms on top of Andrea's car roof and smiled.

"Yes, Rainbow Woman," he said softly. "Did I speak of her, too?"

"Yes."

"I never met her; I only know of her. The rainbow above her is Chief." Russ looked at Andrea. Her skin looked so soft and her features so fine, a perfect nose. She gave Russ a quick glance, and then turned her attention back to the rainbows. Russ looked away. *It is like being in the presence of a beautiful woman, appreciating her without seeing her as the target of a conquest. It is not easy.* Chief's words echoed in Russ's head. Andrea looked back at Russ, her keys jingling in her hand. She caught Russ in another gaze at her. Her eyes were smiling, but he felt more somber.

"What . . . ?"

He chose his words carefully. "Oh, I was just thinking about something an old friend had said to me once. He was a wise old man. I just want you to know that it is great to have a beautiful friend."

"Hey, my husband's going to start wondering where I am . . ."

"Yep, we better get rolling." Russ stashed his pack in the backseat and slid into the car, closing the door. He kept his eyes on the rainbows until they pulled out of the parking lot and the view became obscured. He contemplated Andrea, the first relationship he had ever felt confident with. He had passed a test. He settled back in the seat and let out a sigh of satisfaction. Not a single blister showed for his effort even as he wore his softer skin. Russ felt no need to say more.

Russ and Andrea would refrain from exchanging any more words as they drove toward Route 66. Russ would never violate this new trust. He felt light. He didn't know why exactly, but he felt he had shed his old foundations, formed in his youth. They lay in a cavern somewhere in a desert canyon along with his wall-building tools.

Andrea dropped him off in the parking lot of the Lodge Pole Inn. Their good-byes were brief. Russ gently closed the car door and limped toward the inn without looking back. Andrea looked straight ahead.

It was late morning, before lunchtime, and the place was nearly empty. Russ stood just inside the door, taking time to acclimate his eyes to the dark interior. The smell of stale beer hung heavy from years of absorbed spillage. He approached the bar and the bartender, a burly fellow, heavily tattooed, walked toward him.

"What'll it be, stranger?" the bartender asked.

"Give me a Guinness." Russ watched the bartender let the foam settle for a moment.

"There's a cute blond who works here. Do you know when she comes in?"

"There aren't any cute blonds working here. Sorry, but I'm the cutest thing you got."

"I was in here about three weeks ago, in the evening—and there was a woman working the bar . . ."

"Oh yeah, okay. She dragged up. She headed for Nashville with her boyfriend and his band. She was a great kid, but a wanderer. Her old man comes in here a couple times a week. He might tell you how to contact her. He's a good guy. I have no idea, though. Is it something important?"

"No, not really, I just wanted to tell her about my hike and a mutual friend we had." Really though, he had hoped to verify that he had in fact been in this bar and that there had been an old Indian with him. That was why he had stopped, not for a beer but for validation.

The bartender shrugged and pressed a wet towel to the bar, working his way away from Russ. He showed no further interest. Russ picked up his beer and strolled over to the wall where the pictures of the frontiersmen and Native Americans hung. He walked slowly and perused them until one in particular caught his attention. It was of Chief, a younger version of an adult of maybe twenty years old. The date said 1926. Maybe it was the father of Chief, or Chief was older than he had said.

Russ looked toward the bar and started to form a word but stopped. He looked at the hulking bartender who continued to wipe the bar and decided not to converse with him. Instead, Russ dropped into the closest chair, held his beer up in a toast, and said a brief prayer.

"The truth is the truth whether we know it or not. Right, Chief?" Russ couldn't explain any of it, but knew it didn't matter. Had it all been delusion or illusion? Russ knew even that didn't matter, and he also knew that for the first time in his adult life he was at peace with himself. He chose to accept it without question.

When his beer was done, he walked out to old Route 66. He looked down this remnant of the historical road, and although he saw vehicular traffic, it generated loneliness. It was as if a nostalgic mist wept from the trees lining the motorway—Route 66, "The Mother Road" from *The Grapes of Wrath*.

Russ pondered his options. He could call a taxi, catch a bus, or walk, but it just seemed fitting to end his journey the way it had started so many years ago, during the summer of love.

A thought occurred to him, and he sat his backpack on the ground. He unzipped it and moved its contents around until he exposed an inner pocket. From it he removed a folded piece of rawhide. He held it in his palm and rubbed his thumb over it. He felt several bumps. He hesitated. The significance of it was in the gift, not the content. He felt that it was almost a sacrilege of sorts to know what it contained.

Finally, he opened the folds. Ten blue-white diamonds sparkled on the tan hide. He wished he hadn't looked and stashed it back in his pack.

He walked with traffic, holding out his thumb. An old relic of a pickup slammed to a halt, only one of its brake lights lit. Russ could make out the silhouette of a cowboy hat on the driver's side. He opened the passenger door and slid in.

"Where ya headed?" the driver drawled.

"I'm heading for Phoenix, or as far as you can take me," Russ replied.

"Not going that far. I am going to Sedona, though. Phoenix, there ain't nothin' in Phoenix."

"I've got a nephew there. I just want to check on him before I head home." Russ's voice faded as he raised one eyebrow. He had a strange feeling of *déjà vu*.

The pickup rattled back onto the road, letting out a whiny groan as it accelerated. The driver lifted an open bottle of beer that had been held between his knees and gulped several mouthfuls before securing it again between his legs. The driver glanced over at Russ and then again more thoughtfully; his cheek formed a dimple, and his eyes became slits. Russ returned the glance, and the cowboy looked straight ahead, grabbing his beer bottle and chugging it dry. He tossed the spent vessel on the floor at Russ's feet.

"Excuse me, but I don't litter; ticks me off when I see trash along the road." He gave Russ a good long glance, a dangerously long glance, for when he finally looked to see where they were going, he had to jerk the wheel to avoid a head-on with a dump truck. He was unshaken by the near miss. It was as if it were all part of his normal routine. "You look familiar, mister," the cowboy said, looking back at Russ more intently this time. "Say—you're that fella on the road to the canyon. Remember me? I was working on the fence. It is you, isn't it?"

Russ looked over at the driver and studied his hat. He hadn't seen much of his face that day. Then Russ took a better look at the truck. But the clincher came when he mulled the words "ain't nothin' in Phoenix." Sure enough, it *was* the stranger from the dirt road.

"Yes, I guess we *have* met before."

"Dang, I figured you for being stranded on that old dirt road to nowhere all alone, dying of thirst and drying up with that rental car of yours stuck axle deep in dust. Did you make it all the way through?" The cowboy became animated and reached down to the driver's-side floor to pick another bottle out of a six-pack carton.

"Yes." Russ watched as the cowboy popped the lid of the beer bottle on the steering wheel ring. It was amazing. Russ had never seen such a smooth one-handed opening. It was an often-practiced craft.

"Good for you. I'll bet I was right, though. Didn't find nothin' out there, did ya? Nothin' but Injuns and dust. Hey, want a beer?" The cowboy motioned with the hand that held his beer.

In a very weird way, Russ had his validation. "You know the answer to that better than me—and no, I'll pass on the beer." Russ closed his eyes and slouched in the seat.

He was going home.

ABOUT THE AUTHORS

William A. Wright (Bill) and Dale Ann Edmiston are a husband-and-wife writing team who live in Pennsylvania. Bill gets the ideas, discusses them with Dale, and writes up the draft; Dale then works on the content and line edits. Havasupai is not their only novel; a second (St. Croix) is completed; a third (Paper Alley) is three-fourths completed; and a short story ("Hitchers") is awaiting expansion. Bill has won awards for his flash fiction.

Most of Bill's inspiration comes from life experience. Havasupai was inspired by his own solo excursion into the Havasupai region of the Grand Canyon; his friendship and interaction with Native Americans (including one he met at a bar the night before Havasupai who inspired the character of Chief); and time spent with his uncle, a Native American activist and former prison warden, who lived in Lake Havasu City.
Both Bill and Dale are adventurers who have backpacked and motorcycled all over North America and Europe. And, like Havasupai's Russ, Bill is no stranger to pain. The loss of his five-year-old son to cancer shaped his life. These experiences and others have given Bill's writing depth and grit.

Bill's education is in nuclear quality assurance and electrical engineering technology, and he worked his way up from being a scrapyard worker and truck driver to controlling Pittsburgh's electrical grid; he also worked for NASA. Dale is an Air Force veteran who performed maintenance on F-16s; currently, she's an early childhood educator/preschool director at a high school. Combined, the couple have four living children and six grandchildren. As writers, the two of them have found a rhythm that works, and they continue to hone their skills. When not writing, they enjoy traveling, working on the dream home they designed, and gardening.

GLOSSARY AND WORD LIST

Darkness------- John 1:5
1 John 1:5-10

Demons-------- Luke 9-37-43
Luke 9:28-44
Luke 9:49-51
Mark 5: 1-20

Gold, Treasure- Psalm 119:119-128

Redemption----- Isaiah 35:7-9

Salvation-------- Luke 9:50
1 Peter 1:2

Transformation- Philippians 3:21

Wanderers--------Hebrews 11:38-40

Devil's claw- A term used for several species of desert plants

Esplanade sandstone- Cliff forming, resistant sandstone found in the Grand Canyon

Hoodoos – A tall, thin spire of rock that protrudes from the bottom of an arid basin

Mescal- 1. A cactus, having button-like outgrowths that are dried and chewed as a drug. 2. Liquor distilled from the fermented juice of certain species of agave

Paisisvai – A red river, the Colorado

Parry's agave- A variety of a fleshy-leaved desert plant

Permian Sea- An ancient sea basin in the U. S. Southwest

Red wall limestone- A layer of limestone in the Grand Canyon

Sinyala fault- A geological fault line in the Grand Canyon

Travertine- A form of limestone deposited by mineral springs

Made in the USA
Middletown, DE
05 July 2016